A MUCH KNEADED UNION

A Much Kneaded Union

K.E. Monteith

Also by K.E. Monteith

A Snowfall Valley Novel

A Much Kneaded Union

K.E. Monteith

ASIN: B0CXLLLM4K
ISBN: 9798869314826

First Printing, 2024

Contents

For the girlies who want things that don't fit some types of "feminist"

Content Warnings

Please be aware that this book contains sexually explicit content and mentions of traumatic loss of parents at a young age and subsequent PTSD (involving storms and drinking)

The Playlist

- Like a Rodeo - Kane Brown
- In The Kitchen - Renee Rapp
- Bye Bye Baby - Taylor Swift
- If I Didn't Care - Hunter Hayes
- Here You Come Again - Dolly Parton
- Rumor - Lee Brice
- More - Hunter Hayes
- Tell Me Why - Taylor Swift
- Somebody Like that - Tenille Arts
- What Ifs - Kane Brown, Lauren Alaina
- Last Night - Morgan Wallen
- Found You - Kane Brown
- The Other Side Of The Door - Taylor Swift
- Tenessee Whiskey - Chris Stapleton
- Addict - Don Louis
- Worship You- Kane Brown
- That's when - Taylor Swift, Keith Urban

ICYMI

The Snowfall Valley Series is a set of interconnected standalones. You don't have to read them in order if you don't want to. Here's all you need to know for Ashley & Mason's story:

- Ashley's cafe, Tost-Ka, is right across the street from Mason's cafe, The Pub, yes this caused some confusion
- At the church turned community center, there's a betting board for when Ashley & Mason will go out on a date, Ashley doesn't know about this
- Ashey & Mason prank each other on a regular basis, including: sending a mariachi band during sleeping hours, taping over windows with cardboard, & more
- Ashley claims she hates Mason, Mason just sort of grumbles when asked about her

1

Whiskey Cake

Ashley

Three years ago

I was sitting at a bar, alone, in the middle of nowhere North Carolina, because I didn't have anyone to celebrate my accomplishments with. No one to call or text to say I did it, I signed the lease and I'm opening a bakery in just a few short months.

It was my own fault.

I never went to the after-work happy hours or the break room birthdays. I didn't hang out around the coffee station to chit-chat. I was at work to work, not to make friends. Making friends wasn't going to make me partner.

And being partner was all I cared about until —

"Any chance you're looking for some company?"

I was so wrapped up in my little pity party that I hadn't noticed the man saddle up next to me. And when I say saddle, I mean he had cowboy boots and all, leaning against the bar like he should be out in a field chewing on wheat. Tilting my head to the side I considered this cowboy character. He had a nice smile, crooked like he could tell I was assessing him, and straight, sparkling teeth. I did like a man with good hygiene. I could give him some of my time.

And while I would deny it until my last breath, I loved those Hallmark movies where the big city lawyer came to a small town and fell in love with the gruff farmer and learned to let go of perfectionism. And I sure as hell was a big-city lawyer. And this guy looked like he could play the part of my gruff farmer.

"I could be convinced." I turned in my seat, angling to face him and he immediately turned to me, one arm on the bar, blue eyes sparkling.

"I do like a woman who makes me work for it." He had that Southern twang that could make a girl weak in the knees. The part of me that wasn't completely bitter, the part of me that hoped this bakery would change all parts of my life, lit up for this stranger's charm.

"Is that what those boots are for?" I asked nodding to his shoes. He rested one boot on its heel, tilting it back and forth.

"Nah, I don't get to wear my working boots much anymore and they sure as hell aren't suited for going out to a restaurant."

"Ooh, that dirty, huh?" I teased.

"Yeah, I can get pretty dirty if ya like, sweetheart." He gave me that flirtatious smirk that made my cheeks burn. But I wasn't turning away. I was eating that shit up. Why shouldn't I?

"Ashley Bowen." I offered my hand and the cowboy gave me a firm shake.

"Mason Foster," he said, still holding onto my hand, those baby blue eyes eating me up like I was the most delicious of desserts. Which everyone would agree is whiskey cake. Or maybe mini red velvet bundt cakes.

"I'm guessin' you're not from around here, are ya, Miss. Bowen?"

"What gave it away?" We were still holding hands, even as our arms relaxed, our hands suspended in the space between us. We were checking off all the Hallmark tropes one after another.

"The suit. Doesn't look all that comfortable." His eyes traveled down the well-ironed lines of my blazer, drifting ever so quickly over where I'd undone a few buttons when I sat down at the bar. "Not to say it doesn't suit you."

"Ha!" I threw my head back, incidentally letting go of his hand. "I'm so damn tired of these fucking monkey suits. I can't wait to toss them all out. My mom was one of those 'you have to dress professionally, even for school' types. Everything I owned up until now was black, white, or navy. And always had a collar."

Mason cringed on my behalf, likely remembering a similar story from his own school and how there was always that one kid who took everything too seriously and dressed like they were already working a nine-to-five. Had I been picked on? Maybe. But back then, I thought taking everything seriously made me better than them. That not slacking off in high school or college would leave me better off in the long term.

Fat load of bullshit that was.

"What's changing so you can toss those suits?" Mason asked and the bubbly excitement of finally, *finally*, getting to tell someone about my bakery rose in my chest. I would *not* let that bubbly feeling die just because the first person who asked was a stranger.

"I'm opening a cafe in town. Down ..." I swiveled on my stool and pointed in the direction I'd driven from to get here. "That way. Or actually, maybe it was more that way." I moved my hand 40-ish degrees.

"That's amazing, congratulations." Mason's smile was bright and genuine and too damn charming. Or maybe it was charming because it was the first time someone congratulated me. My mother sure as hell hadn't when I'd told her I was quitting the firm to pursue my dream of opening a bakery.

Her criticism might not have changed my mind completely. But it did make me reconsider a few things. Like changing my place from a bakery to a cafe. With the wider appeal, it was a safer financial bet and I could always change things later on.

"Do you have a name yet?"

"Tost-Ka." I didn't expect him to know the reference, but if he did ...

"I'm getting the toast pun, but you'll have to explain the rest for me, sweetheart."

"Toska is a Russian word for spiritual anguish, melancholia. So at Tost-Ka, you can chase away your toska."

"So like ennui?"

"Yeah, sorta. How do you know that word but not toska?"

"My mom was *very* into Gilmore Girls. I remember that French guy saying it and for some reason, it stuck." Why was the idea of this gruff-looking man sitting with his mother to watch Gilmore Girls so damn endearing? "So is toska why you're quitting your suit job and opening a cafe?"

I looked at Mason, at his plaid and cowboy boots and scruffy beard, and thought if this man could read me so well, why could no one else? Or maybe that's why the Hallmark girl always falls for the countryman. He knows how to read a woman differently than the city boys.

"Yeah. I'm doing the whole quarter-life crisis thing, changing my job, moving to a new place where I don't know anybody, to chase away my toska."

"Well, now you know somebody," Mason said, giving me a more sheepish smile. Like he might be worried he was coming on too forward. Then he shrugged the look away and added, "Well, I live in the next town over, but still. You won't be entirely alone when you officially move down here."

"Hmm, is that the Southern hospitality I've heard so much about?" I teased and Mason flashed me the most charming smile yet.

"Nah. Southern hospitality is watching out for a neighbor, welcoming you to town with casseroles, that sorta stuff. Offering to be here for ya before you've even moved in, that's just me being smitten by a pretty face."

"Are you trying to charm me, Mr. Foster?" I liked this Hallmark movie of myself. I could see the ending now, Mason and I on a wrap-around porch, him rocking a baby while I sipped at lemonade. It was a fanciful vision, one I'd had before Mason saddled up here. The life I pictured myself living once I moved down South. But damn if Mason didn't fit that vision perfectly.

"Only if it's working, ma'am."

I looked at Mason and he looked at me and I think we both knew I was gonna be spending the night in his bed.

"How about we chase away that toska, sweetheart?"

"And how do you expect we do that?" If he said going back to his place … well I wouldn't say no, but it would dull his charm some.

"Let's start with a dance and see where we go from there." Mason set his drink aside, pushed away from the bar, and held a hand out for me.

For a second, I considered what my mother would say. How I was letting a pretty face and an impractical dream sway me. How if I was really going to do this cafe thing, I shouldn't be starting anything that would distract me.

But there was a reason I was moving five states away from her.

So I took his hand.

2

Lemon Raspberry Bars

Ashley

Present day

"Pssst," Rosie whispered, sitting at my counter on a rare day off from her diner. "It's just us, dear. You can be honest."

It only took a millisecond to understand what she was referencing. *He* was the only thing people asked me cryptic questions about.

Mason Foster, the bastard who gave me hope of an idyllic life in Snowfall and has been ruining it at every fucking turn since. Fuck. Him.

I looked over at the bastard's bastardization of a cafe and there he was, smiling at customers on the patio like he was the most gentlemanly host there ever was. It was a fat load of crap.

"No," I said, keeping my voice stern. One of these days people would stop seeing my hatred for a Mason as a cover for any other emotion.

"Oh come on, can't you at least admit you find him attractive?"

"No." I refocused my energy on preparing her cinnamon rolls. She was getting a batch for a family event later today, so it was a pretty large order. I had some dough thawed out in the back, so it might be worth setting her up a kit instead of boxing up the ones in the case. Plus one of my regulars, Louis, hadn't stopped by to get his yet and I'd hate for him to miss out or have to wait for another batch to be ready. "Would you be all right baking the rolls yourself?"

"Oh, yes. That's a great idea. Thank you." She kept quiet for just long enough for me to pull out a sheet of paper to write down the roll instructions. "The scruff really doesn't do it for you?"

I stopped writing to glare at her.

"Why don't you date him then?"

Rosie threw her head back and cackled like a witch. Too bad Mason wasn't here to hear that rejection.

The bell over my door rang and the devil incarnate stepped in. Given how often he stepped in right when I was talking about him or having some sort of problem I didn't want him witnessing, I was convinced he had a sixth sense. Or maybe he bugged my cafe. I wouldn't put it past him.

"Hey there, Rosie. Laughing about how bad the coffee here is? I've got your caramel macchiato with almond milk waiting for you at the Pub." Mason gave Rosie a friendly smile, throwing a thumb over his shoulder to his mockery of a cafe. A cafe named the Pub, with all the decor of a pub too. Ridiculous. He even had a menu item called 'nacho scones'. Disgusting.

"Oh, thank you, Mason. That's kind of you. You've been doing all right?"

While my friend engaged in small talk with my worst enemy, I ducked into the back to pack up her cinnamon roll dough and icing. When I came back out, Mason was leaning on my glass case, raising an eyebrow at me.

"You know you're supposed to bake those before serving them, right?" he said, pointing at the box of raw dough. I set the box in front of Rosie and flipped him off.

"Thank you, Ashley," Rosie intruded, tapping her card on my middle finger before sliding it between my knuckles. I took the card over to the register and rang her up, not breaking my glare at Mason. For all I knew he was planning to break my display case or cause some other sort of chaos.

Last week he'd set one of those fake puke plastics in front of my door and I had to watch several folks approach my door and then immediately turn away. I spent at least three hours trying to figure out what I'd done wrong before I thought to check outside. And when I did step out and saw what he'd done, I caught him giggling on his patio as he watched me try to sweep it up.

He was such a childish prick. I returned the favor by putting one of those fake balls in the window things on his door.

I suppose our pranks were starting to get a little repetitive. I'd have to —

Another ring of the front door shook me away from any revenge planning as Louis walked in.

"Afternoon, Louis. Two of the specials like usual?" I asked him, already grabbing the box for his to-go order. Louis was one of the older gentlemen in town, a local, the kind of grumbly man who complained anytime something changed. Which made it all the more special that he was *my* regular.

"Yes, thank you," Louis grumbled, then added, "Unless you've got any more of those cinnamon rolls."

"For you, always." I smiled at Louis before moving away from the register to gather his baked goods. This was the nice part of owning a cafe. Serving the same people every day, being able to give them a little something to make their day special. It fed my soul in a way that being a lawyer never did.

Then I caught Mason giving me a look and it was all ruined.

"What are you still doing here?" I asked him. If there was one good thing about this small town being in everybody's business, it was that if you had beef with someone, everyone knew and didn't judge when you hashed that beef out in public. Though I do think most of that was because they were enjoying the show and convinced we'd get together at some point.

Thank god no one saw me sneaking out of his apartment three years ago. I'd never hear the end of it if anyone found out about that night.

"I wanted to warn you I'm stepping out today, seeing as last time I left my cafe, you chose to trash my apartment."

Rosie shrunk in on herself, looking away from Mason guiltily. I simply rolled my eyes. I hadn't *trashed* his apartment. I'd just trashed a couple of things. All because I'd spent all day bracing to be in the same room as him, bracing for the comments, preparing comebacks. And he wasn't even there. Out on a date or some other bullshit.

"I don't know why you think I care. I just happened to be there when you were out and took the opportunity."

"Yeah and how'd you know how to get in my apartment?" he asked, arms crossed, hip resting on my display. He did this every once in a while. Threw out a reminder of what a dumbass I'd been. Tormenting me with it and never letting me forget. It was a dick move.

"Lucky guess," I murmured, returning my focus on finishing up Louis' order. "Enjoy, Louis. See you next week. I'm thinking of lemon squares."

"Oh you mean chess pie?" Rosie perked up.

"What?"

"Tsk, what kind of baker doesn't even know what chess pie is," Mason grumbled. Louis nudged his arm and held out his box of goods. My breath caught. For all his trash talk about my coffee and lack of, presumably, Southern desserts, he'd never actually tried anything of mine.

Despite myself, I wanted to know what he thought.

But he pressed his lips in a fine line and shook his head, the movement so small I wouldn't have caught it if I hadn't been looking directly at him.

Louis grumbled something under his breath to Mason and left. Rosie took the opportunity to sneak out with him. Leaving Mason and me alone.

I expected him to make a snide comment and go, but he stood in place, chewing on his lip, staring at me.

It was criminal that such a devil of a man should have such pretty blue eyes.

"If that's all you came to say, you can —"

"I can't have you harassing my staff every time I step out. This thing between us ..." He waved a hand through the air. "Let's keep it between us."

"You don't keep it between us," I spat. His eyes were so damn piercing. I hated the way they pinned me down, how they sparkled as that dumb ass smirk spread across his lips.

"You gonna tell me what you mean by that? I wouldn't consider myself a smart fella, so you'll have to spell that one out for me."

Mason Foster was many things, but dumb was not one of them. He saw the slip for what it was. Too bad for him I didn't actually mean anything. I didn't give a single fuck what he did or with whom. I just wanted him to leave me alone, ideally because his business went bankrupt and he had to leave town.

"I won't bother Travis while you're out. There, are you happy? Will you go now?" I grabbed a wash rag and spray bottle from under the counter and started wiping down tables. I'd already cleaned them after my last guests left, but there was no harm in doubling over.

"You promise not to bother him and anybody else in my shop even when I'm gone to manage the new storefront?"

My hand stopped circling the table, screeching to a halt like a record.

"What new storefront?" I gritted out. How the hell could Mason afford to open a new store? Business in Snowfall wasn't exactly prosperous, the only way I was making ends meet was those little festivals Ms. Taylor obsessed over. They brought in a good deal of tourists and tourists loved local cafes and Instagram worth treats. There was no way Mason was making enough with his shitty decor and trashy desserts to get a *second* store while I could barely afford one part-time employee.

"Touring this place that opened up near 64 today. In Mayberry. You know the town, right? Shop used to be a Subway."

If looks could kill, I'd have to hide a body.

Mayberry was where that stupid ass bar was.

And 64 was one of the bigger routes running through the area. The sort of road folks took to avoid traffic on the main highways. It'd be right in the way of tourists instead of off the beaten trail. The perfect shop location if sales were all you cared about. And I could really use some sales.

I needed those sales. I needed that shop. It couldn't be that expensive if Mason was looking into it. And I bet there were some small business grants I could apply for. I could steal this shop right out from under him.

"That shop is going to need someone with a much better sense of decor than you to go from a Subway to a proper cafe. You're in over your head."

"You think you could do better?" he taunted with that stupid ass smirk.

I tossed the wet rag at him. It landed with a splat at the center of his chest then slid to the floor. The wet line from chest to crotch was satisfyingly embarrassing.

"Yes. I do." I crossed over to pick up my rag, bending over nice and slowly. It was hot as fuck in the kitchen, so I kept to light, linen sundresses, this one featuring sunflowers. And it was rather short to be bending over in. But if he wanted to taunt me with that mistake of a night, then I could remind him of all the things he fucked up by leaving out a vastly important detail about his career. "You should go change before your tour. You wouldn't want to make a bad first impression."

3

Cortado

Mason

I walked back into the Pub, holding out my shirt to keep the cleaner smell from killing me. I was a complete and utter dumbass for taunting her when she had anything in her hands. Pretty sure she'd throw a freshly decorated cake at my head if I said the wrong thing, no matter how many hours she'd put into it. That's how dedicated she was to this hating me thing.

And yet, I kept provoking her.

There was no reason for me to go over and blab about the shop. No reason for me to open my dumb mouth and tell her exactly where it was either. Or that I was going to tour it today.

I didn't even want this shop. I was only checking it out because Travis said it'd be a good idea to expand, give him a position to manage one of the shops. Hell, he deserved it and I had the money to do it. But fuck if it didn't feel like pulling teeth.

Especially since it meant I wouldn't see Ashley as often.

So I went and ran my fucking mouth and provoked her about that night and about Mayberry and the second shop because it got a response from her. Picking a fight was the only time I ever got a response from her.

God, I was sick in the head.

"Why do you smell like cleaner, boy?" Louis grumbled from the bar. I rounded the counter, joining Travis and grabbed one of the spare staff shirts.

"Ashley threw her wash rag at me," I mumbled, quickly changing shirts.

"Speaking of your girl." Louis pushed his box of baked goods from Tost-Ka across the counter. We had a deal about him getting me her weekly specials since Ashley first picked a fight with me. Louis had been a good friend of my uncle's, pretty much another uncle to me growing up, so he happily helped me out. But in the last few months, his patience was growing thin. Pretty sure he wanted to rat me out with the way he offered me the box in front of Ashley.

"Thanks." I snatched the box up and hid it under the bar. The rest of town was having their fun with the betting board, I didn't need to add any fuel to it.

"Why'd you even go over there this time?" Travis asked.

"Told her not to hassle you when I'm gone." I snuck out a scone from the box. Raspberry and white chocolate was this week's flavor, a part of her regular rotation. It was damn delicious and it pissed me off.

"Why'd you tell her?" Travis groaned. "She gonna do some dumb bullshit to mess it up."

I turned to my employee and quieted him with a sharp glare.

It was one thing for me to complain about all the pranks and bullshit between us. I knew we did shit that pissed others off, disturbed the town's peace, but it was between us and everybody else should learn to shut their mouths. Besides they were all enjoying the show anyways.

"Okay, all right. No bad-mouthing our competition that regularly makes your life hell. Understood." Travis held up his hands in defeat and walked off to a table in the far corner occupied by an older couple.

"Just marry her already," Louis grumbled right when Dennis came in and sat beside him. I considered Dennis a friend, though we hadn't been close in high school. But he was also dating one of Ashley's friends and I assumed he'd tell his girl anything he knew, especially if it involved one of her girls. So I definitely didn't want Louis blabbing in front of him.

"Who're you marrying now?" Dennis asked, taking the stool next to Louis.

"No one," I said, just as Louis said, "Ashley."

"Ha!" Dennis laughed, loud enough to draw eyes from across the restaurant. "Yeah, I don't think you could get her to marry you if you were the last man on Earth and offering a million dollars."

"What makes you say that?" I asked, probably sounding a little too defensive. But I was nearing the end of my rope. There was only so long a man could swing from wanting to murder a woman for being so deliberately, astoundingly stubborn and petty to wanting to bring her to bed until she was so tired and satisfied she couldn't fight us any longer.

According to Dennis though, it'd be a cold day in hell before that happened.

"You mean you haven't picked up on the fact that she hates your guts?" Dennis asked, cocking an eyebrow. I grumbled some noncommittal response and moved away to fix his usual order, a long black.

"Seriously, though, why are you guys so ... at each other's throats? I get that the shops are sort of in direct competition, but your specialties are —"

I set his order down a smidge too hard, sending drops of coffee flying everywhere.

"He's a little sensitive about his thing with Ashley," Travis remarked, straddling the stool on the other side of Dennis. "Won't tell anyone how this whole thing started. It's like they just woke up one day and decided they were enemies."

"Really? Ashley won't say anything either," Dennis said, eyeing me for a moment before leaning closer. "Why is it that neither of you will say why you're fighting?"

All of them were on the edge of their seats, including Louis, who knew the whole story. After that night, I'd told him I'd met the woman of my dreams and she was even opening a cafe in the town next door.

That's what I get for counting my chickens before they hatch.

"Y'all need to find better things to worry yourself over. I've got a tour to get to." Through the Pub windows, I could just see the flash of Ashley's store sign flipping over. She was going to crash my tour.

That's my girl.

Fuck, if only. There was no way I could get her to stop hating me. If I could've thought of a way to get her, I would've thought about it by now.

"Wait, Denny, didn't Olivia hate you back in school before y'all started dating?" It was a long shot of an idea. I mean, the way they bickered in high school was nothing compared to what Ashley and I do, but still ...

"I wouldn't say she hated me, we just ... I was a dumb kid picking on the girl I liked. That's all." Dennis had the good sense to act ashamed of what he'd done in high school. I should be ashamed of all the dumbass pranks I'd pulled on Ashley, but I'd do them all again in a fucking heartbeat just to get her to speak to me.

"What changed?" *Something* needed to change, something needed to shift our relationship. Fuck, I was desperate enough to consider simply leaving her alone for a month to see if she'd seek me out.

Not sure I could even last a week though.

"Look, you can't tell anyone all right," Dennis said after looking around the bar. That got me curious. I leaned over and Dennis whispered, "I may have pretended I needed her to fake date me so Nana would get off my case about fitting into town."

"Seriously?" I pulled back, surprised.

"Oh please, you can't be surprised about that when you paid a whole ass mariachi band to serenade Ash."

"You did what now?" Travis asked.

"I didn't pay 'em. I called in a favor. Went to cowboy camp with one of the guys."

"You went to what?" Travis asked while Dennis mumbled, "Of course, there's a cowboy camp here."

"He won a trophy for his lassoing too," Louis added, unhelpfully.

Pushing back embarrassing memories, I tried to think of a scenario in which I could convince Ashley to fake date me. I just needed something to get through her stubbornness, then maybe we could get back to what we had that first night. We'd *had* something, I know she felt it, knew she'd been doing her best to ignore it ever since.

"I'd have to do something a lot more drastic than getting her to fake date me," I grumbled, pushing away from the bar and the men who were making various noises of agreement. The best thing I could think of was this married couple's business grant I saw while researching the costs of a new shop. It came with a good chunk of money, though I doubt there was enough money in the world that would tempt her into marrying me.

4

Mango Blackberry Cheesecake

Ashley

My application was admittedly rushed. I only had last month's statement on hand and no letters of recommendation, but it should be enough to prevent Mason from signing for this Subway shop right away.

Honestly, who did he think he was trying to open a second shop? He had no taste, his desserts were grainy, and he had no business drive. The man barely advertised the Pub, how was he going to bring in business to this new shop? He couldn't count on Snowfall townies coming here to support him. Some folks would sooner starve than leave the city for something.

This plan of his, whatever it was, was going to fail. It'd be good of me to take this store off his hands before he falls into financial ruin. Though it would be fun to watch.

When I stop my car in front of the store, I'm … unimpressed. The store was off a main road, so traffic getting in was a pain. As for the exterior, it was incredibly lacking. The walls hadn't been cleaned since the Subway sign had been taken down, so there was an outline of grime. And there wasn't any room for outdoor seating and the sidewalks were uneven.

Those weren't complete deal-breakers, but it did make me wonder why Mason would even look at this shop. Sure he had no taste, but he valued the community and his Pub's place in it. This shop was completely lacking in any sort of community atmosphere.

Inside, Mason was already speaking with the realtor. When he caught me staring that stupid smirk spread across his face, it wrinkled all that damn scruff and crinkled his eyes. The realtor followed his gaze and, when she saw me, waved. I gathered up all the customer service charm I possessed to return her smile and scrambled out of the car and into the shop.

"Hello, Ms. Burnett, thank you for fitting me in on such short notice," I said once I'd gotten through the door, and moved to shake her hand. Mason might have rolled his eyes at the extra sweetness I put into my voice, but the realtor ate it up. She was around our age, maybe even a little younger. She had a bright, enthusiastic smile and a light handshake. Her whole demeanor reminded me of the type of new lawyer that had graduated thinking they were going to make a difference in someone's life only to be completely disillusioned and change careers within a year.

"No trouble at all. I should be thanking you, two showings in one saves me a trip." Her good-naturedness gave my sad little application hope. I could talk her into a deal and maybe a little bit off rent for the poorly maintained storefront.

"Now, of course, this is your main space." Ms. Burnett started her sales spiel for the shop, stepping into the center, gesturing around as she put a spin on the abysmal features.

"You really couldn't help yourself, huh?" Mason stepped beside me, just close enough for the smell of coffee beans to wash over me. The smell wasn't just coffee, but *rustic* coffee, the kind that you knew had a story to it.

"I don't know what you mean. There's no reason for me not to check out any available storefronts for expansion." I kept my head high, turning ever so slightly so I didn't have to breathe in all the coffee aroma.

"Mm-hmm, had nothing to do with how much you'd miss me if I got another shop, did it?"

I took a hesitant look at him from the corner of my eye. That was *not* the kind of response I was expecting. I would've thought he'd taunt me about my slow business, about not having the money or staff for a second shop. The flirtatious taunt, coupled with his earlier reminder of that night, put me off balance.

"Well," he sighed, "It's not like we don't both know you can't afford this place. You're just wasting your time."

Now *that* was more like what I expected.

"I've already gotten my application together, have you?"

"Of course I do." He tapped at a manila envelope on the counter beside us. A decently sized envelope. Thicker than it had any right to be. "Applied for the small business grant too."

"Shit, what grant?" I hissed.

"Hmm, I don't think I'm gonna tell you."

"Oh, are you talking about the individual small business for Mayberry? That no longer applies for this property," Ms. Burnett chimed in, her smile shining an extra wattage.

"Why's that now?" Mason asked, arms crossing over his chest, shoulders tense.

"The board re-coded this area since it gets so much traffic. Travelers are more likely to stop at a place with a familiar name, so they reworked things to discourage small businesses."

"So they'd rather a union-busting ass of a corporation take up this space than a local business that'll put money back into the community?" Mason asked, his voice edging on an irritated anger I was more familiar with. Though usually it was directed at me. "Isn't there some ordinance about how many shops a business can have in one city? There's already one in the Target, isn't there?"

"God, Mason, don't pretend to be such a hillbilly. Most cities have a couple of Starbuckses. Fuck, you couldn't go more than a few blocks —"

"This isn't New York, Ashley. And the Board shouldn't act like it is or that anybody wants it to be."

Ms. Burnett's smile grew tense and she gave a little nod.

"I understand the frustration. The owner isn't partially keen on leasing to ... well, yes Starbucks. The owner would prefer a small business taking up the space, but they ... have certain upcoming expenses that might necessitate overriding that preference."

"That's a long ass way to say they need the money," I grumbled and, surprisingly, Mason grunted in agreement.

"What grants are still available then?" Mason asked. Ms. Burnett nodded and walked over to the counter where she sifted through a binder.

"Well, Mr. Foster, you might be eligible for a few business grants. I'm not sure if they'll be enough to make the price we spoke about on the phone match what Starbucks is offering." Mason hissed at the news, pacing in a circle while Ms. Burnett turned to me. "You mentioned you had a basic application completed, may I?"

Suddenly I was very ashamed of the bare-bones application in my hand. I tucked it behind my back and started to say, "Well, given the news about the grant, I'm going to have to revisit a few —"

Mason snatched the application from behind me, holding it up just high enough that I couldn't grab it back. His eyes narrowed as he scanned through the application, his smirk turning into a frown.

"Is this seriously —"

"Mr. Foster, please," Ms. Burnett said, voice going stern. She held out her hand and Mason gave her the application. I could feel his eyes on me, so I dug my nails into my hands to keep the nerves from showing. Like hell I was going to let him think he had something on me by seeing that application. There was still a chance I could get —

"I'm sorry, ma'am, but in my experience, applications like this one aren't likely to get many business loans for a second shop. Though you do have a high-value collateral. You aren't by any chance married? There's a grant for married couples that run a business together that won't be affected by the recoding. It's sort of an antiquated grant, but if you have a partner that can be added to the books, so to speak, you'd be eligible."

"Ha," Mason barked and I seethed. I could easily place the blame for my lack of a love life on him. No man in Snowfall would want anything to do with the woman so brazenly in a battle of wills against another man. Hell, everyone in town was convinced we'd get some stupid, ass Hallmark ending. But that wasn't the only thing scaring away potential suitors. I never went out past nine, could barely even stay up that late, and I never took time off work. You could take the law out of the lawyer and move her several hundred miles from New York, but you couldn't change her workaholic ways so easily. I wanted love, I just didn't have the time to look for it.

"No, I don't have a partner." I plucked my application from her hands. It was delusional of me to think I stood a chance of taking this place from Mason. I barely had enough business to keep myself afloat. Maybe that was a sign that my whole quit being a lawyer to run a small town bakery was a bust. If I wasn't doing well by now, then maybe I should call it quits. "Thank you for your time, Ms. Burnett. I'll leave you two to continue the tour. Have a good evening."

I gave Ms. Burnett a tight smile and turned to leave. I could hear her start to speak but Mason said something along the lines of not bothering. Whatever. He was right about one thing, good for him. I'm sure he'll have fun ponying up a shit ton of money in order to outbid Starbucks.

Fuck, if I did close shop, he'd probably throw a party. Beyond my friends, I'm not sure anybody would care much if I closed.

"Hey, hold up." Mason manifested at my side. Or maybe I was too focused on my damn pity party. Fuck, I could do better than this.

"What was that back there?" he asked, tilting his head.

"I don't know what you're so angry about. I admit defeat this time. The shop's all yours if you can afford it." I moved to open my car door but Mason slammed it shut. "The fuck?"

"You can't just give up like that."

"I'm sorry I cut your fun short. But you heard her. There's no way I can afford this place."

"She gave you an option." Mason inched forward, hand still on the door, nearly caging me against my car.

"Ha! You mean find some poor shmuck to marry me? Yeah, sure, I'll get right on that. After I get pigs to fly."

"It could happen." Mason's brow furrowed and those bright blues peered into my soul. I could feel him assessing me, seeing those pathetic thoughts and how badly I just wanted … that vision of a perfect life I had when I first moved here.

"What? Are you offering?" I snarked, not expecting Mason to inch even closer. And certainly not expecting him to lean down to whisper in my ear.

"And if I am?" The things that rough tone did to my body were unfair. The full body shivers, the heat, the quickening of my breath.

"Why would I ever consider that?"

"Because it's the only way either of us could get this shop. Because if Starbucks comes into the area, it's only a matter of time before they come to Snowfall and steal both our businesses. Because I know you can make one hell of a prenup that would leave me broke and in a gutter if I so much as crossed you once. Because it'd be fake, just for show."

"For show?" I repeated, stunned.

"I mean, if you want all the benefits of marriage, I'm happy to oblige. I know you're not gettin' a lot of offers." Before that stupid smirk had a chance to widen, I shoved at his chest. Mason stumbled back and I got into my car, leaving him dumbfounded as I took off.

5

Mexican Mocha

Mason

I played the whole fake marriage thing poorly yesterday. Since the realtor had brought it up, I got excited. I thought maybe if I offered fast enough, she'd get swept away with the idea.

And that might've been the case if I hadn't opened my dumb mouth and ruined everything. I just couldn't help myself, one little whisper, one implication, got her all flushed and I needed her to know that everything she could ever fucking want was on the table. If I could get her to marry me, I sure as fuck wasn't gonna waste the opportunity. Except the first opportunity I offered was fucking her.

She was right to shove me.

But at least I'd planted the seed.

And I was hoping one night was all it took for it to sprout. Because for this to work in the technical sense, for the shop, we'd need to start acting like a couple yesterday. Thankfully the whole town was already convinced we were madly in love, so a quick engagement wasn't going to raise any suspicions. But the paperwork of getting married, getting the grant, and all that shit would need to be sorted out quickly for us to get the shop.

So I walked over to Tost-Ka with a heavy stack of papers, details on the couple's grant, a mock-up of what our application would look like together, and a mildly well-organized spreadsheet on how we'd split expenses and the shop's income. I was prepared to make my argument in a way that Ashley would understand, pure logic.

What I wasn't prepared for was Grant fucking Hines to be there talking up my girl.

"So this is what you do when you're not causing trouble with your friends?" he said, giving Ashley a shit-ass grin that he probably thought was charming. The fucking punk.

"Well, it's a living." Ashley shrugged, that polite, customer smile softening.

"It sure should be. Your decorating skills are amazing." At that her smile widened, beaming. All directed at that asshole. I had half a mind to rat her out to Zoey. I'm sure her friend wouldn't be too happy about Ashley hitting on her cheating ex's cousin.

"Too bad that's the only skill you'll ever be privy to," I said, letting the door swing closed behind me, setting off the loud clang of the bells. Grant had the sense to move away from Ashley, but he kept his arm on the counter like he intended to go right back to flirting with her as soon as he got rid of me.

"Mason, get the fuck out of my shop," Ashley seethed at me, eyes narrowing, arms crossed over her chest. Good. Her focus should be on me, not this prick.

But then her eyes flicked back to him and I could feel every organ in my body burn and twist. I recognized that little look. The assessment. The interest.

She could use him instead of me.

The thought was a kick to the chest. Because fuck she could. She could marry Grant, play off that he helped with recipe development or some other chef bullshit, get the money for the shop, and probably fall for the asshole through it all. He didn't have a habit of picking fights with her. Their careers were compatible without being in direct competition.

They would make sense. And Ashley loved to fall back on logic.

Fuck that. I had logic on my side. The town already loved us as a couple. There was also the fact that she knew I could make her come.

I just needed to remind her of those little tidbits.

"The fuck are you —" Ashley started when I rounded the counter. As gently as I could manage with all the anger boiling my senses, I took her by the shoulders and moved her away from the register. I didn't miss the way her breath hitched as I manhandled her, but I needed this prick gone before I could analyze it.

"Cash or card?" I asked him while I finished up closing the box Ashley had packed his order in. She had these nice little stickers to go over the tab. I put two on and smoothed them over. Fuck him for being able to openly get her desserts. And double fuck him for considering asking for more.

"I'm sorry, what?" Grant looked at me then at Ashley. For once, she remained quiet. My fingers gripped at the register, my whole body itching to turn to look at her.

"Cash. Or. Card?" I gritted out. Grant finally took the hint, sighing as he took out his wallet and handed me a twenty.

"Keep the change, dickhead." He snatched the box up and was out the door before I could seriously consider grabbing him by the collar and kicking him out.

"Mason, what —" I held up my hand and Ashley quieted. She must be in a special sort of mood to not immediately jump down my throat. And I certainly shouldn't push her. Which is why I took my time entering the last of the order to get my jealousy in control. If I wanted a chance at this shop, with her, then I had to avoid pressing her buttons too hard.

But the look she gave me when I turned to face her pushed my buttons.

Ashley may look freer in her colorful dresses, one that had my cock twitching like a needy bastard, but she'd never lose that sharp lawyer look. Which unfortunately had a similar effect on my dick. She was giving me a look that said she was waiting for a good explanation for my behavior but didn't expect to get one.

It felt like a challenge.

Keeping her eyes on me was a challenge. Everything with her was a challenge. And I could never turn down a challenge from her.

"Were you actually considering him?" I asked, stepping closer so her ass hit the back counter.

"So what if I was?"

There was a moment of silence. A stare down. The silent question, 'So what are you going to do about it?' hung in the air.

It was almost as palpable as the strawberry shortcake in the display case.

I needed a taste of it.

The way my mouth crashed to hers reminded me of those magnet lessons in elementary school. On one side, the magnets couldn't go near each other. They'd rather fling one another off a bridge than touch. But if just one of them turns, if there was just one little change, they're instantly together, not a speck of space between them.

And like hell I was gonna let us get turned around again when her mouth felt so perfect against mine.

When our lips first met, Ashley gasped, a hand fisting in my shirt. I gave her five seconds to push me away. In those five seconds, she pulled me closer, tilted her head, and parted her lips. Even with those signs, even as I licked into her mouth and tasted fresh strawberries, I braced myself. Because any moment now, she'd snap to her senses and kick my ass.

But instead, she practically growled at me, pulling me even closer and dragging me back into the kitchen.

"If you're going to kiss me, Mason, *fucking kiss me.*"

I didn't have to be told twice. Fuck, I needed to hear her say it though. Needed to hear the desperation, the desire in her voice. Especially after seeing her check out that prick. I needed something to convince myself I wasn't the only one going crazy.

I grabbed her thighs, digging my fingers into the soft flesh and dragging them up until I slid under her dress. Then I tightened my grip to pull her up and onto a counter. Nipping at her lips, because I wanted it to be clear when she stepped out of this kitchen that she'd been thoroughly kissed, I slid my hand down her inner thigh and *gripped*. My other hand went just as roughly into her hair, pulling so I could kiss a spot on her collarbone that I knew would make her body melt into mine.

I don't know if time dulled my memory or if it's been just as long for her as it has for me, but the sound she made when my lips met that spot damn near made me come my pants. Her voice cracked as she took a sharp breath in, leaning her head in a way that didn't block my access but pulled her hair tighter.

"You want it rougher, huh? Should have figured that," I murmured to myself, sinking my teeth into that spot and sucking.

No one was going to hit on my girl again.

"What — what makes you say that?" she stuttered. Her hands were in my shirt, my hair, fluttering all around like she didn't know what to do.

"Because I have to get rowdy to get your attention, don't I? Maybe that's where everything went wrong in the beginning. I tried to welcome you to town with a gift basket. I should've just stormed in and kissed you." I dragged her ass to the edge of the counter and gripped both sides of her underwear, pulling until the rip joined the symphony of Ashley's heavy pants. Her eyes widened as I tossed the fabric away.

"That was from you?" she asked, voice quiet, hesitant. It sure as hell wasn't what I expected to come out of her mouth, but that basket has been sitting, bitterly on my mind for years. I couldn't drop it.

"Yeah, it was from me. I hadn't realized you'd bought the shop til the sign went up, so I had something delivered. And then when I finally got a chance to talk to you, you —"

Ashley's hands cupped my face and I shut up. Her finger made small movements, scratching the scruff of my beard. I might as well be her dog with the way my body lit up in response.

"Have you been tested since —"

"Yes." I didn't try to hide my eagerness. There was no reason to with the way I was tenting my pants. Fuck it, I just started undoing my buckle right then and there.

"Fuck," she hissed as my cocked bobbed out of my underwear. I settled back between her legs and she wrapped around me, pulling me closer. "Now, Mason."

"But I don't have a —"

"I don't care. Now." Her voice was so sharp, I just knee-jerk rammed into her. It was the best feeling in the whole fucking world. Honestly, if you'd told me she had killed me right then and this was what heaven felt like, I'd believe it. She was so damn hot, so perfect, better than I'd remembered, and a helluva lot better than the fist I've been using these past few years.

Which was also going to be my downfall. Because *fuck*, she felt too good and it'd been too long. And Ashley had me in a vice grip, her arms and legs and that sweet pussy, all of her holding me too tight for me to breathe, let alone hold on.

"Fuck, sweetheart, this was not the right move." I didn't miss the way she pulsed around me at the use of the term. I hadn't called her that since that night. I simply couldn't after everything had happened. Saying it now and that instant response gave me hope.

"If you don't slow down, sweetheart, I'm gonna come before you. It's been too damn long and you feel too damn good."

"Don't you fucking dare, Mason. I will chop off your balls and feed it to that damn deer everyone is obsessed over." Her threat didn't sound hollow, but with the way her hips moved, I was having trouble seeing straight.

"I won't leave you hanging, sweetheart. I promise. After I've filled you up, I'll happily get down on my knees for you. I've been dying to see what tastes better, your desserts or you." I gave up on my endeavor to hold back since Ashley sure as hell wasn't slowing down. I rammed into her, using the little bit of sense I had left to angle her so I could grind against her G-spot and stroke her clit.

But my girl was just too responsive. She squeezed me for all I was worth. I saw stars as I spilled into her, my body heating like I'd been pushed into a volcano.

Ashley looked like she wanted to push me into one.

"I'm going to murder you," she gritted. She let go of one of the hands behind my head to finish herself off but I smacked it away.

"I told you I'm not leaving you hanging, sweetheart." I stuffed myself back in my pants with one hand and started fingering her with the other, pushing my come back where it belonged. Then I sank to my knees, spread her legs, and —

The bell over her front door rang as someone stepped in. Ashley hissed out a curse, pushing me away to hop off the counter. I stood, stunned, watching her straighten her clothes and wash her hands before rounding out to the front.

Without Ashley in sight, my brain started to regain function. And god fucking damn it, did I fuck this whole thing up.

Quickly, I straightened out my clothes, washed my hands and the counter that had a beautiful imprint of her ass, then stepped out to join Ashley by the register. She was packing up a handful of chocolate croissants and other desserts for …

"Well, fancy seeing you here, Ms. Burnett," I drawled as the agent's eyes lit up, looking between Ashley and me, specifically at the bruise blooming on Ashley's neck.

"Oh, I knew there was something going on between you too," she crooned.

"There isn't anything —" Ashley started, but I stepped up beside her and grabbed her waist.

"Don't lie just cause you're stubborn, sweetheart." I turned to look at Burnett and added, "Ask anyone in town and they'll tell ya this has been a long time coming. We might be rushing to the altar for the shop, but I'd be rushing her there anyways."

"The shop, fucking of course," Ashley hissed under her breath. The tone was sharp, like how she argued with me. Very different from the softness about the basket or even the desperate threat just moments ago. The tone had my ears ringing. There had to be something I could do to chase that tone away.

"I looked up your shop after you called, Ashley. And it's just as cute as the pictures," Burnett rambled as Ashley took her card and began ringing her up, nodding along with a pleasant smile.

She must still be pissed about me coming first. I'd warned her, assured her I'd make sure she came too, but maybe she needed more than words.

Sliding my hand down, I went from her waist to under her dress. Her thighs were wet, a combination of her and me making her skin slick. I crooked one finger, sliding the wetness up and back inside her. Ashley instantly tensed around my finger and I slowly started pressing against her G-spot. We needed to get this customer out of here, flip the close sign, and lock the doors this time too. I needed —

Ashley slapped my arm so hard that the resounding smack even made Burnett jump back. I pulled my finger out of her pussy and adjusted her skirt. Ashley kept up her customer service smile, handing the woman her card like nothing had happened.

For better or worse, Burnett took in the vibes and ran for the hill. I wondered briefly if she'd bother calling the police when she saw my missing posters.

"Get the fuck out here," Ashley shouted as soon as Burnett was out of sight, smacking at my chest.

"Sweetheart, I warned you I wasn't gonna —"

"Get out!" She started pounding at my chest, sharp little stabs at my heart. Literally and figuratively.

"But I need to finish what I started," I said, taking hold of her wrists so she'd stop the brigade of little punches.

"Finish what? Your little marriage scheme to outbid Starbucks? Well sorry, but you'll have to find someone else to fake marry. Maybe somebody who can finish in two seconds like you." She started to tear from my grip, but I held tight.

"Yeah, I do want to marry you and get that shop, so what? That has nothing to do with how badly I need to make you come right now."

"I'm sorry your ego is bruised, but I don't need you to do *anything* for me." This time when she pulled her hands away, she broke free. Then she knocked into me with her shoulder, moving towards the kitchen.

"You're really not gonna let me finish this?" I asked my voice starting to slip, the hurt showing. I didn't get the shift. Though that shouldn't be so surprising. It took me over a fucking year to realize she was pissed at me because I didn't mention I owned a cafe that night.

"I'm fine. I can finish myself off."

I turned around to face her, doing my best to control my frustration by grinding my nails into my palm.

"That's not my definition of fine," I gritted out, taking slow steps towards her, mind racing to think of what I could say to convince her. But one look at that stubborn set jaw, I knew there was no hope. Whatever was going on in her head was going to keep her gorgeous, stubborn ass away from an orgasm. That stubborn part of her always managed to stun me, but right now it was my worst enemy. "Fine. I won't force you. But you know what, sweetheart?"

"What?" she scoffed. I leaned in closer, watching her chest still as her breath caught.

"I won't offer next time. You're gonna have to beg." I pulled away, just fast enough to catch a glimmer in her eye that I couldn't read. Then I started walking out. But before I opened the door, I pointed at the packet of papers I'd left on the counter. "Take a look when you've gotten your head out of your stubborn ass."

Then I ducked out, just in time for a paper towel roll to hit the door instead of my head.

6

Raspberry Pistachio Tart

Ashley

I can't believe I was such a fucking idiot to think Mason wanted something real with me. Again.

I should've known he was talking about that stupid marriage idea when he asked about Grant. But all those stupid Hallmark movies and the fact that I was ovulating and feeling extra needy said he was stopping this stupid feud and saying he wanted me. That he was waving the white flag because I was worth more than his pride.

I was so fucking stupid.

"So Ashley," Shea started, pushing her milkshake across the diner table to lean forward. We were at Rosie's place, waiting for the others to get here and one of Rosie's staff to take over for her.

"I passed by the Pub on my way over here."

It was like a game between me and the girls now. A contest of wills to see how long I could play nonchalant versus who could find the right thing to say to make me break into a rant. Shea was the best at getting me to rant. She liked to attribute it to the fact that she knew me first since she was the one who showed me my shop. But really it was just because she ate up the drama in a way that made me feel good sharing it. Not that anyone was judging over my thing with Mason, Shea just had the best reactions.

She'd go fucking insane if I ever told her everything.

But I didn't want anyone to see me for the fanciful romantic fool Mason had turned me into. Twice.

"I don't know what you're talking about," I said, taking a sip of my milkshake. Rosie's place had the best milkshakes in the world. No matter who was working, the consistency was always perfect. And since they started that community garden by the not-church, Rosie's been using fresher fruit. That is when Clive didn't traipse around the garden eating or wrecking everything.

"Mhmm. So it's just a coincidence that buckets of paint seemed to be tossed at his front door and spilled all over the patio area?"

It was only fair. He spilled in me without anything in return.

I won't offer next time. You're gonna have to beg.

Ha. That bastard could never get me to beg for him. Especially after that poor performance. What kind of man couldn't hold out for a minute?

It's been too damn long and you feel too damn good.

Bullshit. He'd gone out with someone a couple of months ago. I haven't been with anyone since.

After I've filled you up, I'll happily get down on my knees for you. I've been dying to see what tastes better, your desserts or you.

He would have talked his way out of that somehow. No guy would actually do that.

"You look like you're thinking about murder," Shea noted scooping up her milkshake and leaning back in the booth.

"What about murder?" Roxie asked, coming up from behind me and sliding into the booth next to Shea. As soon as she settled in her eyes narrowed on my neck, right where I'd covered up the hickey. Roxie raised an eyebrow but didn't say anything as she nodded along to Shea's explanation. Once the paint spill at Mason's was mentioned, Roxie's smile widened.

I pointedly focused on my milkshake.

"What did Mason do to provoke you this time?" Roxie asked, that smile twisting into something more mischievous.

"Is this about the Mayberry place?" Shea asked and I nodded eagerly, glad to have a good excuse for my anger. "Well if it makes you feel any better, I don't think he's gonna get."

"Really?" I asked, doing my best to pretend like this information was new *and* I didn't care. In hindsight, Mason must really need that grant to come close to getting the shop if he was willing to marry me. It was probably his only option and I could use that as leverage.

Not that I was considering it. I tossed that packet he'd brought as soon as he left.

It was a fucking ridiculous idea. Faking a marriage for a business grant, just so Starbucks wouldn't get a foot in town, was beyond stupid.

But *both* Olivia and Zoey had fake-dated a dude. So it wasn't *that* ridiculous.

Fuck, I must finally be a local to even be considering some wild romcom solution.

"So the tour didn't go well then?" Rosie asked, taking up the seat next to me and setting a tray full of food on the table. She started divvying things out, but Roxie smacked her hands away and passed things around.

"It's just too expensive to compete with Starbucks," I said with a shrug and Rosie immediately made a sound of disgust.

"That's a *horrible* company. They union bust and underpay and overwork employees and they partner with suppliers that —"

"Rosie, honey, we've heard your grievances before. They are valid and respected and none of us have gone to Starbucks in years," Roxie assured, reaching over the table to take Rosie's hand.

"How much do you need to get the shop from them?" Rosie asked, head turning to me even as Roxie kept her hands in place.

"It is so far out of my price range, it's not even funny."

"Why don't you go for it? I mean, it'd be tiny for a diner, but the folks in Mayberry sure could use your magic shakes," Shea said and I nodded along. Rosie's diner had been in her family for decades, so surely they'd be in a better place to expand.

"No, that won't be possible." Rosie pulled her hand away from Roxie. Shea sat up straighter before leaning forward to ask more. But Zoey and Olivia came in amid a clamoring discussion.

"I really don't think it's worth all the trouble for one —"

"But we haven't done a big trip in *forever*. And it doesn't have to be just for that one thing either. Stephen has to pack his place up too. So y'all have plenty of time to do whatever other boring tourist thing you want to do."

"What's this about now?" Rosie asked and we all readjusted our seating to make room for the other two.

"Zoey wants us all to go to Seattle next week for some car show."

"Not just for the car show," Zoey said with an exaggerated sigh.

"Ooo, Seattle would be fun," Shea said.

"Yeah, I'm down," Roxie added, taking out her phone. "We could meet up with Bailey and then fly out from Charlotte. What day?"

"I can't believe you all are considering traveling across the country with less than a week's notice?"

"It's not less, it's 12 days' notice. That's practically two weeks."

"Hmm, if we're only gone for a long weekend ..." Rosie started to muse, also pulling out her phone.

"Ashley, please tell me you're not considering this too?" Olivia looked at me, eyes pleading.

"No, I don't think so." It wasn't so much a 'think' as a 'know'. There was no way in hell I could afford that trip at the drop of a hat. The shop barely made ends meet as it is and I didn't have anyone to cover for me. Going on vacation would mean closing the shop.

It was impossible. And it was going to be impossible for a long while unless something changed.

7

Dirty Chai

Mason

It was trivia night at the Pub and I'd been yelled at five times already because instead of reading out the questions, I was staring at Tost-Ka. The cafe had long since closed, but the lights were still on. That usually only happened when Ashley was developing a new recipe, which was her first-of-the-month activity, so something must be up.

"Give me that," Travis said, snatching the trivia cards from my hands. There were cheers from the crowd as Travis took over and I flipped them all off. I loved this town and how we can all give each other shit, but I wasn't in the mood for it tonight.

"Mason, bud," Shea said as she pulled up to the bar with a drink in hand, no doubt spiked. She leaned on the countertop, eyeing me for a bit before looking over her shoulder at Tost-Ka. "What was the last thing you did to Ashley? Cause whatever it is, I think it was a step too far."

"What do you mean?" I asked and Shea's eyes immediately snapped to mine with a 'what the fuck' furrowed brow.

"I'm sorry, did you not notice the huge ass paint splatter all over your entrance?"

I shrugged. What else could I do? I deserved the paint splatter. Fuck, I deserved more. You'd think I'd feel better after having sex for the first time in three years with the woman I'd been obsessed with. But no. I felt like shit. If she had just let me finish her off, everything would have been fine. But no, she wanted to be stubborn.

"She's been acting weird too."

"What do you mean? Is she sick or something?" I could just picture it, that stubborn woman asleep at her desk in the back office. She'd work herself to death before she considered closing the shop for a day.

"God, you do such a shit job at pretending you don't care about her," Shea commented. I took out a pint glass and started making Shea an iced latte with a dash of caramel liquor. She happily accepted the drink and, after a long sip, expanded on what was going on with Ashley. "She's definitely not sick. Just … spacey. We were talking about going to Seattle in a couple of weeks and she was completely checked out of the conversation. I don't think she can take the time off from the shop. So if you could ease up on the pranks and stop interfering with her business, that'd be much appreciated."

"You think she's worried about money?" Not being able to afford a second shop was one thing, but not being able to take a vacation with friends was another. None of her pranks, even the police tape thing from last spring, ever made much of an impact on my profits. I assumed that would hold true for her, but you know what they say about assuming.

"Dude, she barely ever hires a part-timer over the summer to run the register. Yeah, she's worried about money. I mean, I don't think it's bad-bad, but it'd probably make her life a helluva lot easier if you eased up. Maybe not retaliate to the whole paint thing."

"I wasn't planning on it," I mumbled honestly. Shea raised an eyebrow and opened her mouth to question me.

But then somebody opened the front door, glass still covered in splotches of paint, and everybody went quiet.

Ashley walked into my shop with her head held high and the packet of papers tucked under one arm. My heart instantly lodged into my throat in a way that made me think I was gonna kill over. Instead of joining her friends in the back, who hollered for her as soon as she stepped in, she walked right up to me.

"Mason," she said, my name strained on her lips. I found myself searching for signs that these possible money troubles were serious. But I didn't see any sign of weight loss or dark circles. She looked fine. Perfect. And she was staring at me, her chest rising with little huffs that she tried to control by biting her lip. Then those light green eyes blinked up at me and I knew whatever she was gonna ask for, I'd give it to her. Fuck, if she told me to get down on my knees and apologize in front of everyone, I would.

"Can we talk upstairs for a second?"

Shea, who was still sitting *right there* and being ignored by her friend, choked on her drink. Pretty sure some coffee came out of her nose too. I looked away from Ashley just long enough to see Travis hand Shea a glass of water and some tissues. Then I nodded.

The crowd immediately burst into chaos as I rounded the bar, placed a hand on the small of Ashley's back, and walked us up to my place. My apartment was just over the Pub, accessible through some stairs back by the restrooms, out of sight from the main floor. Once we'd rounded that corner, I expected the buzz to die down, but it got even louder.

The town hall was gonna be one hell of a time this week.

Once we were out of sight of everybody, Ashley moved away from my hand and sped up the stairs, letting herself into my apartment with the key under the mat.

"I'm the only one you can do this with," she said as soon as I stepped in and closed the door. "I want an extra ten percent of the profits."

Holy fucking shit she's going to marry me.

"What makes you say that?" I asked, trying not to immediately buckle. If I accepted too fast, Ashley might back out. And then my chances with her, my chances to make up for yesterday's poor performance, would be gone for good.

"The whole town is obsessed with us getting together. Exhibit A, the way everybody freaked out when I came in here. I'm the only person you could marry within a few weeks without raising suspicions."

"Sure. But can't the same be said about you?"

"I don't want the shop as bad as you do."

I leaned back against the door and eyed her. I didn't want this shop all that much, I might be able to stretch things to outbid Starbucks, especially if I made Travis an equal partner or some shit. But at this point, I don't even know why I would want to follow through with this stupid plan beyond the opportunity to have her.

"All right. Forty, sixty split. Can I assume that big stack of papers is your version of a prenup?" I asked, nodding to the packet. Ashley moved to sit on my coffee table and laid out the papers in separate piles.

"This one's the NDA. No one is to find out this was planned for the grant, not even friends or family. At least not with both our consent. Neither of us should be seen with another partner —"

"That won't happen," I damn near growled at her. If this whole thing would be about me getting my chance, I wasn't letting any asshole get in the way. "I can take care of anything you need. No 'partners' allowed."

Ashley narrowed her eyes at me and I could see the snarky remark forming in her head. About how I had a chance to take care of her yesterday and failed. But I'd proven myself three years ago, one slip-up shouldn't overwrite that night.

"That's fine. Like I said before, I'm perfectly capable of taking care of myself. I'll edit the clause about partners," Ashley said after shaking away the nasty remark on the tip of her tongue. Then she leaned over the coffee table, to grab a pen I'd left there, and make her edits. "For living arrangements, I think for most nights when you have to work the next morning, no one will question you staying here. For other days, I'll have my guest-room set up for you. I think we should plan two or three dates in the next couple of weeks and then some sort of public proposal and a courthouse wedding. Afterwards, we'll have to keep up some form of facade with the public. But as far as the grant goes, I believe the business shouldn't need it after three years. After that, we can dissolve it and move on as strictly business partners."

I moved over to the coffee table and picked up one of the stacks. Ashley had a clause for every damn possibility, from our deaths to finding the love of our lives and divorcing early. It was beyond thorough. If there was any loophole, I wasn't smart enough to find it.

Which was fine. I wasn't looking for an out.

But I did make Ashley sit there as I slowly read through and signed all the documents that didn't need a witness. Partly because if she was going to put all this red tape up, then the least she could do was sit through an awkward silence. But also because I wanted to look for tells.

Reading through the contract in front of her got me one very important piece of information. She didn't think I'd accept. Now sure, there were some things that I would have fought her on if I didn't care about her the way I did, like making sure extended family of mine wouldn't try to claim the business if I died during our marriage, but none of it was too ridiculous.

And there was distinctly no clause about sex between the two of us, which was also pretty damn interesting.

"There you go, sweetheart. All signed. 'cept the ones that need a notary." I set everything down in front of her in a nice tidy pile. Ashley straightened, nodding to herself.

"Excellent. We can plan our first —"

"I'll pick you up tomorrow. You usually sell out by noon on the weekends, right? So how 'bout 5:00?" I don't know what surprised her about that, but she pulled back dramatically like I'd just told her I was actually a prince or some shit.

"Um, yeah. 5:00 should work. And as for the ring, I think —"

"I'll take care of it."

"I'd rather you not. You don't know my taste and I'd be much more comfortable buying it for myself."

"Absolutely not, Ashley." I set my hands on the coffee table and leaned over so our faces were level. "There're a couple of things you're gonna have to get used to as my wife, sweetheart."

There was something about how her breath caught when I called her sweetheart that gave me hope.

"What's that?" she asked in a whisper.

"When I say I'll take care of something. I will. There's only so much you can keep me from doing."

Ashley's face burned, the blush creeping over her cheeks to her ears and down her neck. There was a spot the blush noticeably didn't touch and I couldn't help but smirk at the thought of that hickey she'd covered up showing.

"We should make out before you go down. You leaving with your hair all mussed up and lips swollen will really help us sell the story." I leaned forward so my lips could brush her cheek, unable to keep from teasing her. She shoved me back.

Ashley stood, running her hand through her hair, floofing up her bangs, biting at her lip. Then she licked her thumb and swiped away the makeup covering the hickey.

Fuck. I could barely stand seeing that love bite on her. What's it gonna feel like seeing her with my ring on?

"There, happy?" she asked, cocking her head to the side and giving me a sickeningly sweet smile.

"I can think of a way we can both be happier." Her smile immediately dropped and she scooped up the papers, rushing to the door and giving me a hard shove as she passed.

At the door, she paused to take a deep breath, then turned to face me.

"There won't be a repeat of yesterday. Everything from here on will be for show, nothing else."

8

Lemon Truffles

Ashley

The second I rounded the corner from the stairwell into the dining area, I was jumped on. Not literally, but that's what it felt like with the way questions were hurled at me.

"What was that about?"

"Are y'all together now?"

"You didn't murder him up there, did you?"

"Did you already go out on a date or is there still time to get our bets in?"

"Can we get back to trivia already? Seriously." The last comment came from Travis, who was immediately booed. But with all eyes turned on him, my girls took the opportunity to rush me out of the restaurant and across the street into my cafe.

And then I was hit with a completely different barrage of questions.

"Did you just have a quickie in the middle of trivia? Was it good?"

"Are y'all fuck buddies now?"

"Fucking finally. Are y'all gonna quit it with the pranks now? I was kinda waiting for the day you trashed his car and I got to fix it."

"I'm so happy for you, sweetie."

"When did this happen? We were together just last night."

"It was definitely before last night. She had that hickey covered up at the diner. I bet Mason did the whole 'I want them to see that you're mine now' thing and licked it off."

"Ew, concealer is not tasty, believe me. I dated this girl whose make-up routine was the whole nine yards and making out was the absolute *worst*."

"Really? Does it get in the way that much? Should I not wear any?"

"Oh no, you're fine. When I say she had a routine, I mean *a routine*. Like full face and neck coverage."

"I always pictured you with someone more ... low maintenance."

"Well, we didn't work out, so maybe that's why."

"I don't think her makeup was the only reason."

As their conversation got off track, their voices began to blur together. I'd thought a dramatic appearance at Mason's trivia would sell the fake marriage, make it look like we'd been dating on the down low for a while before making things public and then immediately getting married.

I underestimated just how quickly the questions would start pouring in.

"All right, no more sidetracks. Dish," Roxie demanded and all the girls took seats at one of the tables, scooting their chairs in and leaning on their elbows.

Great, I hadn't even signed my line on the papers and I already had to lie to my friends.

The worst part is I could probably tell them. Zoey and Olivia had done their share of fake relationships, Rosie is probably making a mental checklist of how to bring Starbucks down, and Roxie would be all for the possibility of hate sex, even though that wasn't happening again. And Shea would get a kick out of the situation.

But I wrote the secrecy clause in because it made sense. The fewer people we told, the fewer chances there were of this getting out of hand. Plus if I told my friends, then Mason would have the right to tell his. If he had any.

"It's not … *just* a sex thing. But — I don't know. Yesterday Grant came in and —"

"Ew," Zoey interrupted, getting an elbow from Olivia.

"Grant came in and was hitting on me."

"Called it," Shea whispered under her breath.

"And Mason came in to gloat about how I couldn't get the shop or some shit. And he — I don't know, he manned up. He confessed everything was a stupid attempt to get my attention and I … liked that he admitted it first." It was the version of the story I'd almost bought, so I figured they would too. And I was right. The girls swooned, softening into their palms and nearly slumping into the table.

It made me feel distinctly better knowing that line of thinking got to them too.

"So you haven't had your first date then?" Rosie asked and for whatever reason, the others started side-eyeing her. Rosie rolled her eyes and added, "I'm not asking because of that."

The others hummed but I brushed it off. Sometimes there was no understanding their quirks.

"He's taking me someplace tomorrow. And if you guys make a big deal of it, then I won't go. Understand?" I pointed a finger at each of them in turn and Shea dramatically held up her hands while the rest smirked, knowing full well I'd follow through on my threat. Or at least I would have if the lie was true and I didn't have a contractual obligation.

"Okay, does that mean we can go back to trivia? Because we sorta left Denny and Stephen behind," Shea said, pointing a thumb over her shoulder.

"Sure, you guys go. I'm gonna get a few things situated in the office, then I'm going home."

"You sure you don't wanna go over and be bombarded by people asking you about Mason?" Roxie asked.

"Oh hell no. He can deal with all that himself." We exchanged hugs and I promised I'd let them know how the date goes and then they were off.

I took my time closing up the front, doing an extra wipe down before turning off the lights and heading to my office. There, I took a deep breath and signed the papers before faxing Mason his copies.

Within two weeks I'd be married to a man I hated, a man who made me feel like a fool and couldn't even hold it together to make me orgasm. Hurray.

9

Caramel Macchiato

Mason

I was more nervous than a sinner in church stepping up to Ashley's door. I was determined not to stick my foot in my mouth this time or make some dumb come-on. Step one of getting a real chance with Ashley was learning how not to be an idiot around her.

Here's hoping this date will help with that.

Ashley had bought possibly the nicest house in Snowfall. It wasn't overly modern or cookie-cutter like most of the new builds these days. It had character. A large yard, wrap-around screened-in porch. The siding had been painted a robin's egg blue and all the trimmings were a clean white. The front door had that top opening so you could yell outside without risking pets getting out. And unless Ashley had taken it down, there was a tree house in the back. It was the ideal Southern home, especially for a family. There had to be at least three bedrooms.

I know she was some rich city lawyer when she moved down here, but it was weird she bought such a big house for herself.

Though knowing her, if the kitchen had been remolded well, she'd splurge for it.

Just as I was about to knock, the door opened.

And holy fucking shit, my plan to simply *not* say some dumb come-on was already being tested. She wore a sleek little black dress, emphasis on the little. The fabric hugged her every curve and the neckline was too damn low for my brain cells to function. And I sure as hell knew shit about makeup, but I knew effort when I saw it. Her lips were a dark maroon and glossed over. Her eyes were dusted with silver, a small flick of eyeliner at the corner.

"You look stunning," I said, struggling to keep my eyes on her face. I was only a man though and my eyes drifted down to amble cleavage, a golden chain dipping down in a path my tongue ached to follow.

Christ, my dick was screaming at me for fucking up earlier and begging to get back in her good graces.

Meanwhile, Ashley was looking me over with a furrowed brow.

"Thank you. And you look … normal. I guess we're not going someplace nice then, huh?" she asked, clicking her tongue.

"Sorry, I didn't expect you to dress up. There's not much in the way of fancy dress places here." I scratched at the back of my head, feeling more awkward than I had picking up my first date. And her dad was cleaning his shotgun then. "If you're comfortable like that, then —"

"Do we have time for me to change or will that make us late for the reservation?" She was already walking back inside, so I followed behind her.

"Reservation?" I repeated, a little distracted as I looked around her place. The front opened into a large living room, a plush couch taking up most of the space and built-ins full of books and board games and pictures filled up the main wall. The TV set in the built-in was larger than my arm span, but it was the only real modern piece in the room. Everything else was cozy tones, warm.

Then there was the kitchen. And it was fucking *huge*. With a large center island and stools neatly tucked under the counter. And a pot filler over the stove. It was the kind of cottage-farm kitchen you'd see in that Texas show. I was kind of jealous of it. And I wasn't sure if that was because Ashley probably spent most of her time in there or because it was just that nice of a kitchen.

"Great, you couldn't even be bothered to get a reservation," Ashley grumbled as she kicked her heels off and into a closet. She slammed the door, then turned to me. "I'll go change. Just wait here."

"Can't I get a tour?" I immediately got a stink eye. But I pressed on because at least I hadn't put my foot in my mouth by asking to watch her change, which was exactly the kind of torment I wanted. "I mean, I'll be living here some. I should know where all the bathrooms are if we ever need to have people over."

Ashley took in one deep breath before nodding.

"Right. Living room, informal dining, and kitchen." She gestured to the areas in the open space before moving to a doorway around the kitchen. I followed. "Formal dining. Mudroom's that way. Half bath under the stairs." There was more pointing before she rounded the railing to go up the steps. Again I followed. "My room. Your room and another guest room. Full bath. Then two other bedrooms with a Jack and Jill bathroom at the far end."

"Christ. Why'd you buy this house? It's way too big for just you. Don't you get lonely?"

I turned to Ashley, who was standing at her bedroom door, glaring daggers at me.

"I got it because I thought —" She stopped herself, seemingly choking back the words. "It's none of your business. I'll be ready to go in a few minutes."

And then she slipped into her room and slammed the door behind her.

With nothing better to do, I meandered back downstairs to further asses her collection in the living room. Surely one of these books or games had the answer to how to win Ashley over. Or at the very least how to stop angering her. But beyond a few bodice rippers, one of which I pocketed, and a vast collection of competitive games, there wasn't much in the way of telling facts. Even the few photos framed and set on piles of books were all recent. None of her parents or from when she was a kid.

The oldest picture was from her opening day. She stood outside Tost-Ka, hair straightened and trimmed right above her shoulders. Even though the apron she wore had some powder on it, the slick skirt and collard shirt were pristine. Her outfit back then was such a sharp contrast from the pink, lace apron and the large pink bow on her store. But she was smiling a lot brighter than she had been recently.

Which got me thinking. She had this huge ass house and rented a storefront on the main strip of downtown. But she never had more than one part-time employee on staff and they only ever ran the register. She was truly doing it all on her own, from scratch. Without cutting living expenses or even renting out space she didn't need. No matter how much she made as a lawyer, any savings she had would be wearing thin when you put it all together.

I heard Ashley come down the steps and I turned, ready to press her on the house thing. Because this was ridiculous, it was way more house than she needed. Between upkeep and property taxes, this place was going to drain away all her money and —

"Daisies," was what fell out of my mouth instead. Because Ashley was wearing her daisy dress. I'm not sure if it was something she realized she was doing or something anyone else noticed, but if the weather was right and there was something she wanted to look good for or needed a confidence booster for, she'd wear this dress. The daisy dress was her feel-good dress. Her favorite dress, the one she saved for special occasions.

And she wore it for our first date.

Fake date.

"What? Is this *too* casual?" she asked, looking down and holding out the full skirt.

"It's perfect, sweetheart." I stepped up in front of her and slid my hands around her waist.

"What are you —"

"Let's go ahead and get it out of your system." Ashley batted those pretty green eyes at me and I struggled to keep going.

"Give me all your insults now, so you're not tempted to do it when we're out in public."

"Okay." She said the word slowly, shoulders relaxing. "But what about the holding?"

"We need to get used to it. Two birds, one stone. You know?" I don't think there was any getting used to holding Ashley. Every fiber of my being was screaming right now, aware of her every breath.

"Are you sure you're not just ogling my tits?" she asked, one brow raised.

"Three birds, one stone." I shrugged.

"Fine." Her arms wrapped around me, fingers hooking into my belt loops.

"Your shop is a tacky TGIFridays. Your cowboy boots look too clean to be real. It's insulting that you couldn't be bothered to find somewhere nice to take me, let alone get a reservation. I'm worried your truck is going to smell and the smell is going to linger on my clothes. That smirk that you do, yes, *that* one, makes me want to kick you in the balls. And I'd say I feel bad, but if you can't last more than a few seconds, your dick's not even fully functioning anyways."

"Sweetheart, if you need me to make up for that failing, all you have to do is say please."

Ashley's breath halted, a blush creeping down her neck and over her chest. And just as the words of hope were forming in my head, those signals were gone and she pushed me away.

"Let's get this over with."

10

Strawberry Cheesecake

Ashley

When Mason parked outside Rosie's diner, I thought it was a joke. When he got out of the car without saying anything, my theory was further supported. But when he opened my door and held out a hand, I ... well I was fucking confused.

"Here?"

"Yes, here. It's the best first date spot." He said that like it was obvious. Like I was the stupid out-of-towner for not knowing that a diner I go to on a regular basis was a hot spot for dates. "Don't give me that face. People'll think we're arguing."

"Couples argue. It'd be more suspicious if I suddenly stopped yelling at you when you did something stupid," I grumbled, undoing my seat belt and taking his hand to hop out. With his free hand, Mason helped straighten out my skirt, his palm sliding over my ass before giving it a little squeeze.

"You're getting too much out of this," I grumbled, walking away from his hold and dragging him by the hand to the diner door.

"Well, it's never been a secret that I find you attractive." Mason let go of my hand to open the door and once inside, he situated himself at my side, his hand at the small of my back.

"Really? I find that hard to believe," I murmured, trying to keep my voice down as we waited for the hostess to come back from seating the couple ahead of us.

"Hard to believe? What about the way we met or what happened the other day makes it hard to believe I want you?" He leaned over to hiss the words into my ear, making me shiver.

"I don't know. It's just — the first night was a fluke, the other day was just ... you needing to get some." Based on everything that came out of this man's mouth, all the stupid pranks, he wasn't interested in me beyond getting his dick wet. I mean, what sane man would want a woman who'd put out an ad with his cafe's phone number as a free sex line?

I only ran the ad for a day but it turns out some folks in this area really needed someone to talk to.

That might've been how he met the girl he went out with at the beginning of the year. He would be the kind of scum that turned a sex call into a date.

"I've got my work cut out for me," Mason grumbled, but before I could ask what he was talking about, the hostess returned. He turned to her, all charming smiles, hand tensing on my back and said, "First date table, please."

The girl beamed like her smile went from headlights to brights. She even bounced in place some as she guided us back to the other side of the diner from where I normally sat with the girls.

"What's the first date table?" I whispered to Mason.

"Rosie never told you about the first date table?" he said with a brow raised.

We were led to one of the few center tables. Mason let go of me to pull out my chair and I sat down in front of a paper placemat that said 'first date memories' in cursive at the top and had a red lace frame around the edges.

"What is this?" I swear, every time I thought I was understanding all the Southern, small town quirks of Snowfall something else popped out of the woodwork.

"Enjoy," was all the hostess said before skipping off.

"*This*," Mason pointed to the placemat, "Is for us to draw on. We take turns. You draw one thing, I add on to it, then you add something, and so on. It's been a tradition since Rosie's grandparents bought the place. Awkward teenagers would come in for their first dates, not talking. So Ms. Loid would slap a kid's placemat down and tell them to draw and trade. Some folks played along, some folks didn't. Those who did lasted though. So it's sorta a sign that you're takin' the date serious."

As he talked, he pulled the mat towards him and opened up a box of crayons that was set amongst the sugar and condiments. When he turned the paper around, I saw a green field with layers of hills and a trail winding up into the horizon.

"That's really sweet." I picked through the pack of crayons, pulling out bright colors to draw flowers along the trail.

"Sweet enough to get me out of the dog house for not taking you someplace nicer?" My eyes snapped to his, expecting to see that stupid smirk. But instead, he was looking down, fiddling with one of the sugar packets. Something about the nervous tic didn't suit Mason. Or at least the version of him I was used to.

Sliding my hand across the table, I plucked the packet from his fingers and set it aside so I could take his hand.

"I like all the small traditions here. I didn't have anything like that growing up. Not even on Christmas."

"Wait, seriously?" Mason asked, sitting up and pulling my hand closer to him.

"No. My folks weren't really ... family-oriented."

"Not even cringey family pictures in match PJs?"

"Ha! No, I don't think my mother would ever think of doing that. Pajamas that could only be worn once a year? Absolutely not. She didn't do impractical or tacky."

"All right, no family traditions. But what about your hometown?"

"Your small town attitude is showing," I teased, pointing a crayon at him. Then I turned the paper towards him. I expected him to drop my hand to draw, but instead, he picked up a crayon with his left hand and started shakily drawing.

"Surely there was a Christmas tree lighting or something."

"Mmm, maybe at a mall or something. But there wasn't anything town-sponsored. I'm not even sure I ever knew my neighbors before moving here. The suburbs aren't exactly built with community in mind."

"That's some sorta bullshit. The reason suburbs are built the way they are is so no community can really grow. And without community, standing up to oppressors becomes nearly impossible. And what're you smirking at me like that for?"

"Nothings. It's just …" I trailed off, finding it hard to describe how the moment reminded me of Rosie and how many stupid Southern stereotypes in my head had been broken since moving here. When he raised a brow and squeezed my hand to prompt me to continue, I gave him a half-truth. "You act like an idiot so often, it's nice to know there're at least a few working brain cells in there."

"Har har," he grumbled, before setting his crayon down and turning the paper around for me. Mason had drawn a tree on the top of one of the hills. I started on a tree house.

"First date milkshake!" an overly enthusiastic Rosie cheered as she set an extra large milkshake glass with two straws in the center of the table, careful not to get the placemat wet. "Have y'all decided on what ya want?"

"I'll just have my usual, Rosie, thanks." I was concentrating on the tree house, drawing a tire swing underneath it. I'd like to add one to the tree house in my backyard but it seemed like a waste of effort since lord knows how long it'll be until I find somebody to have kids with.

"Oh, sweetie, no. You can't do that," Rosie said in a horrified whisper.

"What? Why not? Are you out of something?"

"No, it's just —"

"You don't order your usual on a date," Ms. Lou huffed, appearing out of nowhere in the booth closest to us. She was accompanied by her usual crew of old ladies who sat in the back of events and gossiped and heckled.

"She's lived here for three years, you'd think she'd know better by now," Ms. Douglas commented, pulling out a yarn ball and crochet needle from her bag. Good lord, they weren't even going to bother pretending they were here to eat.

"Out-of-towners never learn," Ms. Stevenson added, holding up the salt shaker and making a move to stash it in her bag. Rosie cleared her throat and the older woman groaned but set the shaker back on the table.

"It's just another silly tradition, sweetheart. Order whatever you want." Mason squeezed my hand. I read the gesture as a sweet and simple 'ignore them'. But I couldn't. I wished that I could, but it was impossible. Their judgment hit too sharply to ignore.

"No, it's fine. I don't want to break tradition." I liked the traditions in Snowfall, it was quirky and sometimes bothersome, but it made it feel like an actual home. It was the accidental missteps about things I didn't know that I didn't like. It made me feel like an idiot. "I'll get the chicken and waffles then."

"And I'll get biscuits and gravy."

Rosie cooed and my eyes shot up to Mason. That was *my* usual order, unless I was here to talk shit with the girls, then it was chicken tenders and fries. But there was no way Mason should know that. Except ...

"Don't be surprised I've been paying attention, sweetheart."

Giggling, Rosie walked off.

"What else do you know?" I turned the place mat around for him and this time he let go of my hand to draw.

I tried not to think anything of it.

"Hmm, I figure I know a lot more about you than you know about me."

"Oh, really? What makes you say that?" I took a sip of the shake. Strawberry and chocolate. I hadn't ever thought to order this combo of flavors, but this was the perfect, just the right balance. I wondered if this was the first date special or if Rosie made this combo specifically for us.

"All right, what's my favorite color?" He let go of the crayon he'd grabbed and leaned back in his chair.

I had no fucking clue what his favorite color was. But I took a long sip of the milkshake trying to make an educated guess. "Navy."

"Nope. Forrest green."

"Okay, well how would I know that? You don't wear green all that often."

"Yeah, but you don't wear your favorite color all that often either, do you?"

"That's ..." I started. He was right. I didn't wear my favorite color all that often, it sort of washed me out.

"Soft pink. Or maybe you'd call it blush pink or something. All of Tost-Ka's little decor things are that color. And your aprons."

"Lucky guess," I grumbled and was met with that stupid smirk.

"Not a lucky guess, sweetheart. I just pay attention when it comes to you."

"Yeah, so you can get under my skin." The smirk widened and the old ladies next to us chuckled.

"Hmm, I was just biding my time til I could get under you in a different way." Mason picked his crayon back up and I kicked his shin under the table.

"We're in public," I hissed.

"What? It's not like everybody in town hasn't clocked our sexual tension."

"This is a first date, Mason. Don't press your luck."

"Mhmm. Are you gonna tell me you're a three date kinda girl? Cause we both know that ain't true." Another kick under the table, but Mason kept grinning at me.

"Keep that up and you'll never find out."

"Is that a challenge?" His brow raised and I hated how my breath started to come in shallow waves, how a part of me ached for him. But I wasn't going to be a fool again. This was a business deal. And I'd keep it that way.

11

Caramel Latte

Mason

I was getting too close to Ashley's line, I could tell by the way her brow wrinkled like she was considering kicking my ass. It was time to find a safe topic. Something that would keep the little gang beside us entertained and buying that we were falling madly in love.

Good thing at least one of us didn't have to act.

"Your folks haven't been down to visit yet, right? Are they ever planning to —"

"No. They'd sooner admit I only went to Harvard for under-grad than take a trip down South." She leaned over the table and snatched the placemat away. I'd drawn a swing set next to the tree house with one of those two-seater swings where the kids had to push back and forth to get air. I'd always wanted one as a kid, but never had somebody to play with.

73

I didn't miss the way Ashley smiled when she saw it. I knew enough to know she was an only child, we'd covered a lot of ground that one night. So that smile felt like a shared thought. She wanted at least two kids. Which would make that Jack and Jill room make sense.

"How many kids ya want?" The way folks quieted to hear us made the shift of vinyl booths all the louder as they leaned in to hear Ashley's answer.

Ashley eyed me for a moment before shrugging.

"I don't think kids are in the cards for me." The disappointed grumbles were instantaneous. Fuck, even my own heart dropped. But that feeling was quickly drowned out by the brigade of never-satisfied ladies next to us making loud and pointed remarks about Ashley's age and other nastier comments.

Typical Southern protocol would say ignore the old ladies and their ramblings because telling them off wouldn't do much good for anybody. You should just pretend it didn't bother you and move on with your life.

But the way Ashley looked down at the swings and clutched her crayon a little tighter, had me standing up.

"Ladies, do you really think your comments are helpin'? That she'll change her mind about bringing a whole human into existence just to make you happy? How would that be fair to —"

Ashley's hand wrapped around my wrist and I let her pull me around and down to her level. Why the fuck wouldn't I?

"Mason, you're making it worse," she whispered. "If I said I wanted kids, they'd be harassing us throughout this whole charade about when we were finally having kids. It's better this than that."

My girl was always so logical. I don't know how she did it. Though I suppose it was an important skill for a lawyer.

"Fine. Just …" We were so far from this conversation if we were in a real relationship and nowhere within the universe of it with me trying to parent trap her into loving me. But I needed to know. "What's the real answer?"

Ashley pulled back, eyes blinking so fast I wondered if I'd short-circuited her somehow. At least her being a robot would explain the whole logic obsession.

"Why do you care?" she finally asked.

"If you don't tell me, I'll make a bigger scene." I had stooped so low as to find any and all excuses to talk to this woman. Picking a fight with some older ladies seemed almost reasonable given the circumstances.

"Ugh, fine. Three. Now sit down."

Ashley let my hand go and I rounded the table to sit back down. But not before eyeing those little old ladies. They weren't intimidated by me, of course, but at least they knew where I stood.

"Good, now what other questions you shouldn't ask on a first date do you have?" Ashley went back to focusing on the drawing, adding a small garden to the other side.

"Hmm. Is there a list or something I should've looked up beforehand? Cause lists seem to be more your thing." Ashley smiled at that, the tiniest, briefest of smiles that had my heart doing all sorts of flips.

"How about your family? I assume they retired down to Florida or something since nobody talks about them. Like they're shunned for leaving town. That seems like something some folks around here would do."

I'm sure Ashley expected some sort of grumbles from our peanut gallery, but this was one thing they wouldn't gossip about.

"Nah, they passed away my sophomore year of high school." One of the more refreshing things about my relationship with Ashley, particularly that first night, was that she didn't tiptoe around anything related to parents. Most folks in town avoided mentioning their parents around me. They could have the shitiest folks ever and they still wouldn't say a word, because at least they were alive. It was frustrating hearing folks backpedal what they wanna say. And it didn't help anyways.

I thought of them damn near every day. And folks feeling like they couldn't talk about their families made me feel like a shit friend.

"Definitely not a first date kind of discussion. That's the sorta baggage you discuss cuddling in bed with a glass of wine."

"Is that how you picture this night ending?" God, that'd be a perfect ending to this date. I'm sure I'd have a hard-on the whole time, but just laying in bed with Ashley sounded like a dream. Even if it was to discuss my dead parents.

"No," she answered, rolling her eyes. She passed the placemat back to me, eyeing me carefully as I started to draw a dog house. "Does their death have something to do with the Pub not being a pub?"

"Nail on the head," I mumbled, not looking up from my drawing. I wasn't sure what sort of dog to draw. Definitely the kind of dog that'd be a kid's best friend and big enough to scare off Clive if he tries to get into the garden.

"Do you wanna expand on that? Or should I keep guessing?"

"Well, you are a lawyer. I'm sure you could figure it out on your own."

"I could," she said, voice confident. I looked back up, expecting to see a challenge sparkling in her eyes. But that look was missing. In its place was a softness I wasn't used to seeing from her. "I'd like to hear it from you though. Unless you're not ready to share —"

"I'm not." I pushed the placemat to Ashley's side, hoping it would pull her attention away from me. It didn't. She stared at me for a long while, only looking away to thank Rosie when she dropped our food off.

I kept my mouth shut by taking a sip of the milkshake. Should have known it'd be chocolate and strawberry.

I knew I should just tell her. It's not like the venue mattered, everyone here knew and as my wife, they'd expect her to know too. But I liked our dynamic and I didn't want it to change just yet. We'll be married for three years, there'll be plenty of time to fill her in later.

"All right, I can wait. No skin off my bone if you don't want me to see you cry on a first date." There's my girl.

"Careful, Ashley. You keep being nice like that, I might think you actually like me."

Ashley snorted and, with a quick look at the table next to us, added, "Well you got me on this date somehow."

Stupid happenstance was what got me this date. It's what was gonna get me her hand in marriage.

I just needed to find a way to make the most of it.

12

Blueberry Chocolate Tart

Ashley

Well, the dumbass had a tragic backstory and an endearing protective streak. It was enough to make a girl swoon.

And if I didn't know it was all for show, I'd probably be swooning too. I mean, damn near everybody in this town let those ladies say whatever they wanted. Even if they were downright mean. But Mason wasn't having any of that shit.

It was stupid that such a simple gesture hit me so hard. He just squashed a little gossip. Any man could do that. Just because no man had done it for me yet, didn't mean anything.

"You've been pouting since we left the diner. Wanna tell me what that's about?" Mason asked once he'd parked in front of my house.

"I'm not pouting," I grumbled. And I *wasn't*. It was just upsetting being treated the way I wanted by the man I didn't want. *Couldn't* want, *didn't* want to want. Whatever. It was a stupid situation I'd gotten myself in all for a little extra money so I didn't have to seriously think about closing shop.

"Yeah, all right. You're not pouting. Look, I know we've made some sort of silent pact to not air out what's happened between us, but for this to work, you're gonna have to tell me what's on your mind at least some of the time."

There was a running list of what was on my mind relating to Mason. None of which I was keen to share. It either involved wanting to hate fuck him, which was a craving he didn't deserve for a plethora of reasons including his poor performance last time but an effect the date had on me nonetheless. Or how badly I wanted to throw him off a cliff for all the ways he irritated me with his teasing.

"The date went well. I think we put on a good show," was what I settled on. Mason turned to face me, a brow raised.

"I think it went good too," he eventually said, though he didn't stop his examination. "I wanna take you out tomorrow night, 4:30. We'll be out a little past your bedtime, that all right?"

"So now you care about my sleep schedule?" I countered. Mason just smirked. When it became apparent he wasn't going to apologize for the mariachi incident, I finally said, "Yeah, sure, that's fine. Just let me know what we're doing this time. I hate looking like an idiot in front of people."

"Idiot? Ashley, I don't think you could tone down your whole smartest person in the room vibe if you tried."

"I didn't know about a tradition at a diner I've been frequent-ing for *three years* now. A diner my *friend* owns. That's pretty idiotic."

When Mason didn't respond with some snarky comment, I chanced a glance at him. He was examining me. A different way this time, like his brain was actually working something out instead of just taking in the obvious.

I didn't trust that look.

"Just tell me what I need to wear."

For a second, I thought he was going to keep staring at me until I gave up and left. But eventually, he shook his head and got out of the car. I was stunned. Was he really not going to tell me something as simple as what to wear? Did he not realize how this whole charade would work best if we weren't on the same page? No one was going to believe we were a couple if I was constantly making a fool of myself because I had no clue what was going on.

Then my door was opened. Mason leaned in, unbuckled my seat belt, then gripped me by the thighs to move me around. He tugged my legs out of the car and stepped between them, one arm braced on the roof of the car as he leaned in.

"One, imma kiss you at the door because this's been a good date and I need the folks peeping from their blinds to know it. That all right?"

"Fine." I tried to grumble the word, but it came out soft. Having him stand between my legs like this was gutting my air supply, making my brain think stupid things like how excited I was to kiss him again.

"Good. There's gonna be a lot of kissing in our future, so think of a way to tell me off without being too obvious so I don't have to sneak you away to ask every time. As for me, you can kiss me whenever you want. Two, you'll need to wear something comfortable, something you can sit in. Maybe do your hair in that cute little braid crown or whatever it's called. We probably won't have to talk to many folks, but they'll be watching us. And expect a lot of cuddling."

"Cuddling?" I repeated but as soon as the word was out of my mouth, Mason took my hand and pulled me out of the car. Mason's arm curled around my waist, keeping me from landing too hard, and guided me up my porch steps. At the door, he spun me around and my heart was in my throat.

"I'll see you tomorrow, sweetheart." He squeezed my hand and pressed a soft kiss to my cheek. Then he pulled away.

"Wait, what?"

Mason turned back to me, that insufferable grin on his face. "I said I'll see you tomorrow, sweetheart. I don't know what sorta city folk you're used to, but that's all you're getting from me on a first date. Though if you said please, I might be convinced."

My cheeks burned with embarrassment. I expected more and he knew it.

Well, fuck him. If he wanted to toy with me, fine. I can toy with him right back.

And he did just say I had permission to kiss him whenever it suited me.

I grabbed the collar of his shirt and pulled him to me. His legs fumbled forward, knocking my ass into the door as I brought our lips together. He tasted like our milkshake, the flavor combo warm on his lips, more … just more. My hands moved up his neck and into his hair, pulling to angle him where I wanted. When I licked into his mouth, Mason groaned like a man getting a taste of food after being starved.

And then his brain caught up and his hands were on my hips, grabbing and pulling me closer. One hand went into my hair while his other arm wrapped around my waist, keeping me pressed against a certain hardening appendage.

"Just say please, sweetheart. Sarcastically if you want, just say the word so I can get a taste of that sweet pussy. Please," he murmured into my mouth, not bothering to pull away to speak. Which meant he was desperate. Just like I wanted him.

"No, thank you," I whispered against his lips before moving my hands to his shoulders and pushing him away. Mason stumbled back, eyes dazed and confused. "I won't beg for an unguaranteed orgasm. I'll see you tomorrow though, unfortunately. Have a good night, Mason."

And before he had the chance to reply, I ran inside, slamming the door in his face.

13

London Fog

Mason

I needed to make a bingo card for this fake marriage thing. The middle square would be blue balls. It damn near killed me walking away last night. All I wanted to do was break down her door, pin her down, and demand a straightforward reason as to why she wouldn't let us be real.

Too bad I tried that approach before and it didn't work out. After never hearing back from gift basket and her avoiding me at every turn, I cornered her after a town hall. Cornered her is a hard way of putting it, but there were folks around and she couldn't outright bolt away so she was as good as cornered. As soon as I tried to say something about our night, she picked a fight and completely changed the subject. She wouldn't let me get a word in edge-wise and baited me into an argument then somehow managed to get me to step in a puddle on our way out.

No, direct talk just led to confrontation. I needed to take this in baby steps.

Expect the baby step I was about to take was proposing.

It was probably an old-fashioned idea, keeping the proposal details a secret. And Ashley clearly wasn't a fan of surprises. But if this was the only chance I'd ever get to propose to her, I wanted to do it right. Or at least my kind of right.

However, in order to do right by any standards, I had to tear my eyes off of Ashley's thighs glistening on the leather of my passenger seat. She'd taken something comfortable to sit in as super short shorts. And a breezy, bubbly off-the-shoulder top. Sure it was June and hotter than all get-up, but I was too damn horny for that kind of outfit. My tongue was too heavy, my brain wasn't functioning, and breathing was difficult. How was any man supposed to get through a proposal with his girl lookin' like that?

And she did her hair like I suggested.

"The drive-in?" Ashley's voice pitched up in excitement as I turned the truck into the line. She even scooted forward in her seat. That had me sitting up straighter.

"You ever been?"

"No. Me and the girls have talked about it, but there always seems to be something else going on. What's playing?"

Dear lord, please let this be something she'll like.

"Pride and Prejudice."

"The '05 one?" she asked, turning in her seat to face me, hands landing with a loud thunk on the console between us.

"I — it's the first one I think. I didn't know it was a series, but there weren't any numbers by the title when I'd bought the ticket." It'd be just my luck to pick a movie she liked but some-how pick one in the middle of a series. Suppose that'd be suitable punishment for enjoying last night's kiss more than I should have. And what I did in the shower afterward. And right when I woke up because haunting my every waking moment wasn't enough for Ashley, she teased me in my dreams too.

"I meant 2005," Ashley said, giggling at me. "BBC made a series in '95 that followed the book more closely, but in '05 they made a movie. It cut out a lot of stuff, but it's just so ... it's ro-mantic." She sighed, moving around in her seat like she couldn't keep still. Then sighed again, "This is a nice date. Good job."

"I'm sorry, what did you just say?" It was stunning to hear the words 'good job' from her lips, and even more stunning was her look of wistfulness.

"Oh shut up and pay attention to the line," she said with a roll of her eyes and a smile she was trying to fight.

For once, I listened to her.

The quiet set in quickly though and past experience said quiet was bad. I'd have to chance saying something stupid just to keep the silence from causing some other sort of trouble.

"So you've seen this movie before?" I asked once we'd passed the ticket line. I'd ordered our tickets online *and* printed them out, so I didn't even need to roll down the window for the kid at the booth.

"Wait, have you not?" she gasped, hand slapping down on my arm. "Mason, this is the most romantic movie."

"I thought the most romantic movie was You've Got Mail," I said through Ashley shaking my arm. I remember watching the movie with my family way back when and Mom absolutely balling. Dad pulled her in real close and mouthed over her head that I'd get it one day.

"Mason." She said my name like I was in trouble for not paying attention in class. "They reference Pride and Prejudice in that movie. It's like allegorious."

"Mhmm. I don't think I know what that word is," I mumbled. Driving through the lot was always a pain in the ass, so I couldn't really concentrate on understanding Ashley and her answering rambles. I needed to find the perfect spot to park so we'd have a good view of the screen and everybody else had a good view of us. All while kids and teenagers were running about all willie-nillie and the older folks stood right in the middle of the road chatting.

When I finally found the right spot, I started backing into it and nearly crashed when Ashley smacked my arm.

"What're you doing? The screens that way." She kept smacking me as I put an arm around her headrest and looked back. The smacking stopped, but I didn't chance looking away to see if it was because I'd gotten closer to her or if she just didn't want to risk fooling around when I might hit someone.

"I'm aware which way the screen is, sweetheart," I said once I'd parked. "We're gonna be sitting in the back."

"The back?" she repeated.

"Stay there," was all I offered as an answer. I'd spent a good few hours gathering up shit and making my truck bed look like some Pinterest scene. I wanted to get it set up and perfect before she saw it.

I hopped out of the truck and folded back the bed's cover. I'd lined the bed with couch cushions and pillows and blankets.

Damn near every soft thing in my house. Then I'd gathered all the movie snacks I could think of into a basket for her picking. It didn't feel like much looking at it now, but hopefully, the effort counted for something.

When I got everything fluffed up, I moved to Ashley's door and opened it to a narrowed set of eyes and crossed arms.

"What was that for?"

"I was getting something ready for you." I tried not to sigh, but I was trying so hard at a million other things, I failed at that one.

"Oh sorry I made this so difficult for you. You know I don't like surprises. For all I know you rigged up something so I'd spill soda all over my shirt or some other embarrassing shit. Or get toilet paper stuck to my shoe. Or maybe you just —" I'd taken Ashley's hand while she rambled on and helped her out of the car. Once we'd rounded the bed, she stopped her rant and put a hand over her mouth.

Like usual, her silence rattled me into speaking more than I should have.

"I know it's not super fancy, I had to make do with what I had lying around the place. But it should be a good deal more comfortable than sitting in the truck. We can spread our legs out, get cozy, you know. I brought some snacks and shit, but I'll get you something from the concession stand if ya want. Then I got some water and cola in the back seat."

Just shut me up already, Ashley, please.

"Oh my god, Mason, shut up. This is adorable." Ashley grabbed at my arm, pulling me down for the softest kiss I'd ever felt. Then she was scrambling into the bed of my truck, making herself comfortable and sorting through my snacks like she didn't just send my heart into a tizzy.

* * *

I'd done just enough research into the movie to know when I needed to drop down to one knee. Some line about one word would silence the dude forever and something about bewitching.

I was struggling to remember the line and keep a lookout for it when watching Ashley was so much more amusing. She mouthed damn near every line. She squealed when the couple barely touched hands. And she sighed and groaned like the world relied on these rich men pulling their shit together.

Ashley was always so stoic, or at least the only emotions I ever got to see were anger or horniness. But she let herself go free watching this movie. And in the few down moments when she wasn't raging at this dude named Wickham, she cuddled into me. Her head fit so damn well on my shoulder, her warmth and weight calming all that buzzing going on in my head.

"Oh this is the best part," she whispered as the music began to swell and Darcy appeared in the sunrise.

Now or never.

I twisted around in the blanket, my feet tangling as I tumbled into a proposal position. Ashley looked at me like I was insane until I pulled out the ring box from my back pocket and then her eyes looked like they were about to pop out of her head.

"I know we haven't been exactly *friendly* since you moved here. But you and I, and the whole town, know it was just a front. I was smitten since the moment I laid eyes on you. And after that first little spat? I was a goner. It might've taken me this long to stop putting my foot in my mouth and get you out on a proper date, but I'm not wasting any more time. We might still fight, get on each other's nerves, and I most certainly will slip up and say some dumb shit from time to time, but no fight is ever gonna overshadow how much I need you."

My heart was hammering in my ears, I wasn't certain I was breathing right, and I was scared as all getup. While folks hadn't been too rowdy during the movie, it was extra quiet now. I could feel all eyes on us, could even see camera flashes out of the corner of my eye.

But I was focused on Ashley. I meant every damn word I just said and I needed to see if any of it struck. I decided sometime this morning that I wasn't going to remind her of the plan or the cafe or Starbucks or any of the other bullshit I was using for an excuse to get to her. Because if she said yes without any of those reminders, if she said yes after me bearing a portion of the truth, then there was a chance this scheme would work out the way I wanted it to.

"Ashley Bowen, will you do me the greatest honor of allowing me to be your husband? Will you marry me?" I opened up the box to present her with my mother's ring. It was a golden band with twisted strands on the sides and a pale green gem in the center, tiny diamonds at each side of the oval. It kinda matched Ashley's eyes.

"Yes," she whispered, hands clutched together over her heart, tears in her eyes. "Yes, Mason Foster, I'll marry you."

The crowd I'd been doing my best to ignore erupted into a series of hoots and hollers and applause. Meanwhile, I fumbled getting the ring out and onto Ashley. It did something funny to my heart seeing it sit so nicely on her finger.

"I really need to kiss you now, sweetheart." I'm not sure I'd be able to breathe again until she kissed me.

"Please," she whispered.

Everything after that was in slow motion. The way we kissed. The way our lips grazed softly, without the usual hunger and need to get as much as I could get. The way we held each other, foreheads pressed together as Darcy's speech finished on the screen behind me.

My thoughts were slow too. Mostly just a cycle of I got the girl I've been dreaming of and drooling over for three years and how I might fuck this up because I didn't do this the right way.

And then everything stopped being slow as our bubble burst and folks started leaning over the truck bed to shake my hand and say their congratulations. People took pictures, had us pose, and had Ashley flash her ring. Several girls nudged their man, pointing at the setup I made.

I loved my community. I loved the way folks were excited to celebrate something on my behalf. I loved how they asked Ashley questions and showered her with compliments. How some fellas shared their engagement stories and how they'd been as nervous as I was.

But about 30 minutes after the credits finished, I was ready to go home and collapse into bed. Honestly, I might not make it to the bed. I might just faceplant on the uncushioned couch.

"I'm sorry to cut this short, but we really do need to get going. Otherwise, you all will be out of two cafes for Monday morning," Ashley said, one arm wrapped around my waist and her hand resting on my chest.

"Oh, we wouldn't want that!" someone in the crowd chuckled before a chorus of good nights and well wishes sounded off.

I guided Ashley back in the car and made quick work of packing up the bed and getting the cover on. Then off we went, a silent car ride all the way to her house, evaporating every last warm bubbly feeling I had from a seemingly successful proposal.

"I know we said three dates and you're not big on surprises, but I just thought —" I started when I parked in front of her house but stopped when she held up a hand.

"It was a good move. I just ..." she trailed off, staring at her hand in her lap, at the ring. "Um, you should probably stay the night. If you wanna go home and grab stuff, I'll have the guest room ready for you."

She moved to open the door, but I grabbed her arm.

"I'm fine doing a walk of shame tomorrow morning. But you gotta let me open the door for you," I said. Ashley rolled her eyes, but the motion was weak and she didn't make a move to fight me. No fighting should be a good thing, but between that and the silent walk into her house, I was on edge waiting for the other shoe to drop.

14

Raspberry Lemon White Chocolate Domes

Ashley

As soon as Mason shut himself in the guest room, I crashed into my own bed and cried.

That fucker really had some goddamn gall proposing like that. During the best part of my favorite movie, saying all the right things. Even the way his leg got caught up in the blankets was endearing.

I'd never have a real moment like that and the thought burned.

Instead of getting ready for bed like I should have, I turned my phone off its automatic bedtime mode and was blasted by texts.

The first new message was a link to some Instagram video of my proposal. Mason looked so nervous, his hands fiddling with the box, foot tapping under the blankets. And I looked like I was eating it all up like I was so totally in love with the man on his knees for me. And based on the views, other people were buying it too. It couldn't have been more than an hour since the proposal and there were already over a million likes and way more views than I could fathom. The comments were equally insane, women fawning over everything Mason had done and his sweet Southern draw, men grumbling about how Mason was whipped or making them look bad.

Shea: Congrats on being an internet sensation

Shea: AND YOUR ENGAGEMENT

Rosie: Oh my goodness, that has to be the sweetest proposal I've ever seen

Rosie: Oh I just noticed the bedding in the truck too

Rosie: And during your favorite movie 🩶

Roxie: Keep it in your pants, Rosie, he's taken

Roxie: But congratulations! I knew the hate sex was gonna be good, but I didn't think it'd be *that* good

Bailey: Excuse me while I watch this video a million times, your reaction is just so sweet, y'all really love each other 🖤 congratulations 👣 👣 👣

Zoey: I thought y'all were exaggerating

Zoey: But that's really fucking cute, I like how Mason got all caught up in the sheets

Olivia: Ahhhh! I'm so excited for you!!! When can we start wedding planning? Ashley, don't you dare consider making your own cake for practicality's sake

Zoey: Oh my god she'd totally do that

Zoey: But don't, we'll make the cake for you if you wanna be that budget friendly

Olivia: Oh, not me though, I'm horrible at baking

Roxie: Seriously? It's just following instructions

Olivia: I know but I get all worried I miscounted or I haven't mixed it long enough, I always end up screwing something up

Olivia: I know but I get all worried I miscounted or I haven't mixed it long enough, I end up screwing something up

Rosie: Have you called your family yet? I know things have been tense since your move, but maybe this will bring y'all back together

Shea: Rosie, I love you, but not all family rifts can heal

Rosie: I'm sorry, sweetie, I know

Olivia: We should get together tomorrow and start planning

Shea: Or better yet, grab a drink to celebrate!

Bailey: Aw fuck, I wish I could come, but next week we're going up for Margo's graduation

Shea: Shit, I forgot that was next week, what am I gonna do without my surrogate family?

Bailey: You're still more than welcome to join

Rosie: Send Margo our love!

Olivia: God I can't believe she's getting her Masters, makes me feel old

I cursed myself for adding the clause to not tell our friends about this whole arrangement. All I wanted to do right now was rage about how it was all a sham. Those pretty words, the fumbling, all of it.

But the desire to shout that didn't outweigh my unwilling-ness to bend the contract. I'd just have to put on a good front with my friends for a couple of years and then I could tell them the whole thing. Given how they reacted to Olivia's past fake dating, I doubt they'd be hurt. We'd get drinks and laugh about my divorce to the most ridiculous man on the planet. It'd be a big joke, one they'd tease me over for years to come.

So with that in mind, I opened up the chat to tell them some generic thing about being busy and I'd talk to them tomorrow. But my screen wasn't on our chat. It was on an incoming call. From my mother. And the last time she had called was … I had fucking no clue.

"Hello, Ashley Bowen speaking," I said once I swiped to answer. Mom always gave me shit if I answered a call without saying my name, even if it was someone whose number I had saved.

"Well, it won't be Bowen for long now, will it?" she asked, voice clipped.

"Pardon?" I was shell-shocked. Was my mother actually calling about my personal life? And how could she have possibly heard about the engagement? She wasn't exactly the type to scroll through Instagram, or even Facebook, in her downtime. That sort of drabble was beneath her.

"Your Aunt Denise saw some Facebook post or some similar nonsense and called to ask about your engagement. I told her that was impossible as you were focused on your bakery. But she forwarded me the video and lo and behold, there was my daughter crying over some hillbilly drivel."

"Mother," I groaned, trying to swallow down the instinct to berate her for calling Mason a hillbilly. It wasn't a hard pill to swallow given how I knew she looked down on those sorts of public displays of emotion. She wasn't so much worried about my association with Mason as about the fact that I cried in public. It did matter that, at least for appearances, it was happy tears. What mattered was that my behavior and random viral video embarrassed her.

I wondered what she was more embarrassed by, not knowing about my relationship status or being proven wrong.

"So, are you really marrying this man? Out of nowhere?"

"Yes, Mom. I am marrying Mason, he's ..." I wish the things he'd said while proposing didn't strike true at all. But if he could admit he was a dumbass, I could admit, at least to myself, that I always wanted something to work out there. Because when push comes to shove, as many pranks and fights as we had, Mason was ...

"He's extremely caring. For me, for this community. There was one time he kept his place open all night because some kids got kicked out by their parents. And another time he —"

"Ashley, I really don't care to hear a list of reasons why you fell in love with this man. You're a grown woman and you've already proven you're going to do whatever you want despite my advice. I simply wanted to ensure you were committed to this man before planning a trip down there."

"Trip?" I repeated. In the three years I've lived here, she hasn't expressed any interest or intent to visit once. Not for Tost-Ka's opening, not to see my new house, not for Christmas, not for anything. And now she was going to visit me because she thought I was getting married?

No, that wasn't it. She was going to visit me because I'd gotten some mild internet fame over my fake proposal and she looked bad not knowing about it. It was all about saving face.

"Of course. I assume you could accommodate us and pick us up from the airport? We'll fly into Charlotte the Friday after next and stay until Tuesday. I don't want to miss out on too much work."

I didn't bother reminding her that I lived a good two hours from Charlotte or that I would have to close my shop and lose out on some much-needed profit in order to pick her up. I just accepted it.

"I'll make that work. Yes, you can stay with us. I've got the guest room all setup."

"Good. I'll send you our flight details shortly. Good night." And then the phone went dead. No love yous or congratulations. No offers to speak to Dad or follow-up questions about my relationship or how my business was going.

I guess I should appreciate that there weren't any parting jabs about me wasting my education.

There was no sense waiting until morning to tell Mason. Might as well get it over with now.

Ugh, we'd have to share a room with my parents here. At least I had the time to look into getting a trundle bed or something. There was no way I was letting that man sleep in my bed.

I knocked on Mason's door. No response. I knocked a little louder and still nothing. I went so far as to press my ear to the door and all I could hear was the sound of the ceiling fan.

"Mason?" I called, opening the door just a crack, waiting to be yelled at or see something that would make me want to slam the door shut.

But instead, all I saw was Mason's feet, still in his boots, dangling over the bed. He'd collapsed, face first, and was already snoring.

I suppose it was good to know now that his snoring wasn't too terrible. And he really did have such a nice ass. If he could be quiet and not try anything, I could grow to enjoy having him around the house.

Except if I was going to have him around, I might as well make sure he doesn't catch a cold sleeping like that.

So I went through the miserable work of undressing him. I don't know if it was the angle I was pulling or if the boots were just *that* stupid, but it took a solid three minutes to tug his shoes off. His pants, poetically, came off easily once I'd rolled him over to undo his belt. As I was pulling them down his legs, he started squirming, knocking me off balance and sending me face-first towards his dick.

I managed to save myself the embarrassment of face-planting onto his cock, by bracing my forearms on either side of his hips. What I didn't save myself from was the smell. He didn't smell bad, because of course, he didn't. He smelled mouth-watering. It made me want to slam my fist onto his dick as punishment for being so tempting.

Pushing away, I yanked his jeans off and tossed them away. As I pushed and pulled his body around to get him under the covers, I couldn't help thinking what he'd say if he woke up. If I told him what his smell did to me, if he'd take care of me this time. If he'd actually eat me out after filling me with his come.

What he would say if I told him about my parents coming and about how my mom made me feel.

No, I knew what he'd do. He'd turn things into sex either way and I'd feel stupid letting him use me like that.

So with my fake fiancee all tucked in, I went off to be alone and empty inside.

15

Caramel Cold Brew

Mason

"You're actually marrying her?" Travis asked for possibly the fifteenth time today. And he wasn't the only one asking. Every single person I'd rung up today asked the same question or some form of it. There was a pretty clear divide in the responses too. Women were swooning over my proposal like I'd done the most romantic thing ever. They tripped over themselves to ask when I'd fallen in love with Ashley, how I knew she was the one, and what they had to do to get their man to act like me.

Men on the other hand were in total disbelief that I'd willingly tie myself to someone who, in their words, tormented me on a regular basis. They didn't understand why I wanted someone with a stick up their ass that couldn't take a joke.

Thankfully those sorts of men ran off when you made it clear you weren't going to laugh at their bullshit.

Unfortunately, Travis didn't fall in line with those men and wasn't so easily warned off.

"She once covered our patio with police tape and you're going to *marry* her? Why? Because you somehow got her to go out on one date?" he asked as I was trying to clear off one of the tables.

"Yes," I answered, slamming a washcloth down. "She gave me a chance and I'll take as much as I can get. If you have a problem with that, take a number."

Travis simply crossed his arms and leaned against the bar, an eyebrow raised. It was the look I'd seen him give Jayson the few times he'd brought the kid into the Pub. And while Jayson was never bothered by it, it was getting under my skin.

"Folks have been on our ass about getting together, have a goddamn betting board in the church, and now I'm getting shit for wanting what everyone knew I wanted in the first place. And their saying rude ass shit about my fiancee too."

Travis sighed and pushed off the bar.

"*That's* not my point. I mean, I sure as hell don't understand it given how much of a pain in the ass it's been to clean up after you two's messes. But my point is you're going too quick. You went from being at each other's throats one day to getting hitched the next. One of you is gonna regret it in a few months, a few years. And it's gonna make both of you feel like shit."

Travis didn't talk much about his wife who passed a few years ago, but I knew enough to know they got married young. And that things weren't going well before her accident.

I couldn't begrudge his advice knowing that.

"I'll make sure she doesn't regret it," I mumbled, picking the washrag back up to finish cleaning. We were just out of the morning rush, so thankfully there wouldn't be much in the way of eavesdroppers until office workers got out for the day. We could talk freely. Or at least as freely as Ashley's NDA would allow.

Not like I planned on telling anyone this whole thing was a charade, it'd be real soon enough anyway.

"What about you though?" Travis asked, following me around the bar.

"What about me?"

"What if you guys settle in and it's not what you thought it'd be? What if you realize you liked just one part of her and the rest you're indifferent to?"

Once I'd gotten things worked out with Ashley, I was gonna find Travis somebody to make him happy. Nobody deserved to be miserable the way Travis made himself.

"That's not gonna happen. I know everything I need to know to love Ashley. I appreciate the concern though." I clapped his shoulder and moved around him, but Travis moved back in my way.

"What's her middle name? Shoe size? Where's her family from?" Travis pressed.

"Grace. Seven. And Watertown, New York. That satisfy ya?" I asked, cocking an eyebrow at him. My patience knowing he meant well was gonna wear thin soon. And truthfully, most of that shit I learned from the night I met Ashley. Not her shoe size though, I was guessing on that part.

But just as Travis was about to open his mouth and really test my patience, the front door clambered open.

Ms. Taylor barged into my restaurant the same way she barged into every place, like she owned the town. Which she most certainly didn't, she wasn't and never has been the mayor or held any sort of official position, and I'm almost certain she didn't own any land or buildings. But she might as well own Snowfall with how she ran the festivals and town halls, the two things that really made Snowfall Snowfall.

But damn could she be obnoxious.

"Mr. Foster, do you have an update for the bid?" she asked, walking up to my bar with her arms crossed.

"I don't see why I need to report anything when you probably got word as soon as we stepped into the diner." It was a delicate balance with Ms. Taylor. If I didn't put up a fight, I'd be her doormat for the week. And if I made life too difficult for her, I'd be nixed from the next festival and miss out on a good chunk of profit. And I needed to be in her good graces so our out-of-town shop didn't catch any shit.

"Then I'm asking for confirmation. And if anyone knew the date beforehand." Her feathers were ruffled over something. Ms. Taylor wasn't one to get straight to it. So that must mean …

"Who won?"

16

Strawberry Glaze Pie

Ashley

"I don't understand why I have to be here for this," I grumbled as the girls pushed me into the church-turned community center. For some unknown reason, Ms. Taylor had called an emergency town hall and my attendance was demanded.

Surely this didn't have anything to do with Mason and I getting together. Fakely. I mean, I got so many damn questions throughout the day, you'd think everybody knew enough to make this meeting pointless.

"Ashley, we have a confession to make," Olivia said, her voice pitching up like it always did when she was anxious. Which was fairly often.

"Don't say it like that. And wait until we're seated," Zoey said, pushing us forward from behind.

"Oh my god, it can't be that important, why do we have to rush to the front."

"Because we're gonna need front-row seats for this one," Shea said, looping her arm around mine and propelling us into the first row of pews.

If they were going to convert this place into a community space, you'd think they'd put a little money into better seats.

"Just tell her now," Dennis, Olivia's man, grumbled as we all shuffled into the pew. Stephen, Zoey's man, took the end, then her and Olivia and Dennis, then Shea, then me.

"Wait, are Rosie and Roxie not coming? Because if they're not here, I shouldn't have to be."

"There you are, sweetheart." I don't know why Mason's Southern drawl stood out more than anyone else's, but it did. His voice made my hair stand on end and I wished I could tell myself that it was only because I was nervous to act as a couple in front of so many people.

"Hey, Mason," I whispered. Not intentionally, that's just how it came out. He sat next to me, an arm wrapping around my neck as he pressed a kiss to my forehead. "So do you know what this is all about?"

"Shit," he hissed, pulling back to look at my friends. "Y'all haven't told her yet?"

Dennis and Stephen shook their heads, pulling back against the seat, clearly not wanting a part of whatever this conversation was turning into.

"Tell me what?" I asked, turning back and forth to look at Mason and the girls.

"Well, after the first time you went to the town hall ..." Olivia started.

"And picked a nasty ass fight with Mason," Zoey chimed in.

"Completely unprompted too. We all felt bad for ya, buddy," Shea added.

"Some folks in town made a betting pool on when you two would go on a date," Olivia finished.

"Excuse me?" I shouted. "You all knew about this and didn't tell me? Has it been going on since then? Did you bet?"

"I wasn't allowed to," Mason snarked and I elbowed him in the stomach, not taking my eyes off my so-called friends.

"We all made bets before we got to know you," Olivia explained.

"My bet was never," Shea said, "Just based on showing ya the space, I got the feeling you were headstrong. Though not too headstrong for this cowboy apparently."

She leaned across me to give Mason a fist bump, which he didn't return. Instead, his eyes locked on Dennis.

"Did you tell them about the lasso thing?" he questioned and I nudged him to quiet down.

"Shut up, Mason. Of course, you can lasso, just look at you." I waved wildly at the man and he grabbed my hand out of the air to press a kiss to my wrist. I pointedly ignored the action, and everything it did to me, and turned to my friends. "Why didn't you tell me afterwards then?"

"Well, that's because …" Olivia started.

"We knew it'd piss you off and we'd lose our leftover goodies privileges," Zoey finished for her and the other two girls nodded solemnly.

"Seriously?"

"Well, we felt bad about it too," Olivia said, shoulders sinking.

It was kind of hard to be pissed at her when I knew Olivia's anxiety was bad enough to eat her up inside. The other two, however ...

"Shea?"

"Okay, fine, I might have thought it was kind of amusing and wanted to see how long it'd take for you to catch on. The betting board has been up since the pool started. They only took it down for that one town hall where Olivia professed her love," Shea said, motioning to a chalkboard at the back end of the stage or whatever the platform was called. The board was filled with dates and initials from the year I moved here up to three years from now.

"You're only allowed to make a new bet if you double your last one. So some folks who only bet the dollar minimum took another date for two, then four, and so on," Shea explained.

"Each one of those bids is at least a dollar? Holy fuck," I whispered, trying to do a quick count of the bids but after 500, I lost count.

"Bidding pool is up to $7543. That's how badly everybody wants to see us together, sweetheart."

"This town is fucking insane. Who won?"

"Excuse me," Rosie's voice chirped from the crowd. A rather large group had started milling around us, no likely trying to get a look at Mason and me, effectively blocking Rosie's path to the front. It took her another three excuse mes to get through the crowd.

"I don't think it I've seen these people so excited about gossip since Ms. Taylor divorced her husband," Rosie said, taking a seat beside Mason.

"You won, didn't you?" I asked, leaning over Mason to get a good look at Rosie. Even after three years of knowing her, I wasn't sure of her tells. And I had a damn good eye for people's tells, it was the only thing that made court bearable.

"Oh, yes, it appears so. But dear, I hope you aren't too upset with us. I made this bet before we'd gotten to know you. And well ... we should have told you, but you were so adamant about hating Mason, we thought it wouldn't really matter."

"And for the sweets," Zoey chimed in.

"Yes, you are a really good baker. Those cinnamon rolls were a hit with my family by the way." It was hard to glare at someone while they were complimenting my desserts. Especially the cinnamon rolls. I'd spent a good long while on the icing recipe to get the best consistency without making it too sweet.

"Where'd Rox go?" Shea asked.

"She's still up in the booth setting up the live stream."

"They're live streaming this?" I asked, flabbergasted that the town cared *that* much about this fake relationship.

How disappointed would they be if they found out this was all fake?

"Stop thinking so hard," Mason whispered, his arm tightening around me.

"Hmph, that's easy for you to say. I actually have a brain capable of complex thoughts."

"There's the mouth I fell in love with."

I might as well have turned to stone right then and there. Because even though I knew it was fake, knew every word out of his mouth when we were around people would be for show, I didn't expect *that.* The first time a man ever told me he loved me and it was fake. How much more pathetic can I get?

"Wait, where's your ring?" Mason asked, snapping me out of my pitiful stupor by pulling on my left hand.

"Oh, sorry. It's safe at the shop. I took it off and locked it in my desk before work and then I got rushed out by these yahoos."

"Hmm." He intertwined our fingers and set our hands gently in my lap. "I liked seeing it on you."

"What?"

"All right, everybody, sit down," Ms. Taylor shouted over the crowd as she stepped up to the podium. And when folks weren't quick enough to scatter, she smacked her podium with enough force to make everyone jump.

"She's pissed Rosie won," Shea whispered.

"Why? It could have been anyone."

"Look at all the initials ending with T. She had her family making a shit ton of bets for her so she wouldn't have to double her bid."

"What a fucking —" I started only to stop when Mason squeezed my side and tilted his head to the front of the room. Where Ms. Taylor was blatantly glaring at me.

"Is there something you'd like to say, Ms. Bowen? Or should I say the future Mrs. Foster?"

I considered how much trouble I'd get into if I were to flip off Ms. Taylor. I'd be kicked off as a vendor for the town festivals, which was a considerable chunk of my revenue. And considering I was broke enough to get into this charade with Mason, I shouldn't take any sort of financial risks. But ...

"Say what you want. I've got your back, sweetheart."

For a second, I considered if I could trust him on that. I mean, if a man can't hold off coming for more than a minute,

I wouldn't say he's reliable in any other aspect of life. But that proposal showed thought, it showed effort.

"Well, I was considering suing the organizer of this betting pool for emotional distress. I could argue for loss of profits too, considering how this situation could be perceived by outside parties."

There was a series of grumbles, but Ms. Taylor held her stare, not showing a single sign of distress or concern.

"But I'll settle for 10% of the pool going to a charity of my choosing. I mean, these town halls are all about building community, right? It's only suitable that any sort of profit made during them gives back to the community."

The bickering was immediate and holy fuck did the church carry voices. There were arguments over whether I should get any say, if the betting pool was too cruel for a newcomer, if I was overreacting by threatening to sue, and anything under the sun that could possibly be related.

"That's my girl," Mason whispered, hugging me closer. I don't know why he bothered, no one could hear him over the bickering. And anyone who wasn't arguing was watching what was going on with popcorn. Lord knows where Shea had that stashed.

"All right," Ms. Taylor shouted, her crackled voice miraculously carrying over the crowd. "Ten percent of the pool will go to the charity of your choosing. *After* you confirm there's been no tampering with the bet."

The crowd immediately went quiet. Except for Shea's munching. All eyes were on me and Mason, expecting us to say something big. Now I wasn't afraid of a little public speaking the way

Olivia was, I'd have never made it as a lawyer if I had her kind of anxiety. But there was a tiny bit of me that knew if I said anything remotely suspicious, Ms. Taylor was the kind of person to dig. And if she found out this whole thing was a sham, everyone in town would know.

"Mason didn't ask me out until the day before our date. Nobody, including us, had more than 24 hours notice."

"And I sure as hell wasn't confident she was gonna say yes when I asked her," Mason added, sitting up straighter. I followed suit. "Nobody knew we were gonna go out that day, so just give Rosie her money and let it be."

Mason didn't break eye contact with Ms. Taylor, though his hand squeezed mine just a smidge tighter.

She stared at us for a moment longer, the crowd behind us becoming restless. And just when I thought the crowd was gonna demand answers, Ms. Taylor shook her head and sighed.

"Fine. Congratulations, Rosalinda Loid, the pot, minus 10%, belongs to you. You can coordinate amongst yourselves how to make the donation." Ms. Taylor hefted a large cash bag from the podium and tossed it at Rosie's feet. A few folks congratulated Rosie, but the vast majority grumbled and immediately shuffled out of the center.

"Wait, is that it? Why did I have to come here for this?" I asked, turning to each of my friends to see if anyone else found it ridiculous that an event of supposed great importance was over in nearly ten minutes.

But of course, everybody was crowded over the money envelope.

"It's fun to make a big deal out of somethin' silly, dontcha think?" Mason asked, tilting into me to give a little knock to my body.

"I wouldn't say fun. I could be home and getting ready for bed if I hadn't been dragged off for this nonsense."

"Ah, so what? Now we've got a fun story to tell the kids. The town believed mom and dad were gonna get together so strongly, they bet thousands of dollars on it."

My gut twisted at the thought of kids, at the life I imagined us having because of one good night. Having a happy family, with him or anybody, was so far from my grasp and I wanted it so badly it made me sick.

So much for a strong independent, feminist woman.

"I need you to stop saying shit like that," I whispered. It came out harshly, but the thoughts swirling in my head were too jaded for my voice to sound like anything else. Mason pulled back to look at me, but I wouldn't meet his gaze. As far as the marriage charade needed to go, it didn't need to involve talking about my dreams for a family.

"Why does talking about —"

"Congratulations on your engagement!" Rosie interrupted, holding out the money pouch, bills poking out the opening. "Minus that 10% donation. That was a very nice touch."

"I don't think I've seen Ms. Taylor so pissed since Zoey and Stephen tagged the town," Shea said.

"That doesn't count as —" Zoey started, only for Stephen to pull her against him and silently nod his head. Zoey rolled her eyes and they exchanged looks, having a silent conversation no one else could decipher.

"That's really nice, Rosie, but I can't —" I started before she literally shoved the bag in my face.

"You can't say no. The money was earned off of you anyways. I know adjusting to life in Snowfall can be ... well, silly. Consider this compensation for all the weird small town quirks. Plus, this will count as your engagement and wedding gift, if it'll make you feel better. But you *have* to keep it, okay sweetie?"

The money was dropped into my lap as she talked and guilt hit me like a bulldozer.

"It's too much. You guessed right, you should keep it. At least some of it, I mean ..."

"Thank you, Rosie. That's mighty kind of you," Mason said, scooping the money off my lap before leaning in to whisper, "This is the part where you say thank you and start thinkin' of ways to sneakily give it back to her later."

I turned my face to his, not expecting him to be so damn close. It made my breath hitch.

"All right, love birds! Y'all have had your chance to celebrate, it's our time with the girl!" Roxie shouted as she ran down the aisle and bum-rushed me into a hug.

"Yes! Girls' time! No boys invited," Shea cheered, shooting out of her seat and dragging Olivia up with her before moving to collect Zoey. Meanwhile, Mason's grip on me tightened.

"Y'all drinkin'?" he asked, specifically looking at Rosie, which was fair, she was the mother figure of the group.

"Just a bit. But we'll be sure to make driving arrangements before we get into it," Rosie said with a soft smile. It struck me then that she knew what had happened with his parents, all the little details and facts. And I'm sure part of the reason she knew was having lived here her whole life. But also they were friends or friendly. Everybody here, minus Dennis and Stephen who weren't locals, knew more about my soon-to-be fake husband than I did.

And I mean, it's not like I couldn't put two and two together. A drunk driver murdered his parents or one of them drove drunk. But I didn't know the real details. If he was close to his parents, where he lived afterwards, who took care of him, what his relationship with alcohol is like now.

"Walk her back to my place when you're done," Mason said, voice sterner than I'd ever heard it. Then he pressed a kiss to my forehead and said, "Have fun, sweetheart."

17

Lemon Meringue Cupcake

Ashley

"All right, you've had a whopping 24 hours, it's time to spill," Roxie said as we crowded into the back corner booth of Rosie's diner.

"There's really not much to say," I grumbled. I needed alcohol, fast, if I had any hope of getting through this evening.

"Sweetie, you're engaged!" Rosie cheered, turning away for just a second to make a series of hand gestures to the woman manning the counter. Three years and I still had no clue what those hand signs meant or how they correlated to the food brought out to us.

"Did you have any idea he was gonna ask you last night?" Olivia asked.

"God, no. The man didn't seem capable of making dinner reservations, let alone planning an engagement like that. It was …" Even when I got to tell the truth, I found myself fumbling for words. And it was embarrassing to flounder over an idiot who once coated the sidewalk in front of my shop with paint that matched the concrete so whenever anyone stepped inside, they left footprints. No, that sort of childish prick could not make my heart ache. "It was surprising is all."

"You don't have to pretend you hate him anymore," Shea said, nudging my side. "But if you don't wanna get gushy about him either, that's fine too."

"Boo," Olivia and Rosie cried in unison, only to be nudged by Zoey and Roxie respectively. Though Roxie was on my side of the booth, so her nudge required a full body lean over the table.

"It's not a crime to want to hear all the sweet details. Some of us are missing out on romance," Rosie said with a small huff. Rosie wasn't one to complain often, and with her huge ass, intrusive family, she had plenty to complain about. So not having somebody must have really been bothering her.

"Sweetie," Roxie crooned. "You'll find you're person soon enough."

"Sure, but I'm not exactly meeting anyone at the diner. I've been considering getting one of those apps, but —"

"No!" Shea and Roxie shouted.

"Apps suck. Like seriously suck. And I'm trying to get a woman," Shea said.

"Men will quite literally talk to you about their dog and then send you a dick pic. Just cause. I mean, it saves me time, but that scene is *not* for you, Rosie," Roxie added and the rest of us nodded in agreement.

"Fine," she grumbled, "But if all of you end up in relationships before me, I'm getting an app."

"Fat chance of that happening," Roxie said, snorting as she threw her head back to laugh.

"You don't think there'll ever be a guy that's worth keeping?" I asked.

"Hmm, I don't want to say never and eat my own words. But I'd put the chances of that happening are a solid 2%."

"Two? Why two?" Olivia asked.

"Well, I go through enough men that a one in 50 chance sounds right."

"Are you even close to 50?" Zoey asked.

"Um." Roxie started counting on her fingers and staring up at the ceiling. And then a thought occurred to me that had my insides in all types of knots.

"Wait, have you ever been with Mason?" It shouldn't bother me. *I* didn't want to be with him. Roxie could have her fun with him for all I cared. But...

"Oh no. I mean, the dude has always had a nice ass, but he had a girlfriend all through high school, which was my hoe-ist days in Snowfall. Plus he's not a fling kinda guy. I'd peg him as a firm three-date rule holder."

Olivia and Zoey nodded along, while Rosie's eyes got sparkly.

"Are you two going to wait until the wedding?"

"Ew," was the immediate reaction from everyone at the table.

"I don't mean like a purity thing, but like a making the build-up more intense. I mean, they've only been on two dates, so ..."

"I'm not going to wait to consummate my wedding," I scoffed, knowing full well the marriage would never be consummated.

"So you two have done it," Roxie said, nudging my arm. "How's that ass under those jeans?"

"Very nice," I mumbled and rolled my eyes. I could see the spark in Roxie's eyes as she lined up her next question. Fortunately, I was saved as our regular array of fries and chicken nuggets and milkshakes arrived and the conversation delved into men's best physical features, which Shea had a surprising number of opinions on, and what alcohol went with milkshakes best.

And I was gonna need all the alcohol in the world to handle when talk turned to wedding plans.

18

Vienna Coffee

Mason

Thunderstorms and knowing people I love were out drinking are my biggest weaknesses. It put me on high alert and no matter what I did, I couldn't relax.

Which explains why I decided tonight was a good time to deep clean the Pub. It gave me a good view of the sidewalk where Ashley would walk down and I'd been meaning to clear out behind the bar anyways. And hand wipe the baseboards. And dust every single framed piece on the walls. Counted them too. I'd inherited a pub with 78 framed pieces. Wonder if my uncle had ever bothered to count them.

The bell above the main door rang and I jumped to attention. Rosie had a very sleepy Ashley around her shoulders, nearly dragging her over to the closest table. Ashley sat, leaning her head on her friend's shoulder, eyes closed.

"Did y'all really drink that much?" I asked, scooping my arms around Ashley so she could remain upright without Rosie having to prop her up.

"Oh no, she didn't even finish her third drink. I think she's just tired since it's so far past her bedtime." Rosie patted her friend on the shoulder before stepping back to the door. "I'll leave her in your care. Have a good night."

I looked down at my girl, her eyes fluttering as Rosie walked out, a hand weakly waving. We were a good four hours past her usual bedtime and I had two options. Take her upstairs to my bed or figure out how to get her home. She'd get more sleep if I just tucked her up in my bed, plus she could sleep in for a few minutes. But she'll be pissed waking up in my bed.

Well, I had an argument to look forward to in the morning, not much different from our every day.

"All right, sweetheart, time for bed." I scooped her up, one hand behind her back and one under her knees. She wrapped her arms around my neck, eyes fluttering until they narrowed to a glare.

"Roxie says you're a three-date guy," she grumbled, voice rough and sleepy.

"Okay?" I said, not sure what that was supposed to mean.

"But you slept with me the night we met. So am I special or do you just pretend to be a relationship guy for the townies?"

I damn near tripped taking the first step up to the apartment. I didn't know what was funnier, Ashley questioning the rate at which I slept with folks or her calling everybody townies.

"So you were asking about me?"

"I just wanted to know if Roxie had slept with you so I could act appropriately. And then she said no because you don't do flings." She'd buried her face into my chest but I would bet anything that her lip was pouting. She was so good at covering her expressions and I wanted to see what couldn't be swept under the rug.

"Well, she's right. Never been a one-and-done sort of fella."

Ashley remained quiet as I took the stairs, but just as I reached out for the door, she pulled back. And dear lord, my girl could still look so sharp tipsy and half asleep.

"Then why'd you sleep with me?"

I bit my tongue, debating. Even though we'd be married soon enough, I didn't get the impression Ashley was mentally ready for me to confess that I wanted her in every single way and the fake marriage was just the first thing I could get my hands on.

But she was looking awfully tired …

"Because I already knew I wouldn't be done with you in just one go." It was a truth, albeit one that she could, and most certainly would, attribute to me just wanting her physically. That is if she remembered it come morning. But at least I got to say something true without using the charade as an excuse.

Ashley immediately buried her face in my chest and grumbled, "I just wanna go to sleep."

"I know, I'll get you there, sweetheart."

"No, you won't," she muttered, giving me a quick pinch.

"*You* didn't give me a chance to," I said, laughing at how grumpy my sleepy girl was. I wonder if she's like this in the morning too. "But you can ask me to prove you wrong any time tomorrow."

"Pft, you wish."

I walked us inside my apartment and straight into the bedroom. Once I set Ashley down on the bed, she immediately started kicking off her shoes and rolling around until she wiggled her way under the covers.

"I need to wash my face," she grumbled and she smeared her face into my pillow, no doubt getting mascara or something all over it. I leaned against the door frame and enjoyed watching her grumblings. After a few tosses and turns, she found a comfortable space and kicked out one leg from under the covers. Then she pulled it back under and started grumbling again.

"I gotta go back downstairs to make sure everything's locked up. You gonna be all right here?"

"This isn't my bed," was the only response I received before she seemed to conk out and her breathing slowed.

I rushed back down to the shop, locking up the doors before returning to the bedroom with a warm, damp face cloth. In my short absence, Ashley had twisted the sheets and had one corner completely pulled out. I did my best to keep my laughter to myself as I knelt down to clean her face.

Asleep, Ashley looked like an angel. No furrowed brows, no squinted eyes, no worries. Lying to her friends tonight was probably hard for her. I'm sure every ounce of excitement they shared doubled her guilt. I'd have to fix that soon.

And step one to make sure all the lies become truths was sleeping on the couch.

19

Almond Scones

Ashley

Mornings were my favorite. The sunrise drifting through my curtains, the way everything was quiet like nature wasn't quiet ready to get up. And I especially liked going into Tost-Ka and getting the shop ready for the day. It was a laborious routine, but the work, most of which was baking, was soothing.

Despite all those things, I couldn't bring myself to open my eyes this morning. There was something about the position I was in or the mix of smells or something that made me so damn comfortable. Plus I had an alarm on my phone set for the rare days I didn't wake up on time. And since that hadn't gone off, I could spend a little more time in this comfort bubble.

Then I heard the click of the door and had just enough thought process to remember Mason was staying in my house.

And if he had the gall to open my door, then he could take a pillow to the face.

Without looking, I reached up for a pillow and tossed it towards the door. But instead of the expected thunk of a pillow meeting a stupid face, there was clanging.

I shot up and suddenly realized several things in a row. I wasn't in my bed. I wasn't at home at all. I was at Mason's place. In his bed.

And the light flickering in from the window indicated it was mid-morning. As in around the time Tost-Ka's doors needed to be opened. As in I was running real fucking late and missing out on profits.

"I can see the freak out forming on your face, but before you do anything rash, let me tell you it's all taken care of," Mason said from the foot of the bed, where he'd bent over to pick up whatever he'd dropped.

"Like I trust you to take care of anything," I spat, scrambling out of bed and looking around for clothes. Except all my clothes from last night, with the exception of my shoes, were in place.

I guess I could breathe a sigh of relief that I didn't get *that* drunk.

"I prepped everything for Tost-Ka myself and Shea is over there running the register. I swear that woman doesn't sleep and barely ever works. She's at Dennis' place damn near every day helpin' him. I'm not sure how she still has a job, but if it helps you out, I ain't gonna complain."

"*You* prepped the food?" I asked, completely baffled. I had my kitchen set up so that, should I somehow be able to afford someone to take a morning shift, they had everything they needed right there. But for Mason to prep everything? Impossible.

I walked around the bed, ready to berate him for daring to go into my kitchen, only to find him picking up a platter of food, all things I'd set up for today's menu.

"I figured you wouldn't take my word for it, so I brought samples of everything. Wasn't expecting a pillow to the face though."

"I thought you were sneaking into my room," I murmured uselessly before sighing and getting down on my knees to help clean up the mess. It was hard to tell if he'd done well with the presentation, but everything smelled right. Amazing even.

We cleaned for a moment in silence, but when I moved to grab the napkins from the tray, Mason's hands caught my wrist.

"What're you thinking?"

"Thinking?" I repeated, trying to tug my hand free so I could finish cleaning this up and get to work.

"Yeah, you woke up and immediately tossed a pillow at my head. And now you're huffing under your breath while you clean. So you're clearly thinking about something." Those blue eyes of his were too damn clear, too attentive over the most mundane shit.

I hadn't even realized I'd been making noises.

"I'm frustrated that I slept in and now I'm anxious to get back to work. That's all. So let's get this cleaned up so I can go home, change, and get to Tost-Ka." I tugged my hand away again, but Mason held firm.

"I told ya Shea's got it. Honestly, with the way she can push property, I'm sure she'll get you more than your usual sales. So let's take a few minutes to talk."

"I don't think there's anything to talk about." I gave up getting my arm back and settled down on the floor. And when my ass hit the hardwood, I remembered that I very badly did need to talk to him. "Shit, my parents."

"What about 'em? Are they all right?" Mason let go of my hand and I slumped back into the side of the bed, dragging my hands over my face.

"No, they're fine. My mom's just … being my mom. Somebody showed her that viral video of your proposal and she got all pissy about it."

"Shit, I'm sorry. Do you want to tell them it's —"

"God no! She's only upset because she finds the internet attention demeaning. And if I told her why we're doing this …" She'd be beyond horrible, the 'I told you so's' would be insufferable and I would never hear the end of how I threw away a perfectly good career for a money pit of a hobby. "I'm not telling her. But because it looks bad on her to *not* know who her daughter is marrying, they're coming down next weekend."

"Shit," Mason hissed, crashing down onto the floor. "Do you wanna wait to get married until they're here?"

I'm pretty sure my blinking made a sound like a god damn cartoon character.

"All right, not close with your family. Duly noted." Mason picked at some crumbled food on his pants, loudly thinking. "But if they're coming all this way because your mom's upset she didn't know me before the engagement, won't she be more upset if she missed the wedding?"

"No," I huffed. "Honestly, she'll probably commend me for making such a practical decision and saving her from having to make two trips. It'll be the one thing she complements me on the whole weekend."

"Now I'm sure that's not true," Mason started, but I waived the consideration away. On a normal day, I would have told him just how wrong he was, but we had other shit to discuss so I could get to work.

"We'll get married and do the loan stuff this week like we planned. The only thing this changes is that I'll have to get you a trundle bed so they don't get suspicious of us not sharing a room."

"That's all?" Mason asked, laughing as he dragged a hand over his face. "I'm just meeting your parents for the first time, having already married their daughter, and all I'm supposed to worry about is not sleeping in the same bed as my wife? I wouldn't say I'm prone to anxiety, but that's not nothing, sweetheart."

"It'll be fine," I said rolling my eyes. "It's not like they care enough to ask questions or even notice if you say the wrong thing about me. So no need to worry about them. It's kind of a blessing actually, since they're coming the same weekend the girls will be going to Seattle. I'll be so stressed and distracted, I won't have FOMO."

"What about Seattle?" Mason asked.

"The girls are going because of this car show Zoey's interested in and I couldn't — never mind. I need to get to the store." One little complaint about my parents and I was ready to spill my guts about all these problems. It must've been the horrible night's rest I got from sleeping in Mason's bed.

Everything would be back to normal once I got home and cleaned up. But first I needed to make sure Shea was doing all right with the morning rush. I know she helped Dennis out at his bike shop, but being able to run one register didn't mean being able to run them all. Plus, if we ran out of any of the stuff Mason made, she wouldn't have the kitchen set up for quick prep.

"Ashley! Have a good night?" Shea said with a wide smirk, serving an older couple at one of the back tables. The restaurant wasn't on fire, there wasn't an impatient line or messy tables. In fact, it looked just as orderly as a normal day.

"Everything looks … fine?" I questioned, looking around like I was just missing something. Once the couple had their food set and didn't need anything, Shea came over to wrap an arm around my shoulder.

"Of course it's fine, ye of little faith. I worked at a couple of cafes throughout high school. And that Subway you're planning to take over. So I'm an old hand at this."

"Oh, I didn't know that. Thank you. Wait, *all* throughout high school? At multiple cafes?" I looked over at Shea, confused. But she just shrugged and walked back to the register.

"Oh right," she said once she'd rounded the counter and held a sheet of paper for me. "You know that TikTok foodie from around here, Jessie? She wants to interview you and Mason about the proposal, your shops, and the new shop y'all are planning to open. I might've added that last bit, but it'll be such a good piece, or video or whatever. She'll be in town this weekend for the carnival, so I've got y'all set up for an interview on Friday at 7. I know you're usually closed by then, but do ya think it'll be a problem for Mason? I'm happy to help out at the Pub if he needs it."

And on and on Shea went. Meanwhile, all I could think about was this was just one more person I had to lie to, one more performance, on top of everything else.

Fuck.

20

Dark Roast

Mason

I 'll acknowledge that a couple's wedding day is more about the bride. Things are marketed to her and all that shit. But I had my own vision of my wedding.

My vision involved a vineyard or some other sort of outdoor venue. Lots of flowers. Little red velvet cupcakes. A D.J. that played the super cheesy songs my bride claimed to hate. And that beautiful bride walking down the aisle in a flowing white gown, making me cry.

I got fucking none of that.

Instead, I had a bride who wouldn't even ride with me to the courthouse. Which was fine, bad luck to see the bride before the wedding anyway. But when she showed up she wasn't even wearing white. She was in the same thing I'd seen her leave the house in, the same thing I watched her work all day in because

I kept anxiously looking over at her shop to see if she'd make a run for it.

And here I was in fucking suit.

"Why are you — what's with the —" Ashley stammered when she reached me at the foot of the stairs. She looked me up and down, eyes darkening ever so slightly. Pretty sure there was some drool happening too, which would serve her right.

"I've heard most people dress up for their weddings. Common courtesy, you know?" The want in her eyes felt good, but not good enough to soothe the irritation of not seeing her in white. I knew for damn sure she had plenty of white sundresses to wear, I dreamed about them often enough. She would've had to go out of her way to choose something not white.

"It's a courthouse wedding. And not," she paused to look around before leaning closer and whispering, "real."

"Uh-huh." Guess I needed that reminder if a dress color was getting my panties in a bunch. But ... "You could've made the effort at least."

I took the steps two at a time and held the door open. Ashley stared at me for a long moment before rushing up the stairs and smacking a hand against my chest.

"Just pretend you're not a little bitch so we can get married, all right?" she grumbled, walking straight into the building and up to the front desk.

I took a deep breath before following after her. In the short seconds she'd had to speak with the woman working there, Ashley had somehow managed to make the woman look confused beyond all belief.

"Oh, so there's the groom," the woman said, relief softening her eyes as I stepped beside Ashley. "Are you his and his partner's witness?"

"No," Ashley said, gritting her teeth. "*I'm* the bride."

"Oh, but you're not ..." the woman trailed off as she waved a hand over Ashley.

"We're not big traditionalists, ma'am," I explained, wrapping an arm around my girl and pulling her against me so I could press a kiss to the top of her head.

"Oh, yes, I'm sorry. I didn't mean to judge," the woman floundered, face turning red as she scrambled with some paperwork.

"Do people really wear white for a court wedding?" Ashley asked herself, her voice so low I thought I was the only one who could hear her. Until the clerk hummed an affirmative. My girl sunk back into my arms.

Well, now I felt like shit.

"I forgot my bag at home and I didn't have time to go back and get it. I didn't think it would matter that much," she murmured, twisting her engagement ring around and around.

I don't know why I'd never seen it before, but Ashley was hard on herself. Too damn hard if you ask me. I'd always thought she was stubborn about things going her way. Turns out she wanted everything to be some nebulous type of perfect and if it wasn't, she took the blame, whether anyone was blaming her or not.

And I sure as fuck was acting like I blamed her for not wearing white.

"Fuck, come here, sweetheart," I murmured, taking her by the elbow and spinning her around to face me. "It's all right that you're not wearing white. Nobody cares."

"You knew it was going to be an issue as soon as you saw me," she retorted. "I figured that was just your usual disgruntledness of having to see me, but no. I broke some unspoken rule again."

"Now, wait a —"

"Would you two like a photographer?" the clerk asked, interrupting what would likely have ended up being a love confession because even though I knew deep down none of those words were ready to be said, I'd say anything to get her to stop blaming herself for stupid little missteps.

"No," Ashley responded, just as I said, "Yes."

"Mason, it's extra money. We don't need to remember this day anyways," she whispered, pulling me by the arm to get closer. I looked into her eyes and did my damnedest to read what was going on in there. Pretty sure I'd lost the ability to read anything, let alone what Ashley was thinking.

"Let's get the pictures. If you hate them, we can toss them. But we'll be better off having them." *I'd* be better off having them, having that proof I could carry around that I'd fumble into marriage with the most beautiful, confounding woman on Earth.

Ashley crossed her arms and turned away from me. Then she gave a little nod to the clerk. The woman, after a long sigh, went to work on her computer and told us to have a seat and she'd call us when they were ready.

We sat in the waiting area, which was just one step up from a DMV lobby. There were a few other folks sitting in the area, none in any clothes that indicated they were getting married today too.

Good, I wanted our wedding day to ourselves.

"Stop that," Ashley whispered, putting a hand on my knee to stop it from bouncing.

"Sorry, nervous habit," I murmured. With sheer force of will, I kept my knee still in the hopes that she'd leave her hand there. She didn't.

"I don't know what you're so nervous for. Most of the folks in this office don't actually live here, so we don't have to act or anything."

My knee started bouncing again. If there'd been somebody local here, I'd have excuses to touch her, to hold her hand, keep her close. Plus a familiar face would be nice. Somebody like …

"Fuck, Louis is gonna be pissed at me when he finds out," I hissed, burying my face in my hands and resting my elbows on my knees.

"One, don't man spread. It's gross," Ashley said, her knee knocking into mine.

"Sorry," I murmured, resituating my legs but not uncovering my face. I was either gonna have to figure out some sort of clever excuse as to why he didn't get to witness the marriage between me and the woman he'd been helping me pine over for years or find a way to convince Ashley to let me tell him the truth.

"Two, why would Louis be pissed at you? He's a good guy and I didn't get the impression he was invested in our … whatever."

"He's my uncle, sorta. Well, like an uncle. After my dad's brother took me in, all his friends sorta helped raise me. I mean, I was 16, so the raising they did was just teasin' the shit out of me if I did something stupid. But the rest of that crew's passed, so Louis is all I've got and … he's gonna whoop my ass when he finds out."

I hadn't uncovered my face while I talked but I could feel Ashley's eyes on me. She stayed quiet for a long while before she leaned back in her seat.

"Well, we've got two options." I looked up to see her looking straight ahead, face set. "We can tell him and have him sign an NDA. Personally, I think the more people we tell, the more likely this will get out of hand, one way or another."

"So you're saying it's a non-option." Her mouth quirked in the shortest of smiles.

"*Or* you can pin the blame on me. Say we needed to hurry because of the grant, which is true. And say that I didn't want a formal wedding because my family wouldn't come, which is also true. And you, being a dutiful soon-to-be husband obsessed with his soon-to-be wife, wanted to elope so that I wouldn't feel bad having a wedding where no one came for me."

I need to kiss my wife so fucking bad right now.

Except she wasn't my wife yet and I had no right to kiss her.

"I'm sure that's not true," I said, keeping my hands balled up at my side.

"Ha! Let's see if you can say that after you meet them next week."

I was gonna have to use every last one of my brain cells observing her and her parents during this visit to figure out what sort of shit they'd done to make her feel like they wouldn't have her back. Because the way I was raised, if you got family getting married, hell even just a family friend, you'd drag your ass all across the world for that wedding. With a smile.

The fact that she was so confident her parents wouldn't, was … not to my liking. Everybody needed family that they could count on for things like this. Blood or not.

"What about your girls? Don't you think they'll be upset about the elopement?"

For just a millisecond, her mask fell and the hurt showed. Her eyes fell to the floor, every muscle in her face sinking before she took a deep breath and pulled everything into place.

"A little, but not so upset that they won't forgive me. They were all talking about us having this huge wedding. In June no less!"

"Not a June wedding girl?"

"Here? Absolutely not. It's too damn hot."

"Well, what kind of wedding do you want?" My fingers itched to grab my phone and start taking notes.

"Hmm, I've never thought about it too much. The usual stuff, sure, but I'd want a wedding that was centered around my partner and I, an event that was *us*. And I haven't had anyone worth considering what that would look like yet."

"What?" I asked, a little too loudly if the turning heads were any indication. But I must not have heard her right, so I sat up and leaned in, lowering my voice. "Are you telling me you didn't dream of your wedding with your high school boyfriend or anyone?"

"We went over this, I took school very seriously." She crossed her arms and kept staring straight ahead. Though at least this time her brow was furrowed just enough that I knew she wasn't masking anything.

"Okay, but what about after school? In college?"

"God, do you really want to hear that no one's ever been in love with me before that badly? I had a stick up my ass my whole life trying to do the right thing and be successful. Guys might've been willing to fuck around with me, but they certainly didn't want a relationship. And I didn't have the time for them anyways. So it didn't matter. *Doesn't* matter."

"It sure sounds like it matters. No wonder you're so stubborn," I murmured to myself, running both hands through my hair. I was gonna need some help breaking through to her, but who could I ask without explaining the whole situation? I mean, here I was, about to marry the woman I'd been pining after for years, a woman I knew I could fall in love with if she just stopped fighting me for a second, and she'd never been in love. Fuck, I'd probably have to spell it out for her to believe it. In fact, I could picture it now, me realizing I'm deeply in love with her and when I confess, she brushes it off as part of the charade. Am I gonna have to wait three years for this arrangement to end for her to finally believe me?

"What do you mean 'no wonder'?"

I simply couldn't answer that question.

Instead, I pulled a box out of my jacket pocket and set it in her lap.

"I didn't mean anything by it, sweetheart. But open this before I say any other dumbshit."

"What is it?"

"Wedding gift," I said, shrugging. Suddenly I was doubting if she'd want it or if it'd be useful. My fingers were itching to snatch it away for fear of failure.

"But this is — I didn't get you anything. No, I can't accept this." She started grabbing at my jacket, trying to shove the box back in my pocket.

"Ashley, would you not fight me on our wedding day at least," I grumbled, grabbing her arms and holding it away from me, the box still in her hand. She stared me down and I met her gaze with narrowed eyes. I wasn't bending on this one. It took me a whole fucking hour just to pick it out. And let's not talk about how much I spent on expedited shipping.

Eventually, her shoulders sank and she lowered her arms. Once I'd let go, she opened the box. Inside, on a velvet cushion was the necklace I'd gotten her. The pendant was shaped like a diamond but with the top cut off. You were supposed to be able to put your rings on the chain in the middle of the pendant thing and loop it around the metal so they'd stay on the necklace.

Ashley traced the metal quietly, eyes somewhere far off.

"It's a —"

"Thank you," she interrupted, pulling the necklace out of the box and fastening it on. The pendant fell perfectly over her collarbone, pointing the way to a delicious path my tongue actually ached to touch.

God, I'm gonna end up jacking off on my wedding night, aren't I?

"It's beautiful, thoughtful, and I —"

"Mason Foster and Ashley Bowen?" some called from the front desk area. Ashley cleared her throat, her hand falling away from the necklace as she stood.

"You ready for this?" she asked, shoulders pulling back, posture straight, like she was going into war.

I stood and took her hand, bringing it to my lips for a small peck and praying I could get away with this much.

"Been ready for a long time now, sweetheart."

21

Key Lime Pie

Ashley

I parked outside my house after getting married to a man I hated, wearing rings and a necklace *he* provided, having sat through personalized vows from *him*, and being far too distracted by the way his arms filled his suit.

I parked outside my house, set my head on the steering wheel, and cried. I cried because I hated the things I wanted, the grand romantic gestures, the sweet wedding speeches, the reassurances. Those weren't things I should desire, not so badly. I should be focused on the success of my business, focused on things I can control. Instead, my gut was getting twisted over a man who didn't even like me.

A knock at my window made me jerk up. Mason.

Once our eyes met, he pulled the door open and leaned into my car. He undid my buckle, holding onto the plastic and slow-ing its return to the panel. His eyes swept over me and I squared my shoulders, readying myself for some stupid remark on how emotional I was or some other bullshit.

"Not how I pictured you crying on our wedding day, but that's all right," he murmured before sliding his arms underneath me.

"What are you —" I started before he pulled me out of the car and my squirming put me at risk of banging my head.

"I'm pretty sure it's customary all throughout America to carry your wife across the threshold. But if you're not familiar, it's a tradition. Not really sure what the purpose is, but it sounds nice and I don't see the harm in it."

"But this is fake," I argued, even as I wrapped my arms around his neck.

"I wanna be a good husband, whether or not it's fake. And my wife coming home after our wedding and immediately crying is a sign I'm already doing a shit job."

"God. Not everything is about you, Mason. I'm crying because I'm an idiot for caring about idiotic things that don't matter."

Mason paused at the front door and I pulled away from his neck to look at him. I'd given him a spare key the other day, but a lot of folks around here kept their doors unlocked, so maybe he wasn't used to carrying his keys around.

But Mason wasn't looking at the door or reaching for his pockets or anything. He was analyzing me again. Eyes narrowed, brow furrowed. If I didn't know any better, I'd say he was doing complex math. *That's* how he looked at me, like he didn't have the foggiest idea of what was going on.

"In my experience, caring makes you a better person." He shifted his hold on me so one hand could dip into his pocket and retrieve his keys. Then, as he unlocked the door, asked, "But enlighten me into what's idiotic to care about?"

"Things that don't matter," I grumbled. I wanted to ask to be put down so I could go off into my room, have a nice bubble bath, and forget everything that was going on. But of course, my neighbors were out on their porches, chatting, watching.

"And who decides what matters?" Mason brought us inside, locking the door before carrying me to the couch. And even though he'd set me down gently, I felt the air in my lungs whoosh out like I'd been kicked in the stomach. The feeling was so unsettling I looked up to Mason for ... something.

He was looking down at me, still confused. But this time his confusion looked sad. Like he was pitying me for having gotten upset over something so illogical he couldn't comprehend it.

And knowing what I was upset over was silly, knowing he was justified in that look, made me snap.

I swung my feet over the edge of the couch, knocking my legs against Mason's so he'd stumble away from me.

"I guess your idiocy is contagious after all. I'm going to quarantine so it doesn't get any worse. Have a good night, *husband*. Don't forget our meeting at the bank tomorrow."

22

Rose Truffles

Ashley

Ten minutes before our meeting, I was irritated that Mason didn't take timeliness for a business meeting seriously.

Ten minutes *after* our scheduled meeting time, I was ready to murder him.

I had all our documentation ready, proof of marriage, applications, etcetera, so his presence wasn't *technically* needed for us to be approved, just for the finalization and signing. But it sure as hell looked bad that my fucking husband and business partner couldn't show up on time.

"I'm so sorry I'm late," Mason murmured, bursting through the office door. When I turned to look at him, my glare shifted to pure confusion. Mason was standing there completely drenched, shivering like a chihuahua.

He exchanged small talk with Devon, the banker, while he shed his top layers. His drenched cowboy hat and jacket were hung on the coat rack, heavy drops falling to the floor.

It'd been raining when I got here, but not *that* badly. Certainly not bad enough to warrant being ten minutes late and showing up like a dog that refused to come inside.

Mason squeezed my shoulder with one freezing hand and pressed a kiss to the top of my head before taking the seat next to me.

"I'm real sorry, sweetheart. I got in over my head."

In over his head? What the hell did that mean? All Mason had to do was show up on time at a building no more than a 10-minute drive from his place.

And still, Devon nodded with a soft smile. "I understand, no need to explain."

It took every single amount of muscle control I had to not straight up gape at them. This was a business meeting, for a large ass sum of money, and Mason was more than ten minutes late and made a puddle on the floor. No amount of good reputation running a local business should override that sort of unprofessionalism.

Not only did he put his own business at risk, but he put mine on the line too. And I was taking enough risks as is.

"Mason, you can't be serious. You're fucking drenched and *late*. Do you really think one little sorry is enough? This is a *business* meeting, for *both* of us and —"

Mason's hands cupped my face, his thumbs stroking my cheeks. And even though he was looking right at me, those blue eyes were somewhere else.

"I messed up, I'm sorry. But let's save the arguing for later so I don't waste any more time. You can yell at me all you want when we get home, all right?"

I took a deep breath in and bit my tongue. This man would not know a moment's peace in my home until he could give me a reasonable explanation for this sort of behavior. I would figure out a way to make his room unbearably hot or cold at my whim, make sure his bathroom never had toilet paper, and only ever leave him the dregs of milk in the morning.

Mason saw it in my eyes, those plans for his misery, and nodded. I took that as him accepting the consequences of his actions and settled back into my chair to face Devon.

"Well, I guess it's nice to see some things will never change," he chuckled, before shuffling some papers around. "Now, let's get you two that shop."

23

Mazagran

Mason

Another thing I liked about Ashley not being from Snow-fall was that she didn't know I'm a punk-ass bitch when it comes to thunderstorms.

Realistically, I knew I wouldn't be able to keep it from her forever. But given that the whole plan was a sort of fake it til you make it thing, I was hoping she'd be in love with me before I confessed that even driving in the rain set me off. Fuck, even just thinking about her driving in the rain made me want to jump in front of a moving vehicle.

But I knew I'd have to come clean and I spent every ounce of energy I had small talking with Devon after everything was finalized to delay the inevitable.

Because what the hell was I gonna say? *I know you already think I'm a dumbass, but wait til you hear this.*

"So?" Ashley said the second we'd stepped out of the bank, turning around to face me with her arms crossed. But then she did a double take of the parking lot. "Wait, where's your truck?"

"I walked here." I shoved my hands in my pockets, which were uncomfortably damp like the rest of me. Though I couldn't say if the clamminess in my hands was from the wet clothes or nerves.

"Why the hell would you walk here? In the rain? Is there something wrong with your truck?"

I shrugged. There sorta was something wrong with my truck, I didn't trust it the second pavement was wet.

"And you couldn't get an Uber or something?"

"Not much in the way of ride-sharing here, sweetheart."

"Fuck you. You could have gotten a ride from Travis or damn near anyone in town. Shit, you could've called any of my friends for a ride. Or, I don't know, you could have fucking called *me.* It might've been a miserable ass drive, but it would have been a hell of a lot better than sitting alone in that bank for 20 fucking minutes. How are we supposed to run a profitable business like this, huh? How do I know you're not gonna show up for a meeting and I have to cover for your bullshit? That's not what I signed up for."

"Sweetheart, please, I —"

"Don't sweetheart me. We are talking business right now. Unlike you, I have only one part-time employee. I can't spend this much time away from my shop without losing business. Your stubbornness to not ask for help is costing me money."

"Oh, you wanna talk about stubbornness now?" I grumbled, running a hand through my hair and pacing around. She's right.

No *shit* she was right. My business was fully established before I was even born. I had a structure that she had to build on her own.

And I'd seen her application. She was doing well for only being in business for three years, but things were still tight. And she certainly didn't have the space to cut corners like I did.

"What do you mean by that?" she challenged.

"I just mean you don't exactly ask for help from anybody either," I fumbled, knowing every word out of my mouth was doing the opposite of helping. But maybe if I was the one to point it out, she'd start asking for help just to prove me wrong. "It's not like you couldn't just as easily get one of your friends to cover you. I mean, Shea's probably worked in a cafe for at least as many hours as you have and Olivia was Zoey's cashier for a bit. They'd all be happy to help cover a few hours for you. But you'd rather pretend that you have it all together. Just like you pretend we didn't —"

I stopped talking. Partly because I could feel myself digging a deeper and deeper grave. But mostly I shut up because Ashley flung her purse into my chest and knocked the wind out of me.

"Fuck. You. Have fun walking home those wet boots."

* * *

The first few nights staying at Ashley's place were relatively peaceful. We'd get home around the same time, kiss on the front porch so the neighbors got their show, and then quietly exist near each other. It wasn't my ideal evening with her, but given that we hadn't been arguing, I'd considered it progress.

But the evening after my fuck up was different. The tenuous peace we'd made through our arrangement was gone and in its place was a litter of chaos.

The carpet that ran down the foyer area had those little fire-cracker shits under it so when I stepped down it felt like a bomb was going off under my boot. She got a real good laugh from that one, cackling from somewhere upstairs.

Then when I tried to run a load of laundry, she had a load in the washer *and* dryer. The coffee I'd brought over had been dumped in the trash. Everything in the guest room had been shifted roughly two inches to the left. And there was plastic wrap over the toilet, which I of course didn't catch before making a mess.

And then just as I slipped into bed, a soft buzzing started. The soft buzzing that, if I didn't think too hard, I could pretend was a toothbrush.

Except nobody was brushing their teeth for more than ten minutes. And I checked, watching the time click on and on from the bedside alarm clock. With each minute that went by, my blood burned hotter and hotter. What kind of toy was she using that I could hear from all the way across the hall? She'd said she could take care of herself, but if she couldn't get there after *this* long with it up *that* high, she must need help. As her husband, I had the responsibility to help her.

I swung out of my bed so fast I'm not sure my body knew where to pump blood. But it knew I needed to move fast because sense was never on my side and I needed to put my wife out of her misery and —

I opened the door to a wand buzzing on the floor. Heart hollering, I bent over to pick it up and turned the toy off. I waited for a beat, not really sure what to do with it before an idea caught.

I was going to keep her toy, fuck I might even stop by while she's at work tomorrow to look for more, and then I was going to work her up until she begged for me to apologize properly. I wanted her hot and needy for me, and since she was officially my wife, there was no reason for me to not act like it.

24

Peach Cobbler

Ashley

Business-wise, everything was going according to plan. We got the grant and business loan finalized. And between Mason's and my equities, we were able to outbid Starbucks and sign a lease on the ex-Subway. With that settled, all we needed to do before opening was some redecorating and staff and stock everything.

I was confident that we would be in good shape for a Fourth of July opening and we'd have an incredibly profitable end of summer. Especially with this TikToker or whatever that was coming to interview us in the next few hours.

However, outside of business, Mason was an absolute menace. He'd taken my wand after I'd left it on in the hallway to keep him up and one by one, my other sex toys were disappearing. And it wasn't like I had them spread about the house for emergencies. They were all in my bedside drawer, like a normal person. And Mason was sneaking into my room at some un-known hour and intentionally taking them one by one. I was down to my most basic dildo with only three speeds.

Normally, I wouldn't notice if my toy drawer was missing something. With the exception of when I was ovulating, I usu-ally didn't feel the need for that sort of self-care on a daily basis. Most days I was too exhausted from work to want anything more than a hot bath. But Mason decided that every second we weren't talking business, he wanted to talk about how he'd like to apologize for being late. And whenever I said he could simply explain the situation and say the words 'I'm sorry', he instead detailed every little thing he'd rather do instead. Including how he'd used all of my stolen toys.

But I would *not* let a bastard who was all talk win me over.

Instead, I've taken my aggression out by removing batteries in every applicable item, slipping grapes into his boots, and pouring all but a third of a glass of every beverage in the house. Plus I had a remote-controlled sleep machine coming in the mail tomorrow and I had the perfect hiding place in mind.

"You planning my downfall, sweetheart?" Mason stepped into my cafe with that infuriating smirk and unearned swagger. He rounded the counter and wrapped his arms around my waist, pulling me back into him and placing a kiss on the top of my head. Then his lips went lower, grazing the shell of my ear as he said, "You already know how to bring me to my knees though. You're welcome to do that whenever you'd like."

Heat swelled inside me at the image of Mason looking up from between my thighs, him in that stupid cowboy hat that I could tilt forward so I didn't have to look at his stupid face.

"You're here early," was all I got out in response.

"I figured you'd be stressed about the interview and could use a hand cleanin' and whatnot." He pressed another kiss to my head before letting go.

"Oh, yeah, thank you, that's …" Exactly what a good business partner would do. Nothing more. "Thanks. If you could start cleaning up the dishes, that would be helpful. And keep an eye on the oven, I've got a batch of cinnamon rolls in there for Jessie. And the scones on the cooling rack are for her too, so don't touch them. Oh, and you should get somebody to bring over your cold brew. The hazelnut one."

Mason paused on his way to the kitchen, eyes flashing to the few customers chatting away in the back corner before flashing me a wide smile. Fuck, the bastard had dimples hiding under that scruff.

"You have a favorite of my coffee?" he asked, arms crossing over his chest as he leaned against the door frame that led to the kitchen.

"The girls have recommended it in the past," I murmured, trying to distract myself by counting up the register and not looking at his stupid face. A year or so ago, Rosie or maybe Shea had offered me up a sip of their drink and I may have gushed about how good it tasted and how well it would pair with my almond scones before they finally told me where it was from.

"Mhmm and did you happen to make your almond scones?" Mason asked, that smile dipping back into a smirk.

"How would you know what kind of scones I make?" I countered.

"I'd be a bad business partner if I didn't do my research." Mason winked before sliding into the kitchen and out of sight.

The bastard.

I spent the next hour wrapping up the front of the store, cleaning tables as the last customers left and making sure the sitting area looked like a Pinterest dream for Jessie. Then I went back in the kitchen to get the samples set up. Mason had iced the cinnamon rolls, unfortunately getting an even coating, leaving me with nothing to complain over. The man himself was nowhere to be seen, but he did leave a note about running back to the Pub to get a coffee flight.

With Mason out of sight, I slipped into my office and printed off a single-page NDA that I'd typed up the other night. I needed him to stop mentioning the two times I was stupid enough to have sex with him. The reminders were killing me, along with the absence of all my vibrators. So I planned to negotiate in the way I knew best, legally binding contracts.

And since I knew he liked to see me squirm, I added something in it for him, promising to never remind him of how he failed to satisfy me. Well, not satisfy, but still. If I don't remind him of things he's ashamed of, he could do the same for me.

So with that set aside for Mason, I focused on plating and setting up the table for Jessie. Scones, cinnamon rolls, a muffin, croissants. It was, hopefully, an amazing spread. And I had a couple of idea boards for the new storefront ready to show too.

"Yeah, I ain't signing this shit, sweetheart." Mason somehow manifests from the kitchen, a tray of coffee shots in one hand and the NDA in the other.

"Why not?" I stumbled on the words, shocked. Did he really like tormenting me that much?

"Because the night we met meant something to me and I'm a little pissed you want to sweep it under the rug with a goddamn NDA. Look if you're pissed about the vibrator thing, just —"

The bell over my door rang and there stood Jessie, biting her lip to keep from laughing because of course she'd walk in just in time to hear Mason mention my vibrator.

"Should I take a lap around the block to give y'all some space or …" she said between giggles. I guess I should thank my lucky stars she only heard the last bit and didn't catch the beginnings of that argument.

"Oh, no, I'm so sorry you had to overhear that," I fumbled, waving my hands around at a complete loss for what to do. How do you come back from an interviewer overhearing a conversation about vibrators?

"Oh my god, don't even worry about it! I'm early and you had the close sign-up and everything, I totally should have thought to knock or something. Consider it completely forgotten."

"Thank you! And I really am sorry, Mason is just a bit of an ill-mannered barbarian at times," I grumbled, smacking Mason's arm.

"Don't complain about me when you're the one who started this whole thing," he said, keeping his arms crossed and his voice low. I couldn't remember the last time I'd heard him like that, like he was really put off and not just frustratedly angry with me.

I didn't have long to think about it though because Jessie was watching our bickering with a wide smile.

"I'd heard y'all argue a lot, but I wasn't gonna take much stock in the rumors," she said.

"We don't —"

"No use pretendin' we don't, sweetheart. There's no shame in having a couple of spats every now and then."

I bit my tongue to keep from huffing. Because to call our arguments, especially the one we were about to have, spats severely trivialized it.

And last I checked, 'spats' didn't normally result in business-halting pranks.

"Spats?" Jessie giggled. "I heard about the paint spill just a couple of weeks ago. I used to live in Mayberry and a few of my friends live in Snowfall now. They keep me up to date with *all* the gossip. They're all super excited about engagement, which congrats by the way! I saw the video and it was the most ador-able thing ever." As she spoke, Jessie took out her phone, taking pictures and videos of the decor and food.

"Yeah, it … it caught me completely by surprise. The whole date with the drive-in and the setup in his pick-up, I didn't suspect any of it." It really would have been the perfect date if it was anyone but Mason. Fuck, it was a perfect date even though it was him.

"How'd you get the idea for that setup, Mason?"

Mason tossed something into the trash, probably the NDA, and crossed over to the table I'd set up to put the coffee flight down. He took a seat there and I followed suit, reminding my-self that I couldn't scoot away, that I'd have to live in the husky smell of roasted coffee and Mason for the sake of our image as a happily married couple.

"I asked a couple of guys and looked on Pinterest," Mason mumbled, arms crossed and looking down. Too bad for him that wasn't enough to cover the blush spreading to his ears.

"Really?" Jessie and I said in unison, though her tone was a squeal of excitement and I was just baffled.

That was a lot of effort for a fake arrangement. Especially for a man I assumed had never logged on to Pinterest before.

But then again, if we'd just been watching the movie in the truck, it wouldn't have been a public proposal. And we needed something public for our marriage to be believable. So the effort was just for that, not because he was a thoughtful man or anything.

"Ashley doesn't like surprises, so I had to make it worth it."

My heart *did not* skip a beat. I was just nervous because the interview could really make our break our opening. We shouldn't waste this chance on inconsequential things like a sweet proposal.

"So how would you like to set up?" I asked and Jessie tilted her head to the side.

"She's a little bashful when it comes to us 'cause of the whole rivals thing," Mason explained, uncrossing his arms to push the coffee flight closer to Jessie. "And she's nervous about making good content for your video so the new shop does well."

"Oh, of course. Yes, let's get to it." Jessie clapped her hands together and pulled out a tripod for her phone. She set that up to frame us, then sat back down. "I'm mostly gonna use this for the audio, but I like having the visual just in case we start talking about a dish or something and can hold it up. So let's start with some basics. Why did you both open our cafes?"

Mason and I looked at each other. I was confident in my ability to speak in front of a camera, but I wasn't sure he was.

"Ladies first," he said with a nod.

"Right. About four years ago, I realized everything I'd done in my life was for somebody else. Nothing about my job or life-style brought me any joy. So I started reassessing my life and determined running a bakery would make me happiest. I had the funds from my previous career, it was something I could build up from scratch, and I could choose anywhere to open up."

"What made you choose Snowfall?" Jessie asked.

"I wanted to live somewhere that had a sense of tradition and community, something everywhere I'd lived before lacked. So I searched for open restaurant properties that suited my vision, then researched the towns. With those two requirements, there weren't that many options. This place was the third property I'd looked at and it was exactly what I'd picture when I thought of my new idyllic life."

"A classic self-search story. Mason?"

Mason looked at me for a moment before nodding and shifting up in his seat.

"Well, the Pub's got a lot of rich history. Supposedly one of my great-grandfathers opened it up in honor of his father who immigrated here from Ireland. Not sure how much stock I put into that story since the number of greats changed every time it was told. But still, it's a family joint. As the name implies, it was actually a proper pub up until I took it over."

"What made you change it?" Jessie asked and I stiffened. If Mason wasn't willing to tell me that story, he certainly would be able to do it in an interview setting.

"That's actually not something he likes to —" I started but Mason put a hand on my thigh and squeezed.

"That's all right, Ash. I can tell it now."

Oh. Good, that saved me from having to awkwardly cover for him.

And if I felt any type of way that he was willing to tell this stranger when he couldn't tell me, then it was just irritation. I mean, how did he expect me to react to a story I should already know?

"My uncle was runnin' the Pub before me and he ... well he didn't take any sort of precautions. Didn't make sure folks sobered up before they left or had a ride home. Then one stormy night during my sophomore year of high school, my parents paid the price. One of my uncle's regulars was too drunk to be on the road, hydroplaned right into my folks and flipped 'em. My uncle and I had very different ways of dealing with our grief. He drank and overworked himself and I'm overly conscious about anybody drinking. So it only made sense that when it came time for me to take over the shop, I made some changes. We still serve some alcohol, particularly Irish coffee, and folks can bring their own stuff for events like trivia, but I've got my staff trained to check on everybody before they leave. Some folks have called me a buzzkill for it, but I think Snowfall is a much safer place this way."

Silence fell over the cafe like a wet blanket, suffocating and uncomfortable. Based on what Mason had said at the diner, I figured it was a drunk driver. But for them to have gotten drunk at the Pub never crossed my mind. That sort of guilt must have eaten his uncle alive. And Mason ...

"You were late because of the rain," I whispered, pieces of his attitude that day suddenly starting to click into place. The refusal to ask for a ride or drive, the way he dug in and wouldn't explain himself or apologize. And I put firecrackers under the front rug and tormented him all week because of it.

Beside me, Mason just shrugged and pushed the coffee flight even further across the table. "I know it's not a fun story, but it matters. Pubs can do their share of taking care of folks, that's what community is for. That's why I made the shift, for my community. Plus I ended up being damn good at making coffee and it's got all the pretentiousness that comes with IPAs too. So it's not that big of a difference."

"Oh, that is absolutely true! The amount of dudes I get in my comments saying the exact same things I see on brewery posts is wild," Jessie said, leaning into the change of subject with en-thusiasm. "Let's get to that coffee though. It smells delicious."

25

Hazelnut Roast

Mason

After my sob story, the interview finally moved on to an actual interview. We talked about the coffee, Ashley's pastries, and our plans for the new shop. And all the while I watched Ashley slip deeper into a customer service mode. She was polite and kind, but not all that personable.

As she talked, she brought up a lot of technical shit about the flavor pallets and how things pair together. It was professional and if I was being honest, a little boring. She was missing that spark she had when we argued and I couldn't figure out if that was because she was nervous about this interview going well or something else.

Knowing my luck, this whole business attitude was cover for her being pissed at me for telling her about my folks like this.

"I think that's everything I need. The food and drinks were seriously delicious though! Once y'all open in Mayberry, I'm gonna have to get my mom to pick up these cinnamon rolls before I come home. They're amazing."

"Thank you," Ashley said, standing to collect the empty plates.

"No, thank you! I can't wait to get this all put together. I should have it posted late next week and I'll make sure to repost it around opening. Have y'all settled on the name?"

"Tost-Ka at the Pub," I answered. "Tost-Ka got its name from some foreign word, toska, that means ennui or something like that. So you chase away your toska at the Pub. I'll admit, Ash is too damn smart for me to follow sometimes, so I might be explainin' it wrong."

"I'm not that smart," she grumbled just before ducking into the back. I watched her go, an eyebrow raised. How many times since our little charade started has she made a comment like that? If it was enough for me to notice, it must've been a lot.

"So are you two going too?" Jessie asked. Apparently, she'd been talking this whole time while I was pondering my wife.

"Pardon?"

"The carnival, are y'all going too? Or do locals skip out the first night so they don't have to deal with the tourists?"

"Oh nah, we're going." Ashley walked back in, her focus on resituating the skirt of her dress. "Besides, this is gonna be our first outing as husband and wife, so I wanna be there for the fireworks and everything."

Ashley's face turned the brightest shade of red, her eyes going wide, and her hand going to the necklace where her rings sat.

"Mason," she hissed, shaking herself out of whatever had been running through her head. "I thought we weren't going to tell anyone yet."

"Well, we're wearing rings, sweetheart. They're gonna put two and two together," I teased. The tension from the past few days was easing now that I'd told Ashley the reason I'd fucked up that meeting. Well, I probably should have told her alone and with a bit more detail, but at least it was out now.

"But I haven't told the girls yet," she said, fiddling with her rings.

"Then we'll tell them together." I was mildly aware of Jessie still in the shop, gathering her things in between giggles, but I was focused on my wife. I needed to determine if she'd let me out of the dog house and I could start making real headway with her again.

"They're gonna be pissed at me. Can't we just wait to tell them next week before they go to Seattle? That way I can prepare them a basket of all their favorite desserts."

"Ashley Grace Bowen, are you really telling me you want to postpone our marriage announcement just so you can bribe your friends with food?"

"Have you told Louis?" she countered and I was grinning like a fucking idiot. These were the kinda arguments we should've been having this whole time. Stupid and harmless. Little jabs that only *we* can make.

"Nah, I haven't. But we'll face their tirades together. Tonight." I paused for a second, considering the effect of Ashley's baking had. "And we'll make some apology baked goods tomorrow."

"Oh no, you're not stealing my thing. Get your own thing."

"We're married now, sweetheart. That means it's *our* thing."

Ashley rolled her eyes at me before the bell over the door had us both spinning. Jessie had gathered her things and slipped out while we weren't paying attention.

"Great, she's gone. I wanted to give her our business cards before she left. What if she thinks we're rude assholes now?" Ashley grumbled, smacking my arm.

"I think she was getting a kick out of it. Don't worry." I slid my arm around hers and guided her into the back, flipping off switches as I went.

"But it was unprofessional."

"Yeah, if you were still a lawyer, it'd be unprofessional, but you're not. Different professions have different ... I dunno, strictness."

"Ha. Like I'd take advice from a man whose biggest word he knows is ennui."

"You got me there. Not even sure I know how to spell it. French words always have silent letters, right?"

"I guess I should be impressed you know that much."

"Back to the Neanderthal jokes, huh? I thought you were more creative than that," I teased. We walked back into her office, where her laptop had that stupid NDA open. Ashley moved away from me to gather her things and I took the opportunity to delete the file. If she wanted to completely forget about that night, she'd need to tell me why. I'll admit I'm a petty stubborn man, especially when it comes to our relationship, but if she directly told me she didn't want us, I'd respect it.

The thing is, I'm pretty sure she hasn't said it directly because she can't.

"I told the girls we had an update. So we're going to be ambushed as soon as we get there. Apparently, Shea has sunk $50 into some carnival game and they're requesting your assistance."

"My assistance?"

Ashley threw her bag over one shoulder and grabbed my arm, leading us out the back. I quite liked her grabbing and moving me around. "There were a number of lasso gifs but no description of the actual game."

"Oh, I know what they're talking about. That game might not be rigged, but it's hard as fuck if you're not lassoing properly. I remember doing it with my folks when I was little. My dad had given me 20 bucks to play games and I wasted it all on that one. Then made a very passionate request to go to cowboy camp the next summer."

Ashley froze just as we'd stepped out of the shop and turned to me, a wild giggle escaping her lips before she asked, "Is there photographic evidence?"

"Nah-huh, I'm not opening myself up to ridicule by showing you those pictures." I tugged our connected arms to pull us forward and around the shop.

The carnival was set up on the drive-in field, so it wasn't a long walk from Main Street. Ms. Taylor had outdone herself this year though. Along with the carnival crew doing their own thing on the field, she'd decorated the street with colorful banners and mini-games and booths. She'd nagged every business along the way to make either a booth or donate some products.

I'd 'donated' damn near a dozen gallons of coffee just so I wouldn't be pressured into manning a booth.

"I wouldn't ridicule you for embarrassing kid photos," Ashley said, with a clear 'but' on the tip of her tongue. "But if you've lost your touch, then I might."

"Oh, game on, sweetheart. But why don't we make this interesting?"

"What do you mean?" Ashley asked, one hand reaching into her purse as we approached the ticket booth. I pulled us over to the side, grabbing her hand to keep it away from her wallet and to slide her rings back on.

"I mean, we'll take turns playing the lasso game. If you win before me, I'll show you every single one of my embarrassing childhood photos and return all your toys."

Ashley bit her lip, eyes glazing over as she considered my offer.

"What happens if you win?"

"I picked your prize, you pick mine."

"And what if I decide your prize is to rub my feet every night for a month?" she challenged.

"While I'd happily oblige, I think you can do better than that."

Ashley's fingers tapped against her arm as she thought, her wedding rings sparkling under the neon lights of the carnival.

"Fine, I'll think of something better," she finally said. "But I want a handicap. You have to win twice for it to count."

Ah, my wife was too damn smart for me. That was a good call. Too bad for her 2:1 still wasn't a fair ratio.

"Game on, wife."

26

Apple Turnovers

I had a mission and I would not be derailed.

I was going to get my vibrators back at any and all costs. I will flirt with this bastard of a man I was married to and throw him off his game just so I could get a reliable orgasm. Fuck it, I might even let him hear just so he knows what he's missing.

"Ashley! Over here," Shea called, waving wildly by one of the game stands.

The carnival was exactly what you expected, but in the way that it was insane that it was stopping in such a small town. This was the sort of carnival you'd see in TV shows, not in real life. The rides looked secure, there wasn't any sketchy swaying or squeaking, and the food smelled insanely good.

"All right," I said as soon as I'd reached the girls. "Mason and I are married. It was a courthouse thing because we had to get the grant to get the Mayberry shop. None of that is important right now because I have to win a prize or whatever in this lasso game before Mason wins two prizes."

For the briefest of seconds, everybody just stared at me, wide eyes blinking in surprise. And then everybody exploded.

"What do you mean you're married?" Olivia shouted.

"That's ... practical, I guess," Zoey said, shrugging.

"Practical, shmactical. You can't just do a courthouse wedding, not with everything that's gone on between you two. You will hold a proper ceremony eventually, right?" Rosie asked.

"Rose, you can't pressure them into having a wedding," Roxie said, nudging at Rosie.

"I don't mean to pressure, I just think —"

"I don't think there's any way hell you're gonna win this game," Shea interrupted, pointing over her shoulder. "I swear the ropes are allergic to forming a circle."

"Shea, that's not what matters right now," Olivia grumbled.

"She literally said the married thing wasn't important right now," Shea argued.

"Of course it's important! How could it not be?" Olivia's voice pitched up.

"We could've at least gone to the courthouse with you," Rosie said, voice edging on a whimper.

"That's my fault," Mason chimed in. "I wasn't inclined to wait given that her sayin' yes still feels like a dream. I was a little afraid she'd come to her senses if I gave her time to think about it."

"Yeah, that tracks," Shea said with a snort.

"Exactly, so," Mason paused to hand me a stack of tickets and kiss my temple. "You get some practice rounds in and I'll go grab some food. Corn dog?"

"Oh, yes. And funnel cake."

"Rodger that, sweetheart." Another kiss and he was off.

"It's still kinda weird to see, ya know?" Roxie said, elbowing Shea, who nodded vehemently.

"Oh shut up and help me beat his ass at this game," I grumbled pushing through the girls and handing over a fistful of tickets. The man behind the counter mumbled some quick speech about how I needed to lasso a duck on the conveyor belt a good ten feet away from the counter.

My first few shots were wildly off. Like not even a couple of feet within the belt. Shea tried to give me some pointers, but given that she'd been at this for over 20 minutes already, I was a little reluctant to try her ideas. But after a solid ten minutes of trying on my own, I gave in.

"Having trouble there, sweetheart?" Mason said, leaning over my shoulder to whisper in my ear just as I was making my 12th or 17th attempt. Mason had bought the tickets, so I wasn't keeping track of the money that I was wasting.

"I'm doing perfectly fine," I mutter, swinging the rope over my head before flinging it towards the ducks. It hit the very edge of the counter with a loud thunk.

"You're making progress. Now open."

I turned to face him, ready to ask what the hell he was talking about when a corn dog was placed in my mouth. Placed, not shoved. Just enough past my lips for the suggestion to be there. Mason smirked, his lips twitching to make some comment.

I bit the tip of the corn dog off and turned back to the game.

Behind me, Mason was laughing like an idiot. I tilted my head ever so slightly to get a look at him. He had such a nice smile and the way his dimple hid amongst scruff was more charming than it had any right to be. And how did he get those biceps? Was lugging around coffee beans really all it took to get that kind of definition?

"You checking out your husband, sweetheart?"

"No." I turned back to the game, again. Then I realized where I was and that we were supposed to look like a husband and wife having a friendly competition. "Fine. I was."

Mason had been setting our food down on the counter of the game booth and nearly knocked it all over when I admitted to looking at him.

"Not used to hearing her admit it?" Rosie teased.

"Not at all. Especially not in public."

"Stop talking, I'm trying to concentrate," I grumbled, tossing the rope again and managing to knock a couple of ducks off. The man held up a hand for me to wait and picked up the ducks. As I waited, the girls all gave me a squeeze and congratulations before peeling off to do their own things.

"Want me to show you how it's done?" Mason asked. I shrugged and handed the rope over.

"Oh, no, no. You're banned," the game attendant said, waving his hands at Mason.

"Wait seriously?" Mason guffawed.

"Yes, seriously. This is you here, right?" The man reached down below the counter and produced a photo of a teenage Mason holding a lasso and a bag of at least ten stuffed animals.

"You can't prove that's me. That had to have been taken over ten years ago," Mason argued.

"If that's not you, then how do you know when it was taken?" the man countered, making a completely valid point. Plus I'm pretty sure Mason was wearing the same cowboy hat as in that photo.

"Come on, man, I'm just trying to play this game with my wife. We've got a bet going on."

"Sounds like you're gonna lose."

"Don't be like that," Mason started, looking around like someone was going to help him out. And while Dennis and Stephen had gotten a little buddy-buddy with Mason in the past few months, they'd left with their girls. I was the only one here to defend his honor.

He was, publicly, my husband. I should always try to defend him. Especially over something as trivial as a carnival game banning.

But I also had vibrators to win back.

"I dunno, *sweetheart*, seems like you should respect the man's rules." I picked the corn dog back up and slid it past my lips, winking at him before biting down.

It was a pretty decent corn dog for the fair. Not super greasy.

Mason watched me, his Adam's apple bobbing. Then he turned back to the man, slapping down another handful of tickets.

"Look, I don't need the prize, I just need to play."

"Then you're taking space away from people who *do* want the prize."

"They'll see me win and think they can do it too. It'll draw customers."

"You'll draw customers that'll get pissed when they can't win. They'll accuse me of using a plant."

"Fine, I'll give you double the tickets per round."

This gave the man pause. I'm not sure how carnival games worked, but I imagined you exchanged the tickets with the manager for cash. And if that was the case, they probably tracked who turned in the most tickets for bonuses or something. Mason might be good, but he probably still needed a round or two to warm up. So the man would get a good dozen tickets out of him.

Plus he was running the risk of me leaving if he rejected Mason.

Though I wouldn't consider the bet won unless I got at least one duck lassoed. But he didn't need to know that.

"Triple," the man eventually said. Mason threw his head back, groaning before straightening to shake the man's hand.

"God, you're so desperate," I mocked, standing beside him to knock my hip into his. "You don't even know what your prize is. Why're you going through so much trouble?"

"Because," Mason paused, picking up the lasso with his left hand and swirling it a few times over his shoulder before flinging it forward. It sailed through the air and wrapped right around one of the ducks. Mason flicked the rope back and undid the duck to set it on the counter, then leaned in close to whisper to me, "I trust you're gonna make it worth it."

27

Matcha Latte

Mason

My wife was the most stunning woman in the whole damn world.

And ever since my first win, she's been using it against me.

All of a sudden her skirt was two inches shorter and her cleavage was just *more*. She'd shimmy as she scooted back to make her throw. And dear fucking lord, whenever it'd finally get to my turn, because I agreed to one round to her three, Ashley'd lean her ass against the counter and watch me, her arms in front of her, pushing her tits up and making me falter.

"You're not playing fair," I grumbled at her.

"I don't know what you're talking about. I'm just watching for tips. Though I'm starting to think that first win was a fluke." She pushed away from the counter and slid the lasso from my hand. "Meanwhile, I'm getting better with every shot."

That she was. My wife was a quick learner. She was already trying to copy the way I twisted my wrist and she nearly had it. Once she got that down and figured out the footing, I'd be out of luck.

But maybe two could play her little game.

I shifted to stand behind her and trailed one hand up her arm. With my other hand on her hip, I shifted her into a better stance. Or at least a decent one. I wasn't gonna put performance over having her body pressed up against mine.

"What're you doing?" she whispered even as her body started to relax in my hold.

"I'm showing you how to do it."

"Mhmm, sounds like you're using this as an excuse to feel me up." Her response lacked her usual bite, but still, I scooted back so I wasn't pressed against her. Ashley moved back with me, pressing her ass right up against my cock and settling in like that was her spot. "I didn't say stop."

Dear lord almighty, this woman was gonna be the death of me.

I had to make this even.

I guided her arm to start swinging the rope then pressed my lips to her neck, gliding them up to that spot that sent shivers down her body. "You know it kills me not knowing what my wife tastes like."

Ashley jerked and the rope went flying straight for the ground.

"That's my turn," I whispered, biting back a smirk. Ashley was good at pretending she didn't feel this thing between us. She was so good, over the past few years, I found myself second-guessing if that night ever happened. So those moments where she slipped, they were damn satisfying.

I reached for the rope and Ashley stepped away, returning to her perch to presumably up the ante after what I'd done. But when her ass hit the counter, her eyes ran over me thoughtfully. She didn't lean her body or bat her eyelashes at me or any of the other dirty tricks she'd been playing.

Too bad for me, she was just as distracting sitting in my line of sight.

I started swinging the lasso over my head, waiting to gain enough momentum when my wife spoke again.

"Why did you tell that story in the interview?"

The rope sailed straight over the conveyor belt.

I took my time reeling it back in to think. There were several reasons I told her right then and there. I needed to rip off the band-aid. I needed to explain what happened with the bank meeting. I needed to clear the air before any of our pranks went too far. But to be honest…

"I was hoping if I was vulnerable about that, you'd tell me why you don't wanna talk about our first night together."

"What? So it was just a matter of getting information out of me?" she huffed, immediately crossing her arms and turning away from me.

Nope, not having none of that. Ashley might not do well with directness sometimes, but there had to be an exception.

With a flick of my wrist, I tossed the lasso over Ashley. She yelped as I tugged just hard enough to tighten the rope and pull her to her feet. Wrapping the rope back up, I walked over to Ashley, keeping my eyes on her for signs that she'd bolt.

"It hurt my feelings seeing that NDA. All the nonsense between us aside, what was so wrong about that night that you want to pretend it never happened? I sure as hell don't want to forget."

"It was a mistake," she murmured, head drooping down. I tucked a finger under her chin and brought her gaze up to meet mine.

"Which part? Because if it's the fact that I didn't tell you about owning a cafe, then I want a do-over. You didn't realize that place was in Mayberry instead of Snowfall and I didn't want to derail your excitement by bringing up my business. You're a smart woman. I'm sure after you were done being pissed about it, you would have figured that out."

"You never confirmed it." Even with me holding her chin, her eyes still drifted away. I wanted to shake some sense into this woman. How could somebody be so smart and so oblivious at the same time?

"Ashley, sweetheart, I have never, for a single second considered that night a mistake. Not after the paint or the trashed room or the cardboard windows or the missing to-go cups. Not a single fucking thing you've ever done or could ever do would make me consider that night a mistake. So why do you think it was?"

"Because it made me want things I shouldn't want. Stupid pointless things that would distract me from my business. I'd already bought a huge fucking house because I was living in la-la land. I'm not making any more mistakes."

She was talking nonsense. And she was saying it like she was only half convinced of her reasonings.

"You know what's stupid and pointless?" I asked while I un-did the rope.

"What?" Ashley huffed, wiggling to get the rope off quicker.

"Denying yourself what you want when it's not harmin' any-one." With Ashley free of the rope, I started spinning it over my head. "And it's especially stupid to call your wants that, when you know damn well I want it too."

I let the lasso sail over her head and she spun just in time to watch the rope settle over the duck.

"So sweetheart." I cupped her chin again and turned her to look at me. Her eyes had gone wide and her breaths came in heavy waves. "What's my prize?"

"Please."

28

Peach and Prosciutto Tart

Ashley

"Please." I wasn't even sure what I was asking for. My head was in a tizzy from trying to vocalize why that night was wrong and something about the confident way Mason handled a rope set everything on fire.

I could see the exact moment Mason realized what I meant. Or at least what he thought I meant since I wasn't sure myself. His eyes had narrowed, assessing me, then went comically wide even as they darkened.

Mason tossed the rope over the counter towards the man and scooped up the remnants of our tickets. Then his hand was around my wrist, pulling me through the crowd and abandoning our food. The man running the game shouted something, but Mason had already dragged me too far away to hear.

"Where are we going?" I hadn't realized how crowded the carnival had gotten since we'd started our game, but it was packed. I remembered something about some country singer doing a show before the fireworks go off, so people were probably heading towards the stage. Mason was dragging us in the opposite direction.

"You said please, I'm gonna deliver," he murmured before stopping us in front of the Ferris wheel. Without a word, Mason pulled out his wallet and handed the dude in front of the line some cash. The man raised a brow but took the money and waved his hand for us to go in front of him.

"Mason, wait a minute. This is —"

The couple in the carriage that just landed exited and the attendant waved us ahead. Mason practically threw me in as bored-looking teen rambled off safety procedures.

As soon as the door was shut, Mason dragged my legs over his lap and slammed his lips to mine.

My first thought was that it was funny that a man who made coffee for a living had such a sweet tooth. During the interview, he'd eaten all the spare cinnamon rolls and scones and since we'd been at the carnival, he'd devoured a fried Oreo and funnel cake. He tasted so sweet, it was going to give me a sugar rush.

Then his hand dipped under the skirt of my dress and the only thought I had was if I didn't get an orgasm this time, I was legitimately going to murder him.

"Did you have fun teasing me all night?" he whispered into my mouth, not pulling away to speak. To be fair, I wouldn't let him. My hands were clutching his T-shirt like I'd die if I let him go. Which was ridiculous, I knew this man had a history of not following through. I shouldn't be trusting him to give me any pleasure now. It's not like anything has changed.

Except for the effort he'd shown to propose. The vulnerability with his past. His refusal to let go of a moment I wished didn't mean anything to me because I thought it didn't mean anything to him.

"Answer your husband, sweetheart. I need to know if all that torment was worth it." Mason's finger grazed up and down the outside of my thigh, sending shivers all through my body. I tensed each time he dipped up, anticipating him reaching for what we both really wanted him to touch. But each time his fingers traced the top part of my thigh, he retreated.

"It will be if you make me come this time."

"Not what I was asking," Mason murmured, nipping at my lip. He pulled back just enough to meet my eyes, his such a dark blue that it felt like I was drowning. "I'm asking if tormenting me, flirting with me when you knew damn well I couldn't do anything back until you said the word, was fun for you? If you got off watching me act like an idiot because I couldn't take my eyes off my wife."

"Find out," I challenged, dropping my outer leg to the floor of the carriage and opening up for him. Mason's eyes didn't leave mine as his fingers *finally* slid over my thigh, dipping down to my underwear. He tugged the fabric aside and slid two fingers down my cunt, the touch gentle, testing.

"Let me tell you what's gonna happen. And just to be clear, if you don't want me to follow through for whatever reason you need to say so before we get any further, all right?" He kept up the slow stroke as he spoke, his free hand digging into the fabric on my back to keep me still as I squirmed in his lap. "I'm not wasting any time, soon as you say yes, these panties are coming off and I'm gonna get down on my knees and finally taste my wife's pretty fucking pussy. I am going to lap you up, sweetheart, 'cause you're fucking drenched for me." Either to prove a point or to get me worked up so he had something to eat, Mason shoved two fingers into me, the noise of my pussy too loud and distinct to deny. "I am going to eat this sweet little pussy until you pull me away or it's time to get off the ride. I am going to make you come so fucking hard on my lips that I'm all you think about when you get your toys back. You understand?"

"Mason, please," I whimpered. I kept clutching and letting go of his shirt, not sure what to do with my hands when he was fingering me and talking like that.

"Please what?"

"Please get on your knees, eat me out, everything you just said, please."

In the blink of an eye, Mason was down on his knees, my panties torn in his hands and my legs draped over his shoulders. I'd never seen a man move so quickly, let alone to eat pussy. But there Mason was, staring at my cunt like a starving man. His eyes had darkened, but the color was still so vibrant as he looked me over.

"God, I've been waiting for this for so fucking long." And then just as quickly as he'd gotten down on his knees, his mouth was on me. The sensation was so sharp, so sudden, I jerked away. Mason gripped at my ass, hard, and dragged me back to the edge of the bench.

"You are not getting away that easy, sweetheart. You taste even better than those peanut butter cookies you make. I didn't think I'd ever have anything tastier than that."

A small part of my brain wanted to ask when he'd had my peanut butter cookies because I only ever served those in the fall.

The rest of my brain was taken over by heat as Mason began to eat me out in earnest. He started with rough, slow licks, just savoring the taste of my arousal before his tongue twisted over my clit. He put more focus on that bundle of nerves than any of the various pranks we'd pulled on each other. And some of those pranks required a lot of forethought.

His tongue traced around my clit like he'd been thinking about how he'd do this for a long ass time.

"Mason." I breathed his name as I tilted my hips and dropped my legs out as far as they could go. His hands, still digging into the fat of my ass burned, the place where his stubble chaffed my thighs stung, but the places his tongue touched ached so deliciously. I needed more of it, all of it.

"I don't know how much noise we can get away with here, so you might want to be careful with those little whimpers of yours." Mason looked up at me from between my shaking thighs, a mischievous glint in his eyes the only warning I had before he sucked at my clit. I threw my arm over my mouth just in time to muffle the scream as he pulled away, dragging his teeth over the sensitive skin.

Tears began to form as he repeated the motion, slower, gentler. I bit down on my arm, desperate to smother any and all words that rose up in my throat. Bits of praise that Mason deserved to hear given what he was doing to my body. But I was too stubborn, too afraid I'd say something I'd regret tomorrow.

That's how it always was with us. Explosive chemistry, heat that could probably engulf us both, and then a moment where it was all proven to be just a moment and nothing more.

Mason reached up and tugged my arm away.

"I'm not smart enough to read your thoughts," he said, trading his mouth for two fingers that easily slid into my cunt and curled to stroke my swollen G-spot. "What does my wife need right now?"

"I'm not really —"

He tugged on my arm again, bringing my mouth to his and shutting me up. His lips were warm, coated in my arousal, the taste overwhelming his sugary kiss from earlier. I was savory on his tongue.

Mason kissed me like he was trying to prove a point. Every sigh, every lean in, every pulse strengthened him, proved him right in some unfathomable way.

"Stop thinking about stupid shit and let me enjoy you. Let yourself enjoy this." Mason's lips left mine, his free hand pushing at my collarbone to make me lean back. I complied, but my eyes flickered to the window. We were on our descent.

"Mason, I don't think —"

"God, are you ever gonna let me take fucking care of you?" he growled, crashing his mouth back to my pussy. While his fingers worked my G-spot, his mouth sucked and twirled my clit with near-lethal aggression, like he was pissed at me for everything our relationship had been thus far and how long he had to wait for this meal.

It was insane.

And I was falling apart.

"Mason," I pleaded, biting down hard on my lip because we were getting far too close to the ground and I didn't want us to end up on the tabloid this town called a newspaper. But everything was burning and twisting inside me and I was going to come on my husband's face in the middle of a fucking carnival. And fuck, this might be the hottest thing a man has ever done for me. Probably the hottest thing a man *will* ever do for me.

Almost like he could hear my thoughts, Mason's teeth sunk into my swollen flesh. Not hard, but with just enough pressure to send a jolt through my whole body.

I looked down at Mason. That stupid cowboy hat had somehow managed to stay on this whole time and was blocking my view of my hungry, desperate man.

I knocked it off.

When those blue eyes met mine, they sparkled. God, men shouldn't be allowed to have such pretty eyes. And they sure as fuck shouldn't glisten like that while doing such dirty things to me.

"Is my wife ready to come for me now?" he asked, his breath tickling the over-swollen flesh. I whimpered some sort of affirmative and nodded my head.

Even with his lips pressed right up against my cunt, I could still see the smirk. And then I wasn't capable of seeing anything because he did something I couldn't even describe. It was like he entered some kind of cheat code and my whole body became so overstimulated that everything went fuzzy. Fuzzy and warm and like a breath of relief.

My body sunk into the seat, my orgasm relaxing parts of my body that I hadn't even realized were tense. The euphoria was so instant, so all-encompassing, I was suddenly contemplating how I could get this feeling every day, damn the consequences.

"The best tasting thing you've ever made," Mason groaned, pressing the flat of his tongue to my cunt like he was liking his plate clean.

The carriage rocked as we made another descent. We were next to get off.

"Mason." I tugged at the shoulder of his shirt, trying to pull him away so we had time to get decent before our door was opened. Mason grumbled, giving my cunt one last lick before moving away. He tucked my tattered underwear into his pocket, put his hat back on, and sat next to me, adjusting my skirt just in time.

"Thank you for riding with us," the teen attendant mumbled as he opened our door and gestured for us to get out. We mumbled a thanks and Mason took my hand, leading us further and further away from the crowd. His hold on my hand was tight, but he didn't say anything. I didn't mind at first, my body still buzzing, all my concentration focused on walking right so nobody could tell I just had a mind-shattering orgasm. But as the quiet stretched, nerves settled in.

One of us had to say something.

"I guess we're even now." It was all that came to mind and given the way Mason stopped and turned to me, it probably wasn't the right thing to say. We were just a few blocks away from my shop, most of the Main Street booths being taken down as folks were drawn to the concert. A few folks waved as they walked by, seemingly unaware of the intense way Mason was staring at me. Almost like he was doing complex math again trying to figure out how to respond.

I was just about to admit I didn't mean anything by it when Mason finally spoke.

"Like hell we're even."

29

White Chocolate Mocha

Mason

I don't know what I had to do to get Ashley to tell me what was going on in her mind, but I had a couple of ideas.

Strike that, I'm not sure she'll ever let go of all her stubbornness, but I did have an idea to make things better.

So once we got home from the carnival, I let her be. Even though the ache in my cock told me to take her to bed, get another taste of that delicious pussy, then consummate our marriage for real. And with the taste of her come on my lips, resisting that was real damn hard.

But through some sort of all-mighty blessing, I refrained. And I refrained on Saturday and Sunday, letting her settle and digest what was *finally* starting to happen between us. Then on Monday night, when she got home from work, I had dinner and a game set up at the kitchen table.

"What is this?" she asked, voice hesitant as her eyes bounced around the kitchen.

"Dinner and a game," I answered simply.

"Okay, but why? Shouldn't you be at work?"

While we both had similar businesses, I was finally starting to see the differences between our stores. While the Pub was technically a cafe, we stayed open through dinner. Tost-Ka only stayed open til the after-work rush or whenever Ashley ran out of goods. So she was home for a timely dinner most nights, while I only got home for dinner if Travis was doing a night shift. And given that Travis had his kid to take care of, I typically didn't ask him to cover those.

But I'd asked him to this week because we had a lot of work to do. With the new shop and her parents coming into town, I needed every available second my girl had.

"Travis is gonna be closing this week so we can focus on the new shop in the afternoons." It was a half-truth. But I was afraid she'd dig in her heels if I told her the other side of things.

Ashley stared at me for a beat longer before sitting at the table. I finished drying off the last pan and joined her. As I settled in, she picked up the instructions for the card game I'd set out. It was one of those get-to-know-each-other games from Ashley's collection. It hadn't been opened yet.

"What's this for?" She picked up the first card and then slid it under the deck. I tsked at her and pulled the card back out.

"I didn't want to sit through silence. This gives us something to do. And you can't just discard a card like that."

"It's a card game, we can play it however we like," she said, rolling her eyes.

"Maintain eye contact for 30 seconds," I read aloud. "We're gonna have some trouble pretending we're happily married if you can't manage to look at me for at least that long."

Ashley's eyes met mine and didn't look away for exactly 30 seconds. Then she took her fork and stabbed into the meatloaf.

"What'd you notice?" I asked, the last line of the card.

"Nothing I hadn't noticed before," she grumbled before taking a bite. As she bit down, she closed her eyes and sighed.

"Family recipe," I told her before I drew my card. "Do I remind you of anyone?"

Ashley opened her eyes and then narrowed them as she assessed me between bites of food.

"No," she finally said. "I'm not sure I'd met anyone like you before."

"Is that a compliment?" I teased.

"That I'd never met anyone as ridiculous or childish as you? No, I don't think so." There was a pause for another bite of food, then she asked, "Who do I remind you of?"

I took just as long as she did to come to the same answer. "No one I can think of."

Even as I said it, I kept wracking my brain for someone to compare her to. Even if there was nobody in my life that matched her wit and attitude, surely there was a fictional character that had those qualities. But no, not a single name came to mind.

"What does my phone wallpaper say about me?" Ashley read from the next card, tossing it into the discard pile before pulling out her phone to show her wallpaper.

It was a picture of the wedding cake she'd made for Ms. Taylor's granddaughter earlier this year.

"You're a romantic."

"What? No, I'm not." She pulled her phone away and set it screen-side down.

"Sure you aren't. You're also proud of the work you've done. As you should be."

"Well, of course. That cake was a pain in the ass to make and transport. I regret letting Ms. Taylor talk me into doing it," she grumbled, even as her shoulders straightened at the compliment.

I drew the next card and smirked.

"God, what is it?"

"What compliment do you think I hear most often?" I set my elbows on the table and leaned forward, eager to hear even an indirect compliment from her.

"Something about your eyes or your ass," she said, not looking up from her food as she continued to eat.

"My ass?" I repeated.

"Don't pretend like you don't know women gawk at your ass in those jeans," she huffed.

"I did not know any such thing. What have folks been saying about my ass?"

Ashley pointedly ignored me and drew the next card. She immediately moved to discard it, but I grabbed her wrist before she could set it down. She sighed and pulled the card back.

"Do you think I was popular in school?"

"My know-it-all, smart-mouth girl? No way. You probably even intimidated some of the teachers." She rolled her eyes, but the way her shoulders stiffened got me thinking she didn't like how she was back then. I remember her telling me about her mom dressing her like an office worker and put two and two together. "You would've been popular if teenagers weren't such dumbasses. I mean, look at you now. Got a tight-knit friend group, the most eligible bachelor with your ring on, folks comin' in from out of town to taste your food. If that ain't popular by adult standards, I don't know what is."

She smiled, a soft movement of her lips. A genuine moment.

"How come you don't really have a friend group here? I mean, with the girls, they all grew up here. I'm surprised you don't have something similar."

Hell, I was surprised she was asking me a question without the prompting of a card. But fuck if I wouldn't take it. Even though this was a far more vulnerable thing to talk about than the things on the cards so far.

"I went to college with most of my high school friends. Given how seriously you treated school, I'm not sure you got this experience, but all anybody wanted to do was party. Sure we'd done our little small town drinking beer and throwing a bonfire on some abandoned farm property, but off at college, it was different. Folks wanted to get wilder. And I became the wet blanket. I didn't want to get drunk and I sure as fuck didn't want to go to parties where folks were being deliberately reckless. Had a lot of arguments and by the time freshman year was over, I wasn't talking to anyone I'd been close with in high school."

I'd started pushing my food across my plate, that anxiety of being pitied or rejected weighed me down just like it did back in college.

"Those fucking assholes," Ashley snarfed. My eyes shot to hers to see a fucking livid woman with a deep-set frown, huffing and looking around like she needed something to beat someone up with. "They knew about what you went through and still expected you to be okay with that sort of behavior?"

Seeing Ashley upset for me felt like something got lodged in my chest. Like a chunk of taffy. Sticky and not going anywhere.

"Yeah. I guess they thought after a few years I'd have gotten over it and loosened up."

"Over your parents' deaths? Who are these fuckers? Do they still live here? We should ban them from our shops." Ashley gathered her empty plate and mine and continued her rant into the kitchen. She talked about things we could do to get back at them, little revenge schemes we could pull off together instead of against each other. All while she washed our dishes.

I sat at the table, silently watching my wife. And probably falling in love with her.

30

Raspberry Cheesecake Tart

Ashley

By pure happenstance, my parents' flight came in right around the time the girls needed to be at the airport for their Seattle trip. Half of them road into Charlotte with Stephen and the other half with me and Mason.

"Are you two sure you don't want us to bring you anything back?" Rosie asked from the back seat for, possibly, the millionth time.

"No, Rosie, we don't need anything. You guys just enjoy the trip."

"It's not gonna be as fun without you," Roxie said, "But we'll do our best."

"Make sure you don't leave a string of broken hearts out there, Rox. I don't need no coffee snob moving here to chase after you," Mason said, not taking his eyes off the road as we entered the crowded area around the airport. In the back, Roxie threw her head back and laughed.

"What? Afraid you wouldn't meet their standards?" she asked.

"Nah. I think they'd be an ever-present fixture in the Pub and be obnoxious as fuck about it."

"I feel like we should be more worried about Shea bringing somebody back. Seattle has quite the queer scene, doesn't it?" Rosie asked, humming to herself as she no doubt thought through several possible meet-cutes for Shea.

I was struck with a wistful sort of envy. They'd only be gone for a few days, but there was so much that could happen. I was going to miss out on a lot.

Mason's hand found my knee, giving me a quick squeeze before returning it to the wheel.

"Too bad y'all are gonna miss out on meeting Ashley's folks," he noted.

"You mean miss out on them beating your ass for marrying their daughter before meeting them?" Roxie asked.

"They're not gonna give a shit," I snorted. I could practically feel the oncoming awkward silence, like a fog rolling in. But Mason spoke up before it could set.

"Of course not, they're gonna fall for my charm the same way Ashley did," Mason said, winking at me as we pulled up to the departure bay.

"Oh sweetie," Rosie started, "If they fall for you the same way Ashley did, you're in for a rough weekend."

"That'd be an understatement," Roxie snorted before we all fumbled out of the car to quickly unpack their things and exchange goodbyes and promises to text.

As they headed into the airport, Mason pulled me into a side hug and kissed the top of my head.

"What's that for?" I asked. Nobody here knew we were married, there was no need for the fake affection.

"You look like you need it." Mason stepped away from me to open the passenger door, a hand out to help me in. "Ya nervous?"

I shrugged as I got in and Mason rolled his eyes before closing my door and getting in on his side.

"You know you don't have to pretend around me, right?" he said. I wanted to laugh, because who was he kidding? One, he kept up the married act when no one else was around. And two, I did need to keep myself together around him and anyone else. Otherwise, they'd see all the failures and mistakes I was covering up.

"Well, I'm nervous," he said, pulling into traffic so we could loop around to arrivals. "I mean, I know you're not close to your folks and I'm sure as hell curious to see what the dynamic is like. But I've got a feeling they're gonna take one look at me and label me as a country bumpkin."

"Hmm," was all I could say because he was absolutely right. "Just go on your Starbucks rant. That'll help with some of the bumpkin accusations."

"I feel like a rant about corporations killing communities and community-building efforts, isn't gonna make the best first impression. Help me out here, sweetheart. What should or shouldn't I say?"

I sighed, looking out the window.

"Try not to say ain't, my mom will silently judge you for it. I'd honestly lose the hat too. And the belt buckle. Really every piece of your outfit that fits into the cowboy stereotype."

"God, you coulda told me that before we left the house this morning."

"Well, I figured it'd be a big ask." I shrugged again and sank into the seat.

"So if I happened to order both of them some hats as a little welcome to Snowfall gift, that wouldn't go over well?"

I snapped up so fast that the seat belt jerked me back.

"You didn't."

"I did." Mason threw his head back to thunk against the headrest. "I thought it'd be a nice little gesture or something. Not the kind of gift they'd get up in New York. Unique, you know?"

Something about the way Mason was scratching at his scruff, wholly distressed that he fucked up something he wasn't required to do, was so sincere. And all I could do in response to that emotion was giggle.

"Yeah, real helpful, Ash," he grumbled.

"Why didn't you just go with food or something more universally liked?"

"Like I said, I wanted it to be special, not some generic crap."

I was still laughing at Mason when I spotted my parents in the crowd.

My laughter immediately died.

"What —oh."

Yeah, my parents were always easy to pick out of a crowd. My father was a tall gentleman, always in a suit and carrying a briefcase. He used it like a masculine version of a purse. Which wouldn't be a problem, except it always made me cringe when we were at the grocery store and he'd pull out his briefcase to get his wallet. The case was just like him though, plain and rigid.

And then there was my mom. Also in a suit, *and* pantie house, her hair slicked back and up into a tight bun. Just looking at her hair like that gave me a headache. At least instead of a briefcase, she carried an ordinary purse, something black and expensive looking. Just like her whole outfit.

"Let's just get this over with," I murmured as Mason parked in front of them. I pulled on my usual customer service smile, though it felt tight and unbearable, and stepped out of the car.

"A pickup truck? Really?" My mother's shrill disappointment was so familiar and unwelcome, I considered turning right back around. Mason wasn't a wholly unreasonable man. If I said I wanted to leave my parents here, he might listen.

"Hello, Mr. and Mrs. Bowen. Pleasure to meet you two. I'm Mason Foster, your daughter's husband." Mason had moved quicker than my rattled brain could manage. Hopping out of the car to deliver the news I hadn't really planned on mentioning and shaking their hands before scooping up their luggage and sliding it into the back of the truck.

"Husband? Why is this the first I'm hearing about this? You better not have told anyone else in the family."

God, just fucking kill me now.

31

Assam Black Tea

Mason

The two-hour car ride back from Charlotte was illuminating, to say the least.

Ashley's dad was a quiet man. As soon as they got settled in the back, he pulled out his tablet from his briefcase and mumbled something about needing to handle some business.

Her mother was something else entirely. She talked damn near the whole time, giving updates about family members and their kids, things happening at Ashley's old office. But instead of sounding like she was catching up with a daughter she hadn't seen in years, it sounded like a business meeting. Everything was stated as fact, delivered in a monotone voice with zero eye contact. And these reports came with little digs. Somebody's kid got promoted to partner at their law firm, similar to the offer Ashley got before she quit and moved. She compared someone baking for their kid's PTA fundraiser to what Ashley did. And she called Tost-Ka a bakery at least five times.

At first, I thought I was reading into things. That the digs weren't on purpose and she just spoke in a matter-of-fact way. But then I noticed how Ashley's shoulders tightened with every comment.

I did my best to derail the criticism by talking about Snowfall. I suggested we go around the carnival and the Main Street booths that got set up during the weekends, but Mrs. Bowen immediately shot down the idea, explaining carnivals were for children and since no children were present, there was no need to go. Then I suggested the Lookout or the park for some hiking and just general enjoyment of nature and Mrs. Bowen pointed out it was far too hot for any sort of outdoor activity. She then asked after a mall or shopping outlet and was disheartened when I informed her the closest Target was almost an hour away from Ashley's place.

"Dear lord, you really did pick the most backwater place to live, didn't you? It's a wonder you get any business at all. Is there *anything* to do here?"

I bit my tongue hard to not mention any of the things she'd already dismissed and tapped my fingers on the steering wheel. We only had about ten or fifteen minutes left in the car, but time was dragging.

"Main Street is similar to an outdoor mall, albeit on a smaller scale. There are our shops, a lovely florist, a bike shop, pizza, a bookstore." Ashley listed the shops off quietly, with the sort of lackluster I'd only seen when she pretended to not be interested in me.

"That's nothing," Mrs. Bowen dismissed. "You do have decent Wi-Fi at your house, yes? If there's nothing interesting to do in town, I can at least get some work done."

"Yes, Mother. The Wi-Fi works just fine here."

"Good." She was quiet for one blissful second before tacking on, "I hope you weren't planning on sending out a registry with your wedding announcement. It's tacky to ask for gifts without hosting a party. Though I agree that it's much more practical to go to the courthouse and have everything done."

She continued her list on why a courthouse wedding was a practical choice then went into a lengthy Q and A on our prenup.

"Welcome to our home," I damn near shouted as I parked in Ashley's driveway. I rushed out and around the car to open Ashley's door and help her out, then did the same for her mom.

"This is the place you bought?" her mother asked, tone incredulous.

I focused on getting their luggage out of the back.

"Yes, Mom. This is my home."

"It's huge. What do you need this much property for?" A handful of folks were out on their porches, like normal, and I waved, trying to hide a grimace. Based on their hesitant waves back, I'd guess I wasn't too successful.

"Lord, I hope you're not thinking of filling this house with children." Apparently, my retrieval of the bags didn't take long enough. "Children are an absolute waste of time. They're expensive, do whatever they please, and they take such a toll on your body. Plus you're both small business owners, opening a new shop no less. Children would ruin all of that."

Ashley was a damn good actor. Even after watching her, carefully, these past three years, I still couldn't read when I was getting under her skin until a towel hit my face. She could probably murder someone without changing her expression.

But right now, with her mom talking about kids being a bad decision, to her daughter no less, Ashley's face dropped. I'd upset her enough times to recognize when it's bad. And this was bad.

I let go of the luggage and rushed to my wife without a clue in the world how to help, just knowing I needed to hold her. I stepped in front of Mrs. Bowen and took my girl's face in hand, stroking her cheeks and looking into eyes that were trying very hard not to cry. From behind me, I heard her mom say something about being dramatic and then giving her husband orders to grab the bags before she headed up the porch.

"What can I do to make this better for you, sweetheart?" I asked, keeping my voice low. Ashley was one of the few folks in town who locked her house, so her parents were just sitting on the porch swing, presumably looking at work emails on their phones. "I'm afraid anything I say will make it worse."

"I just — it's fine, really. I ... my periods coming soon, so I'm over sensitive." She tried to knock my arm away but I wasn't having any of that.

"That's bullshit and we both know it. Your period isn't until next week and before you spout PMS shit on me, let's also acknowledge that I've said some stupid, insensitive shit to you and it's never landed this hard. On your period or not."

"God, why do you know when my period is?" She half laughed, but the noise came out low and insincere.

"Because I pay attention to my wife. Now tell me what's up?"

Ashley's bottom lip wobbled for just a second before she shook it away.

"She's right. The house is too big and having kids — if we were real, having kids could be disastrous for our businesses. And they really can destroy a woman's body. I don't need them to have a fulfilling life and —"

"And nothing. You want kids. You want three kids to fill up this big house with their laughter and shouts. And a dog runnin' around after them."

"I never said anything about a dog," she grumbled even as tears were wobbling at the corners of her eyes.

"You didn't have to. We're on the same page for once." Her eyes jerked to mine and since I knew there was no way for me to read her thoughts, I put all my focus into showing her I was being earnest here.

Ashley stilled and I knew she saw it, knew she recognized what I was trying to say, what I wanted to provide her. But she shook it away.

"No, we're not. My mother is right. Kids would just be trouble. Impractical trouble." The steadfast mask slid back into place and she pushed me away. "You're causing a scene over nothing. Let's move on."

Yeah, like hell I was moving on from this. We were on the same page about some pretty damn important things for our relationship and I wasn't gonna let her mother's remarks rattle Ashley into closing the book.

We were gonna work this out one way or another.

The only question was how.

32

Lemon Cream Puffs

Ashley

Unsurprisingly, the whole evening was exhaustive.

Mom made several comments that sounded like they were simple facts but always came with a heavy undertone of criticism. Dad didn't say a damn thing and just mumbled and nodded the whole time. And Mason was somehow the worst of all.

I'd figured him meeting my parents would involve butting heads But I assumed it would result in my mother including Mason in her judgmental notes. Instead, every time my mother said anything, even something as benign as the quality of the toilet paper in the bathroom, Mason countered her. Not aggressively. He still pulled off that Southern gentleman demeanor. But I could see it. The way his muscles tensed, eyes narrowed, the way he didn't say ma'am every other sentence.

I hadn't expected him to be … upset or whatever was happening in that caveman brain. And I especially hadn't expected him to notice anything my mother said bothered me. I pride myself on keeping a straight face. In court or with wild customers, no one could ever tell what I was thinking. That's I liked it.

But somehow Mason saw the exact moment my mother managed to say the one thing I couldn't hear her criticize. And his reaction to seeing me break wasn't to poke fun or keep it in mind for a later date. No, he quite literally dropped what he was doing to be at my side.

And now I had to share my bedroom with him.

Mason stepped out of the en suite, a toothbrush sticking out of his mouth and no shirt. It was obscene.

"I'm just realizing I never saw the trundle you ordered. Did you already set it up or is it hiding somewhere?" he asked.

"Crap." I kicked at a pile of Mason's crap that he scooped out of the guest room and dumped onto my floor this morning.

"Crap as in you didn't put it together yet and it's late and you just want to go to bed or crap like it didn't get here in time?"

"Crap as in I forgot to even order the damn thing." I kicked at his shit again then moved to my dresser to pull out my pajamas. Mason hummed before returning to the bathroom to finish brushing his teeth. I took the opportunity to change as fast as possible.

"So, what are you thinking?"

"What?" I turned to see Mason leaning against the bathroom door. He'd put on a shirt thankfully, but he'd stripped down to his boxers.

"Are we gonna take the easy path and share the bed or are you gonna make me take the floor?"

I looked at the bed, pretending I didn't feel the way his eyes drifted down my body. I had a King bed and a long body pillow to snuggle. We probably wouldn't even touch. And if we did, so what? It's not like a little spooning would lead to anything else. Plus, setting up some sort of floor bed could be risky if my parents needed to enter my room for some reason.

It was safer for our act to just share the bed.

"I like sleeping next to the door," I murmured before sliding into bed.

"That's what you wear to bed?" he asked, eyes wide as he took slow steps to the bed, hand tapping against his thigh.

"Uh, yeah? What's wrong with it? You're in literal under-wear," I pointed out. My pajamas were light cotton, shorts and a button-up with a collar. It was cute, maybe on the short side, but the nights got hot. But with the way Mason was acting, you'd think I was wearing lingerie.

"I guess. I — you're right." He shook his whole body, arms waggling at his side like a dog shaking off the rain, then he slid into bed. He stayed upright while I resituated my pillows. And I somehow managed to resist the urge to shove my body pillow in between us.

"Ashley?"

I twisted under the sheets to face Mason, still seated, looking down at me. He was assessing, clearly about to rehash the child incident. I don't know why he cared about it so much, it's not like me deciding to be practical over dreamy would affect our business deal.

"I know you were planning to work some tomorrow, but I want to handle it. Will you trust me with that?"

I jerked up. That was so far away from what I was bracing for my mind was doing cartwheels trying to rearrange my thoughts.

"What?" was all I got out in the end.

"I know Saturdays are your high earners and I also know you're stubborn and controlling about your business and don't wanna lose out on any money, especially with the time you've had to take off today."

"… that's true."

"We're partners, Ashley. Your success is my success and vice versa. I don't want your shop going under any less than you do. So my resources are yours. I've got the staff to manage both our places for tomorrow. Plus you've left such detailed instructions and recipes, anyone who can read could run your shop. I want you to take tomorrow off and spend the day with your parents, even though I don't like them much."

"You don't like my parents?" It was a stupid question to ask after everything he'd just said. If I were to even consider his offer, there were at least a dozen things we'd need to go over.

But for some reason, that was what my brain focused on.

Probably a result of my bedtime routine being thrown off.

"I don't like the way your mother talks to you. Figured I'd made that much clear already," he grumbled, shifting around in bed before sliding down.

"I mean, I don't think my mother noticed given how she doesn't know you usually call women her age ma'am with every breath." I resituated in bed to lay down, facing Mason.

"Well, she lost my respect pretty early in the evening." Mason pulled a pillow between his arm and head, settling down, still looking at me. He was definitely searching for something.

I realized this was probably the moment to thank him for today's incident. Even if his comfort was unnecessary, it was still a kind gesture. A kind gesture not necessary for our little ruse.

"So what do you say? Let me run things for tomorrow?"

The moment to thank him was gone. I'd taken too long.

"Yeah, sure, do whatever."

33

Con Panna

Mason

> **Me:** All right, she's all right with us covering for tomorrow

> **Travis:** Do I really have to be the one to run her shop? She seems like the kind of person who would murder me if I accidentally put something back wrong

> **Travis:** Though I'll admit Jayson loves her cupcakes

Me: Hey that's my wife you're talking about

Dennis: How hard did she fight you on it?

Me: Not at all, which kinda has me worried

Dennis: Well she likes practicality and she doesn't get to see her folks a lot, so I'm sure she's relieved you offered

Me: Nah, her folks suck

Me: Her mother spouted some bullshit about how kids ruin your life right in front of her daughter

Travis: Fuck that, kids are great

Travis: Wouldn't encourage you two to have them right away though

Dennis: Does it matter? Ashley doesn't seem like she wants kids

Me: Oh she wants kids, trust me. And her mom spitting that bullshit stung

Travis: Don't start too soon, I mean it

Me: Why? You worried I'll ask you to babysit?

Dennis: I don't think you'll ever have to ask anyone to babysit, the girls will be all over that shit

Stephen: Can confirm Zoey would very much like to hold a baby at the earliest possible moment.

34

Banana Bread

Ashley

Mason had somehow slipped out of bed without waking me up. He'd also turned off my usual alarm and set one for 7, presumably because my mother mentioned wanting to grab breakfast at 8.

So without much fuss, I ushered my mother and father out to Tost-Ka at 8:00 on the dot.

Despite the shop being only half a mile from my house and the weather clear, Mother insisted on being driven into town. With her in the front seat and Dad in the back *still* checking emails, we drove into town. It was a silent, awkward drive, made worse when we drove down Main Street looking for parking and folks would stop dead in the middle of the street to gawk at my car.

"Are people always so distracted here?" Mother tsked.

"They're not distracted." My fingers tensed over the wheel to keep my irritation out of my face as I smiled at someone crossing the street in front of us. "They're all very perceptive actually. They know I don't usually drive in, so they're worried something's wrong."

"Worried? Sounds like they're just busybodies," she huffed.

I bit my tongue and parked a few shops down from Tost-Ka, getting out of the car and leading the way without a word. If it was anyone else, I'd fill the short walk with small talk. I'd have pointed out the shops we passed and my favorite things about them.

With my mother, I didn't bother. She either wouldn't listen or find something to belittle. And given that I needed all the strength I had left to withstand her critiquing my shop, I remained quiet.

"Welcome to Tost-Ka," Travis called when we entered the shop. I stalled in the doorway, surprised to see him. I figured Mason would be the one manning my shop, especially given that Travis seemed to hate me for all the pranks Mason and I have pulled over the years.

But whether he actually hated me or not, he took care of my shop. The tables were mostly full, usual for a Saturday morning, but the few unoccupied tables were pristine and the display case was missing its usual grubby fingerprints from kids pointing out which dessert they wanted. It was kind of impressive how clean he managed to keep everything, especially impressive that the display case was nearly empty already.

"Ashley!" Travis rounded the counter and wrapped his arms around my shoulders for a quick hug. "I take back everything I have ever said about you having a stick up your ass. You have the most efficient and logical set of instructions I have ever seen. Please, please, please set up the new shop exactly like this. Everything is so much easier to run here. Mason's register system drives me insane, it's five years too old and requires manager input after every three transactions."

"Oh, yeah, thanks. I guess?" It was weird to see Travis' attitude shift so sharply. Though to be fair, I had an excellent system set up so that in the event I needed to onboard anyone, it could be done with the utmost ease.

"It's quite small, isn't it? And still, the tables aren't full," Mother murmured, her nose crinkling as she looked around.

"You always this rude when you enter a shop?" Travis remarked, stepping away from me to cross his arms and assess my mother. "Because if that's the case, you can just go. I'm already out of our sour tarts today."

"Tarts weren't on today's menu," I noted before shaking my head. That was irrelevant. I shifted focus, gesturing to my parents, and said, "Travis, these are my parents. Mom, Dad, this is Travis, one of Mason's managers at the Pub."

"Pub? I thought you said he said he owned a restaurant too?" Mom had completely dismissed Travis and his early comment. The man rolled his eyes and returned to the register, mumbling something about things being explained.

"The name of his cafe is called the Pub," I explained.

"So not only did you marry the competition, you married an idiot that named his restaurant after a *different* type of restaurant?"

"Mother." The word came out sharper than I intended, surprising myself and my parents. Mother gave me a confused look, brow furrowed as if she had no earthly idea why I'd snap at her like that. As if she didn't just call my supposed husband an idiot.

From the other side of the counter, Travis raised an eyebrow. I chose to ignore the look.

"I'd appreciate if you refrained from commenting on my husband like that." I looked at my mother, eyes blurring so I didn't have to see her or her reaction. Then I stepped around her to get to the counter. "We'll do the sample box, please. And your piping work looks great."

"Ah, I can't take credit for that," Travis said, moving about to get the box set. "Mason came in and got most of the baking done for me. You can ask Jayson, I suck at decorating. His cake last year was supposed to have Godzilla on it and it turned out more like Flubber."

Behind me mother huffed, likely readying a comment about the staff not having all the skills necessary for running a bakery. But I wasn't going to give her the opportunity to speak.

"When's his birthday? I'll make the next cake for you."

"Really?" Travis asked skeptically. I suppose it was a fair question given how … abrasively I'd treated Travis in the past just because he worked for Mason. It seemed fair before, I mean, I hadn't directed any of my pranks toward him. But now …

"Yes, Travis, I'll make your kid a cake. No need to make a big deal out of it," I grumbled, shame heating my cheeks.

"Oh, I am one hundred percent going to make a big deal about it. Texting Mason right away." Travis held out the sample box and my father grabbed it with a mumbled thanks and headed straight for a table. Mother grumbled and followed behind.

"They're a real piece of work. No wonder you came to town with a stick up your ass," Travis said once they were out of earshot.

"I'm sorry about —"

"Nah, don't mention it. Mason warned me your folks were coming by and to be prepared for turbulence."

Something about the idea of Mason talking about my parents with Travis made me nervous. For all I knew, he could be complaining about all the bullshit my parents said and resenting that he had to put up with it on top of all the other fake marriage bullshit. I trusted him not to blab about our little scheme, but...

"What did he say?" I found myself asking, wiping down invisible crumbles off the counter.

"Honestly? He sounded pretty pissed," Travis said and my eyes shot up to him, gut-twisting. Of course, Mason hated this, he had to act more than our usual arrangement and share a bed. Plus he'd gone through all the work to cover things so I could take today off. There'd been nothing but work for him and our relationship had just gotten started.

"The way they talk to you is getting under his skin and I can see why."

"Wait what?"

"Aw don't tell me you're pissed he ranted to us about what they said, he just needed some advice. You should be thankful he spoke to us instead of causing a scene. Your mom looks like the kind of woman who'd walk out immediately if somebody stood up to her." Travis was looking away from me now, nervously wiping down the counter as he spoke, the words coming out in a rush.

"I'm not pissed, I just — what exactly did he say?" This wasn't making any sense. Mason wouldn't have to go on some rant to make our lie believable in a text to Travis. All he really needed to do was ask Travis to cover my shop and say my parents were in town, maybe add something about making a good impression. A rant didn't make sense, it was unnecessary.

"He mentioned they said something about how kids weren't a good idea and the comment hit a nerve. That's all. I mean, that and all the lowball criticism they threw his way, but he didn't seem too bothered by any of that."

"Oh." Mason must've really been bothered by it. Not as part of our act.

But of course, he would. Despite our thing, whatever it is or was, he was a good guy. He helped my friends out on a regular basis and was a big part of the community. Seeing someone being belittled by their parents probably struck his community-driven heart.

It was just a looking out for your neighbor kind of thing. That's all.

35

Lungo

Mason

Monday night was our last evening with Ashley's parents before driving them back into Charlotte and hopefully not seeing them again for a good long while.

Ashley's mother had a comment for every damn thing under the sun. Ashley's bodice ripper books, her board games, the way she'd organized the kitchen, my boots, my accent, the decor of the Pub, the way so many shops in Snowfall were named after their purpose. Anything in her line of sight was fair game as far as Mrs. Bowen was concerned and it was driving me insane.

And while I was starting to hear nails on a chalkboard, Ashley was as cool as a cucumber. There were no more breaks in her armor. She derailed her mom with ease and, more often than not, set up food so her mother wouldn't speak.

It was baffling how she could be so calm in the face of constant criticism. I wanted to kick her mom out for all the shit she'd said about my wife. But Ashley spent the whole weekend in a thoughtful quiet. I tried to get her to rant about her mom, about how her dad had barely said a word the whole weekend, but Ashley softly brushed me off, apologizing for anything her mom said about *me* throughout the day.

I was getting to the end of my rope with the whole visit.

"Ashley, a spot at your old firm opened up. It seems like the Jameson boy couldn't cut it. I do hope you'll consider applying. You weren't raised for this … quaint type of life," her mother said, eating dinner while not looking up from her phone, not even to address her daughter. That was enough to tick me off, the things that actually came out of her mouth were just a shit topping to it all.

"Mother, I explained this to you already. I wasn't happy as a lawyer and have no intention of returning." Ashley didn't look up from her plate but she was far from being dismissive. Under the table, I gave her thigh a gentle squeeze. Her hand came down to meet mine and I started to pull away, afraid I'd crossed our fake marriage line. But she rested her hand on mine, keeping me in place and giving me a little squeeze in return.

"You're being impractical. That bakery is nothing but a money pit. And if you insist on filling this house with children, you'll need a stable source of income. Plus all that baking has gone to your ass, making those little dresses of yours all the more ridiculous. And the weight gaining will only get worse if you insist on bearing a child. Afterwards, you won't have the time to work out and maintain your figure without the money for lipo and —"

"All right, that's my limit." I pushed away from the table and grabbed the Bowens' plates, snatching the silverware right from their hands. "Look, I work in a restaurant, so I don't like cooking after work. But I do it for the folks I care about. I care about Ashley and you're her family. So I've been making y'all dinner despite every little spiteful comment you've said since your plane landed. But apparently, you don't give a rat's ass about Ashley given what you just said or *didn't* say." I make a pointed look at her father who, for once, was looking up from his tablet. "So y'all can kindly fuck off for the rest of this evening. For the rest of our lives for all I care. Because if that's the way you talk to family, *your own daughter*, I don't want no part of it. Y'all should be ashamed of yourselves."

I dumped the food in the trash and set the dishes in the sink. Then I went back to the table to grab my wife and dragged her up to our room.

Though thankfully she didn't need to be dragged, she stumbled along after me in a daze.

Once we were in our room with the door shut, I let go of her arm and paced around. She was gonna be pissed at me once her senses kicked in and I wanted to get ahead of it

"Look, I know I overstepped there," I started, finally looking over to Ashley. She'd leaned back against the closed door, arms crossed, head cocked. She was wearing her daisy sundress again, probably to fortify herself against her mother. And damn, maybe I should've pulled her aside this morning when I first saw the dress. I was always catching on to these things a moment too late.

"You did," Ashley said when I didn't keep going, her voice flat and unreadable.

"I know, but I'm not sorry. Your mother is a real fucking piece of work. I get her not liking me, I'm some country bumpkin shaking up with her daughter out of nowhere. She has every right to say some bullshit about me. But the shit she's been saying about you all weekend? The little digs about you changing your life to make yourself *happy*, comments about your weight of all things. That's my line, Ashley. I can't handle that shit. I saw how happy you were after signing the lease, I saw the change between then and now. There's so much more life in you. You love it here and for her not to see that is insane."

I was pacing again, unable to tell if my explanation was worth anything to her or not.

"Look, if you want me to apologize, I will. I won't pretend I like it or them, but I'll do it for you if that's what you want. I just — I can't stand seein' her talk to you like that. I can't do it anymore, all right?"

Ashley stood there, not saying anything, just making my nerves boil.

"Would it make you feel better if I let you shave me bald?" I offered. It was the only idea I had left. "Though if you want to shave my beard, I'll warn you it takes ten years off me."

The edge of her mouth tilted up and suddenly breathing was so much easier.

"You'd really let me shave you?" she asked, her voice shaking on the edges to keep from laughing.

"You can do whatever you want to me, sweetheart."

Her eyes dipped down my body and I was suddenly aware of the innuendo. I tried to keep a straight face as she assessed me, just so she'd know I didn't do it on purpose that time.

When her eyes met my face, she softened. Her shoulders relaxed, she uncrossed her arms and walked over to me. I stayed still, still not sure what to expect. But when she reached me, she pushed up to her tiptoes and pressed a kiss to my cheek.

"Thank you, sweetheart."

36

Cheesecake Brownies

Ashley

Things were shifting and I wasn't sure how to wrap my head around it.

After Mason said his peace last night, I went back down to inform my parents they could manage on their own for the rest of the evening and any follow-up discussion was unnecessary.

I might have said that because I didn't want to endure the endless barrage of my father's silence and my mother's nagging that I couldn't handle criticism. But I also meant it in the way that I had everything I needed from a family in Snowfall. I had my girls and Mason.

Even if I didn't know how Mason fit into everything.

He wasn't my rival or the embarrassing one-night stand anymore. But I couldn't exactly call him a friend either.

Either way, since he dealt with my parents all weekend, picked up my business, and even drove them to the airport after that spat, I needed to do something for him. And the something I decided on was to bake.

"I didn't murder your mother, sweetheart. But I did fantasize about pushing her out of the car a time or two on the drive. And holy hell, what exploded in here?" Mason said as he stepped into the kitchen.

"Exploded? Don't be so dramatic, I just did a little baking." I wiped my hands down my apron looking everywhere but at Mason. What he'd said last night about not cooking outside of work unless it was for someone you cared for rang true. These days I only baked if someone really needed me. And for Mason, I guess.

"A little? Ashley, there's a good dozen cookies just in my line of sight. Lord knows what you've got cooling in the fridge."

"Well, you said you liked my peanut butter cookies. So … here." I scooped up a plate of cooled cookies and shoved them at Mason's chest. "Since we need to finalize the new shop's base menu, I figured I'd fine-tune this recipe and add it. There really wasn't any reason I kept it as a fall rotational, just that peanut butter reminds me of school starting. Based on that, I made one batch with raisins, another I put a jam topping on. I've been wanting to make my own jam, but the strawberries I planted in the community garden aren't ripe yet. So I don't think those are going to turn out as good, but —"

A cookie was plopped into my mouth.

"Mason," I grumbled around the cookie, looking up at the man with the biggest smirk on his face.

"You made me cookies," he said. A statement, not a question.

Mason slid the plate of cookies aside before scooping up me to set my ass on the counter beside them.

"What'd you make me cookies for, sweetheart?" Mason asked as he pulled at my knees and settled between them. It wasn't a sexual movement, it was too intimate and warm for that, which somehow made the ache inside me even worse.

"I told you, I'm testing new recipes for the shop." I kept my eyes down, staring at the Pub's logo on his chest, trying to figure out how we could merge our logos or if we'd need to get Olivia to make us a new one.

"Nah-uh," Mason said, clicking his tongue dramatically. The crook of his pointer finger hooked under my chin and forced my gaze to meet his. I wanted to poke the dimple peeking out from under his scruff. "I remember there being something about open honesty in that prenup of yours."

"That was in case either of us wanted to seek out physical intimacy from some—"

"Yeah, that's not happening, sweetheart. You're my wife, nobody else is gonna be providing you physical intimacy but me. Even if that means we're celibate for another three years."

"Another?" I repeated.

"I told you, there's been nobody else since you."

"But that one —" I started, only for Mason to bop a finger on my lips.

"Wasn't a date. Just happened to go out with a friend from high school that night. I haven't been out with anybody, for a date or just sex, since you."

"Why?" It was suddenly a very important question, that single word. I gripped at his biceps and pulled myself closer so I could hear the answer.

Mason's eyes searched mine for a long time. Long enough that I was starting to feel like an idiot. The answer had nothing to do with me, I was just reading into it with everything else going on with our fake marriage.

"Never mind, it's none of my business," I said, pulling away from him and placing a hand on his chest to push him out of the way so I could get down.

"No." Mason moved my hand over his heart, the organ beating wildly. "It is your business." He paused, eyes still roaming over my face like he was looking for something. But he bit his lip, shaking his head before saying, "But you're not ready to hear it."

Suddenly his hands were under my ass and I was being carried over to the couch.

"Mason," I grumbled, falling into his chest and holding on as he dropped into the cushions.

"Look, sweetheart, I spent two long-ass hours with your parents, holding my tongue the whole time. I need to decompress before I can truly enjoy your desserts." He laid down on the couch, keeping me tucked against his chest. "Let's just talk."

"Uh, about what?" I asked, my voice muffled against his chest.

"Was your mom always like that? All dismissive and shit?" Mason's grip around me tightened. With the turn of the conversation, I was grateful he couldn't see my face. I didn't talk about my parents because it stung that they didn't love me the way I would love my future kids. But I felt safe here, cuddled on the couch, the smell of fresh cookies filling the air. And I probably owed him after everything he put up with.

"Not really. I mean, maybe? Looking back on it, I'd only get praised over academic things, so I leaned into it. I was doing everything 'right' according to my mother. Up until I decided to quit that is."

Mason shuffled back, pressing to the back of the couch, arms still around my waist as he looked down at me.

"What was the catalyst for that? I know you weren't happy, but was there something specific that pushed you to make the change?"

"Um," I murmured, chewing at my lip.

"It wasn't some asshole, was it?" Mason asked, jaw tightening.

"Ha, I wish," I laughed. Because the real reason was so stupid, I'd never live it down.

"Ash, you're acting like some asshole breaking your heart would be preferable. And with that limited amount of information, my brain can get *very* creative. And if you don't tell me and I start gettin' worried, I'm apt to do something very stupid. Like, call your parents to find out what happened. Hell, I'll drive right up to New York and —"

"It was a commercial, god," I rushed out to say because I truly believed Mason was stubborn enough to follow through on every word.

"A commercial?" he repeated.

I took a deep breath, looking him in the eye before burying my face in his chest.

"You know those Pillsbury cinnamon roll commercials? The ones where the family is making the rolls together and then it's the kid's kids. I saw that commercial and I just ... I wanted that life."

"The life in the commercial?"

I pulled back, eyes narrowed at Mason who was fighting back a smile.

"You're making fun of me," I grumbled, smacking at his arms and trying to pull out of his hold. He held on tighter.

"No, almost laughing does not count as making fun of you. And for the record, neither do giggles or any other knee-jerk reactions. Now tell me more about this commercial, what'd you find so appealing about premade dough?"

"It wasn't the cinnamon rolls," I grumbled, smacking at his arm again. "It was the tradition, the family. I didn't have any of that. I didn't even have friends back then. I was miserable and had no human connection. My family was no more than 30 minutes away, but I barely even saw them, even on holidays. I saw the commercial and it just ... I dunno, it clicked. *That* was the kind of life I wanted. And once I realized that, everything that didn't fit needed to go."

"Like those suit skirts?" he teased, the corner of his mouth pulling up.

"Yup. All off to the donation bin." I twisted in Mason's arms and snuggled back into him. Over the weekend, I'd woken up a few times and snuggled just like this. It was comforting.

"Shame. Those would've done wonders for my sexy librarian fantasy."

My elbow went straight back into his stomach and through heavy coughs, Mason spouted claims that he was just kidding.

"In all seriousness though," he said once he'd recovered from the blow. "Are you closer to the life you wanted?"

"Closer, yeah," I whispered. "But parts of it feel impossible to get some days."

"The kids?"

"The kids," I confirmed. Mason's arms tightened around me, pulling me flat up against him. I waited for a come-on, for him to grind into me or offer himself up as a sperm donor. But none of that came. Instead, he held me closer, pressed a kiss to the top of my head, and whispered into my hair, "I want that too."

37

Banana Pudding

Ashley

My girls were back from Seattle, Bailey included, filling up my cafe with their stories and laughter. And unlike when they left, I wasn't bemoaning not being able to go. I was earnestly happy to listen because I had Mason to keep me company while they were gone. And when I talked about how Mason and I managed with my parents, I didn't have to lie or embellish our relationship.

"He did not?" Shea questioned, throwing back her head to laugh. "Aw, shit, I can totally picture that. Fuck. I want a girl to shit talk my parents for me."

Bailey's hand went to Shea's, a big, knowing smile lighting her face. "I think you'll find someone soon."

"Uh-huh, sure. You're just saying that because you've got museum boy tripping all over himself to keep your attention," Shea said, rolling her eyes and pushing off her best friend's arm.

"He's not tripping over himself."

"Dude called you like seven times during the *fight*," Zoey pointed out.

"Was it really that many?" Olivia asked, eyes wide.

"Mm-hmm," Shea said. "I wouldn't be surprised if he tried to propose to you by Christmas."

"That's nonsense." Bailey shook her head, long hair going everywhere. I couldn't tell if she was nervous about the possibility in a good or bad way.

"Are the boys over at the Pub?" I asked, craning my neck over the counter to see if I could catch a glimpse of them through the windows.

"Yeah. Apparently, Mason's coffee is better than Stephen's 'usual' place. We went back and he just stared at his cup after one sip like it had gone bad. He even asked the staff if they changed the recipe," Zoey said, smiling as she talked about her man.

"I'm glad they're all friends. Mason needs them. He told me about his high school buddies and I —" I realized that that part of our conversation might have just been between us. It was probably common knowledge Mason fell out of touch with them, but I didn't want to share things like that without him confirming it was okay. "I'm just glad is all."

"Oof, speaking of high school," Shea huffed, looking out of the window as a blond woman walked into Mason's shop. "That was Danielle, wasn't it?"

Every single one of their heads snapped to attention.

"No way," Zoey whispered.

"What a bitch," Roxie murmured.

"Now come on, we don't know why she's in town. She could just be stopping by to say hello," Rosie said, her soft voice a touch hesitant.

"Or she heard Mason got married and wants to remind her backup plan he's *her* backup plan," Roxie scoffed and for once Rosie didn't chastise her. Which was more than enough to worry me.

"Should I be concerned? Who is she?" I asked, pushing on my tiptoes to see into the Pub. I could see the blonde in question at the counter but I couldn't make out who she was talking to.

"She was Mason's girl all throughout high school, then they broke up in college," Roxie explained.

"I think they just grew apart," Rosie added.

"She was always kinda a bitch though," Shea said and various noises of shock slipped from the other girls. Shea just shrugged and said, "She was one of those, 'I don't care if you're gay just don't hit on me' girls. Gave me the ick."

"Really? Why didn't you tell me?" Bailey asked, her mouth dipping into an uncharacteristic frown. Shea just shrugged away her concern and leaned over the counter.

"Do you want us to do some reconnaissance? Or I can cover the register and you can go see what's up, stake your claim and all that shit."

"I'm texting Dennis," Olivia said and the rest started nodding in agreement. Stephen was over there too, but the man only looked at his phone when he needed it. He and Zoey didn't have a doom scroll problem like most of us.

"He says Mason took the woman to the side to talk." Olivia looked up at me, eyes so wide I thought they might fall out of her head. She was the anxious one of the group, so of course she was jumping to conclusions.

The problem was she wasn't the only one this time.

It wasn't hard to picture Mason's high school sweetheart hearing he'd gotten married and come back trying to prove they belonged together. Fuck, even I was beginning to find Mason attractive. Of course, she'd come to get him back. And the only thing stopping them from reuniting is a couple of papers and a rather impulsive business decision.

If he really wanted to get back with her, I had no right to deny him that.

"Nothing's going to happen, sweetie," Rosie assured, stretching her arm across the counter to give me an encouraging squeeze. "He's head over heels for you. You know that, right?"

"Right," I said, then immediately repeated it to reassure myself. "Right. I trust Mason, it's fine. You all should go home though and get some rest."

I started shooing them out of my shop, packed with boxes of treats to bring home before they inevitably conked out. Stephen and Dennis met them out on the curb and everyone dutifully left.

Except Shea.

"Are you sure you don't want me to duck my head in? I really don't mind."

I looked across the street again, unable to make out Mason or the girl.

"Is it that obvious I'm anxious about it or are you just looking for excuses not to go home?"

"Both," Shea said, running a hand through the long side of her stark red hair. "It's hard to go from all of us hanging out to quiet sometimes, ya know?"

"Yeah." I thought about my house, how I used to spend every night with the TV on or music playing. And how recently, I didn't need to because Mason would drag me into a conversation about how hard it'd be to literally rip off a proper bodice. He'd looked it up apparently. "Yeah. I get that. You're always welcome at my place though."

"And interrupt y'all's newlywed sexcapades? No way."

We shared a laugh and Shea went on home, with an extra scone for her offer to be my spy.

The day went on and I focused on work. I baked, I served customers, and I went through paint samples for the new shop. Through all of that I successfully only thought about Mason and that girl every few seconds.

I hadn't caught her exiting the store and that fact repeated over and over in my head like a broken record.

"Not my business," I muttered to myself. I was just being stupid. The lines had gotten blurred, but they were still there. Mason and I were just fake married and on friendlier terms. That was all.

But when I got home that night, I found myself dumping the leftover peanut butter cookies in the trash. I stared at them, feeling stupid for caring, for not just stopping by the Pub to ask Mason what happened, for thinking things might be changing between us, for thinking that and then letting some little incident ruin it.

I'll just call him now. I needed to know if he was going to be back for dinner anyway. He had the closing shift today, but he didn't always do a deep clean on weeknights, so his time home was variable. But if he was going to be home in the next hour or so, then we'd eat dinner together. Because that's what sensible adults living together do.

I paced around the kitchen as the phone rang, my mind racing with possibilities. The Pub was closed, she could have snuck back in and gone up to his apartment, waiting for him. As long as he hid it, it'd be within our contract. I couldn't be mad at him if he followed those rules, but —

"Ashley?" Mason said, voice surprised and rough.

"You sound out of breath." I didn't want him to be out of breath. I wanted him bored and lonely, wiping down the counters and counting the minutes till he could come home to me.

"Uh, yeah. I was hefting up the chairs to mop. Something wrong, sweetheart?"

"I just — well I saw that — the girls saw —" I hated this, this feeling of not knowing what was going on, of how it weighed my heart down. "You know what? I'm being stupid. I shouldn't have called. It doesn't matter anyway, so just forget it. I was ... being an idiot."

I could hear Mason start to talk, but I couldn't process it. If I heard his explanation, I'd just keep acting like an idiot. I'd do more than toss the cookies in the trash, that's for sure. It was best for everyone involved that I turned my phone to bedtime mode and went to my room. I'd just sit in the quiet and reorder everything in my mind so I wouldn't wish for anything else.

And that's what I did, until three sharp, demanding knocks shook my door.

38

Mexican Hot Chocolate

Mason

After a shit day, I was excited to see my wife call me. For once, she was reaching out to me. Maybe wondering when I'd get home, hoping we could have dinner together, asking for some sort of connection.

She almost did. Or at least that's what I thought was gonna happen until she pulled away and started bad-mouthing herself again.

And I was absolutely through with that shit.

I locked up the restaurant faster than if I'd been told my home was on fire, the mop bucket sitting in the middle of the room, a pile of trash swept to one corner, and the radio playing. Travis was gonna be pissed when he clocked in tomorrow morning, but like fuck was I gonna let all the progress we made this weekend fizzle out because she got caught up in ... whatever it was she'd been trying to say.

Well, she wasn't getting away with pushing me out this time. We were gonna talk this shit through whatever it was.

After breaking several speeding limits, I parked outside our home and marched straight to her room, knocking hard enough to rattle the wood. Then, without waiting for a response, I opened the door to see my wife sitting on the bed, dried tears on her cheeks.

It took all my restraint to walk over to the side of the bed slowly, all my restraint to just drag her ass to the edge of the bed instead of laying her down and caging her in. I stood over her, hands braced on the bed next to her thighs, fingers digging into the sheets.

I was done not talking about us, but I was still scared of pushing for too much too soon. I needed to keep this simple. One issue at a time kind of simple.

"Why're you upset, sweetheart?" I asked, my voice angrier than I meant it to sound. But hell, my wife was crying over something and that sort of thing pissed me off apparently.

Ashley straightened, her features falling into place one by one. Her throat cleared, her shoulders pulled back, and her mouth settled into an unbothered, flat line.

"I understand your ... first love stopped by today. And I'm sure that brought up some old feelings. Dennis said you two talked, so we should discuss —"

I lost control of every damn nerve in my body. One hand went up to grab a fistful of her hair so I could slam her lips to mine. Ashley gasped and I took every advantage that gave me. This woman was too damn frustrating to kiss with anything but every desperate need I felt for her. And she tasted like peanut butter.

"You've been eating my cookies," I noted, not pulling away from her lips. I deepened the kiss, leaning her down until her back hit the mattress.

"Mason," she whined, hands coming to my shoulders. She didn't push me away, but she didn't pull me in either. So I stayed there, waiting for her to move.

"I don't understand what you're doing here. But I told you before, we can make arrangements if you want to get back together with Danielle."

"I don't want any arrangements other than the ones I have with you," I growled. "I talked with Dani for all of ten minutes, maybe even less. She asked if I was happy and I said yes because I have the most stunning wife in the whole goddamn world." I slammed my lips back to hers for a rough but quick kiss. Too many words were flooding my head and I needed the right ones to come out first because I somehow knew this was not the moment to stick my foot in my mouth. "A wife who is driving me insane with all this stupid, idiot talk."

"What?" she stuttered, eyes sparkling and wide, cheeks flushing.

"You call yourself stupid and an idiot way too much for my liking." I moved her hands around my neck, yanking her up the bed so I could crawl on and place one knee between her thighs.

"I don't understand." Her voice was getting breathy, her eyes bouncing all over my face.

How much clearer can I make this without scaring her away?

"That's right, you don't understand." Another rough, short kiss. This time she hummed into me, her hips rising up to grind on the front of my thigh. "There are so many damn things we need to get cleared up in this relationship, sweetheart. But let's start with these two."

I pulled away from her and she let out the sweetest little whimper that would have gotten me to do anything she wanted on any other day. But I was focused on fulfilling the half-baked plan cooking in the back of my head. I grabbed my girl's hips and twisted her onto her stomach before pulling her up to her knees, back pressed against my chest. Then I took her chin and pointed her face at the standing mirror in the corner of the room, where she was now on full display.

"One. *You* are my wife. You are mine to have and to hold. And I will be faithful to you and you alone."

"But this is —" she started, jaw wobbling. But I interrupted with a thrust of my aching cock against her ass.

"*You are my wife,*" I repeated. "I don't know how many times I've got to say it before your stubborn ass gets it."

Keeping one hand on her chin, I started undoing the buttons of her sleep shirt. With each button undone her breath caught until she damn near stilled.

"Two, I don't take too kindly to folks insulting what's mine, even when it comes from you. And I've noticed you calling yourself names too many damn times for me to let slide."

"I'm not yours," she huffed as the final button came undone. The shirt slid open and caught on her breast in a way that was deliciously teasing.

"It's a sentiment, sweetheart. You know what I mean by it." I kissed the sensitive spot just above her collarbone before giving it a little nip. "But maybe you need a little more proof, huh?"

"Proof?" she repeated, head lulling to the side so I could keep at her. Since the act felt like a request, I obliged. Nipping and kissing up her neck.

"Yeah. You are the smartest, most successful woman I have ever met. And it's a shame you don't realize that." Goosebumps spread across her neck as my breath skated over her skin. Then she huffed and shook the effect away.

"I'm not successful. You saw my application, I'm barely making ends meet."

I jerked her body up, hand on her chin forcing her gaze to meet mine in the mirror.

"Not successful? You think anyone can just waltz into a small town, a tight-knit community like Snowfall, and turn a profit? Even steal profits from a local business that's been around for decades? You've charmed everyone in town, Ashley. *Everyone.* When everything was set up against you, *you* drew everybody in. What you've accomplished so far is nothing short of a miracle. Stop selling yourself short."

"I've considered selling." She whispered the admission and my heart damn near gave out.

"What?" She started sinking back into me and real panic set in. Panic as bad as during thunderstorms. "Why would you ever consider that?"

"I'm barely keeping even. I bought a house too big for me. I can barely pay for part-time help. It's getting too much on my own."

"Well, good thing you're not alone anymore." Her eyes re-focused on me, searching and questioning and probably mis-construing every word out of my mouth. Well then, I might as well just stop talking and show her. "I'm gonna punish you, sweetheart."

"Punish?" she said, but the word swooped out of her mouth as I twisted her waist around and tossed her onto the bed. The move had fully opened her shirt and fucking Christ, I'd forgot-ten how perfect those tits were. I crawled over her, kissing up her stomach and nipping at the underside of her breast.

"This is how tonight is gonna go, sweetheart. Unless you want me to stop, you only speak when I tell you to. Given how argumentative you are, that should be punishment enough." I looked up at her, hands gliding up her waist. There was a lot going on behind those gorgeous eyes, but one thought was clear from her raised eyebrow. She heard the 'but' and wanted answers. I could oblige her that much.

"*But* you like quick and rough, so we'll be going nice and slow this time." I kissed my way over the curve of her breast, only letting my lips brush over her nipple before moving to the other side. Ashley huffed, but the sound transformed into a moan when I sunk my teeth into her skin.

"I can't wait to find out every single noise you make, sweet-heart. But do you agree to take your punishment like a good girl?"

"Yes," she panted, her breath hitching as one of my hands trailed down her side and tucked into her shorts. She lifted her hips but I made no move to take off her shorts. There'd be time for that.

"Condom?"

"No," she answered quickly.

"And why's that?" I stroked my thumb over her hip bone, careful not to pull her shorts down any further, and swirled my tongue over her hardening nipple. She arched up and I pinned her right back down. "Tell me, sweetheart. Why don't I have to wear a condom when I fill up this sweet pussy?"

"Because I'm fine with getting pregnant."

I sucked hard, pulling away so her nipple popped out of my mouth. She watched as I moved to the other side, keeping my eyes on her so she knew I didn't believe her half-truth. But I'd accept it for now.

"And how did you feel when you thought I was with some other woman?"

"Scared." The word was possibly the softest thing she'd ever said to me and it shattered me to pieces. This woman, brave and stubborn, should never feel scared of a damn thing. And most certainly not when it came to me.

"Scared? Sweetheart, I was going for jealous there." I pressed soft kisses up her body until I was right over her, showering her face with more kisses, at a loss for what else to do. "What part of it scared you?"

"I don't know. But It's not like I have a right to be jealous either." Her head fell to the side, eyes going out of focus.

I don't think I've ever been so emotionally wrecked while still being as hard as a flag pole. Her body was warm and soft underneath me and she was so lost in her head that none of it mattered. I needed to pull her out of those thoughts.

Grabbing her waist again, I flipped us around, me on my back and Ashley straddled over me. Her face was flushed, shock and movement draining her of color. But she almost immediately resituated herself to grind against my cock, a soft sigh escaping her lips.

"That's yours, sweetheart. It has been for a long ass time." I thrusted up and was rewarded with a strangled cry of my name. "And it's not like you haven't gotten jealous over me before, right? Tell me, you trash any of my shit tonight?"

She bit her lip but a grin was fighting through.

"Those were two different situations," she argued. The light was coming back to her eyes, the green sharpening into focus

"Not really. You, wrongly, thought I wanted someone else and acted out. Last time it was my apartment, this time you took digs at yourself. So tell me what else took a hit so I can start fixing things up."

"Your cookies might've ended up in the trash," she admitted sheepishly, a smile pulling her lips up. And fuck, the loss of the cookies she baked me was a real shame but I'd sacrifice every damn thing I've ever owned to get her to smile after a bad spell like that.

"That's my girl."

Her smile stretched ear to ear and she was absolutely glowing.

"So," she said, rocking her hips against me. "Are we still gonna do the whole punishment thing?"

"We sorta circled around a whole emotional thing there. Doesn't feel right to punish you now," I murmured as I pushed to sit up and wrapped my arms around her, keeping her close. "What does my wife feel like doing?"

"My husband."

39

Apple Cheddar Galette

Ashley

Before I could fully process what had just slipped out of my mouth, I was flipped on my back again.

Head still spinning, Mason's body collapsed onto mine, pressing hot and sloppy kisses against my neck. With his arms bracketing my head, his hands sank into my hair, pulling me so he could kiss the spot that gave me full-body chills.

I had to give Mason credit, once he learned how to make my body melt, he didn't forget. Even that time Tost-Ka, he went right back to that spot, despite having years to forget about it.

"Say it again." His voice had gone through several types of gruffness since he barged into my room. This one was my favorite. A roughness of desperation. All because he wanted me to call him mine.

The thought tugged at a chord tucked deep in my heart.

"I want my husband." His response was immediate, a deep, satisfied groan and his hips grinding in between my thighs at the exact perfect angle.

"How do you want him, sweetheart?" he asked, still rocking into me. It was so hard for my brain to hold on to words with the way my body buzzed. All I really knew was that what he'd been talking about earlier sounded nice. Different from the usual we were starting to build.

"Nice and slow," I said, even as my hands pulled at his tucked-in shirt, desperate to feel his skin on mine. Once the fabric was loose, I dragged my nails up his back, resting my hands on his shoulders and pulling him closer. He came willingly, his weight resting on me like a blanket.

"You're gonna be the death of me, you know that, sweetheart?" he whispered into my ear, hands beginning to pull at my open shirt.

"Hmm, if you die and they can't prove it's me, do I get the Pub?" Mason was so warm, his weight against me so comforting, my eyes flitted closed and my hips raised. I wanted to be encompassed by him, have him occupy every single one of my senses. I *needed* it.

"You get everything, sweetheart." His hands slid under my now bare back and pulled me up so I felt every hard inch of him. I was very well aware of what we were working with in terms of Mason's dick. But there was something about feeling him be *this* hard after our conversation twisted back and forth from sex to vulnerability. He hadn't been turned off by it. In fact, it seemed like he liked our little talk *a lot*.

"Mason." I tugged at his shirt, pulling it as far off him as I could, though that was only up to his shoulders. He grumbled some nonsense before pushing up to his knees and grabbed the shirt from the back collar to pull it off.

Heat pooled between my thighs.

Then he crawled off the bed, his hands eagerly tearing his jeans down. But as he pushed them past his thighs, his eyes caught mine and he slowed. I immediately groaned, making Mason chuckle.

"You asked for nice and slow, don't be mad at me for following instructions." With his jeans finally gone, Mason stood at the edge of my bed with nothing but a pair of boxer briefs on. Grey, with little donuts on them. And a stick straight boned underneath them.

"What're you thinking?" he asked, one knee resting on the bed as he leaned over me. His hands slid up my body, from waist to breasts, kneading my skin in a way that dissolved all my tension. His grip softened as his fingers met my nipples, grazing the raised skin too gently. He pressed the pad of his thumb, smoothing out the skin, teasing me. "I wanna know what had you licking your lips like that."

"Donuts sound good right now," I murmured. The slow pace of his fingers on me wasn't all that bad. Like sitting in front of a fire on a summer night, you know it's going to get to be too much soon, but you wanna enjoy it for as long as you can.

Mason chuckled, his eyes flying briefly down to his underwear to confirm what he had on. "You know, I don't think I've ever made donuts before. Have you?"

"Mhmm." The way his hands massaged into my breast was heaven. And just as I was lulling into the rhythm, he pinched my nipples and my back arched in a sharp needy thrust.

"We should make some together," he said, a playful smirk pulling his lips up. "You got a home fryer?"

"Uh-huh," I answered with a whine as he pulled at my nipples before kissing the sting away.

"What kind should we make?" Mason's hands slid to my back and down my shorts, grabbing at my ass and kneading the skin. I arched into it, my hands going to the band to strip the remainder of my clothes.

"Chocolate. Chocolate cake donuts are the best." It was a wildly foreign thought, but I was utterly grateful Mason didn't stop me from taking my pants off. There was only so much slow I could take after having been worked up so much already.

"Hmm. Chocolate cake is all right, but I'm more partial to blueberry." He moved away from my breast to kiss my lips again. His kiss was languid, thorough and slow in a way we'd never really had the opportunity for. I returned his kiss with the same energy, exploring the taste of him, noting the way he reacted to each movement.

"We can make chocolate with blueberries," I murmured into his mouth.

"Hmm, marriage is all about compromise, huh?" Mason used the knee braced on the bed to shove my legs apart, dancing his fingers up and down my stomach.

"Can we compromise on your definition of slow too? I only meant slow enough to make sure I could come first."

Mason bit my lip and dragged his teeth over my skin.

"You're never gonna let that go, are you?" His fingers dipped down, finally sliding over my cunt. "No wonder you were anxious to get going. You're real worked up, aren't you?"

"It's your fault," I grumbled, arching up to try to get him to finger me. But he was either dense or deliberately torturing me. "And edging me won't make me forget, if that's what you're going for."

"Well, you didn't let me do any foreplay that time and then destroyed my patio. I've learned my lesson." His lips found that spot on my neck again and his fingers *finally* slid inside me. Just having his fingers in me eased some tension in my body. I sunk into the bed, head rolling back with a heavy sigh.

"I didn't destroy your patio because you came first," I murmured, not wholly aware of what I was confessing. I was just so soothed by the way he was treating my body, the way I could feel the warm build-up in every cell of my body. "I did it because you fucked me under false pretenses. I thought you wanted me but you just wanted the shop."

Mason's lips on mine paused for a moment before slamming into me. The kisses took a hard turn from exploration to claiming.

"That is *not* what happened," he growled into my lips as his fingers changed from slow strokes to hard passes over my G-spot, his palm grinding into my overly swollen clit. "Every time I touch you, it's because I want you so fucking bad, it hurts. Seeing you flirt with Grant drove me fucking crazy. No way in hell he wants you as bad as I do, as bad as I always have. I fucked you then cause I couldn't help myself. It had jack shit to do with the shop. And if I said anything that implied that, it was an excuse to get you to give me the time of day. Just like every single prank has been."

As Mason spoke, his fingers coaxed out a sort of twisting heat I didn't know my body was capable of. It was stormy and all-encompassing and summoned a flood of warmth that spasmed through my body like a tsunami. It was too much, but also perfect. Like that first sip of hot chocolate on a cold day, where it burns your tongue just as much as it warms you up.

"God, my wife is so fucking stunning," Mason murmured, his eyes flitting all over my body. From my flushed face to the goosebumps along my arms. From my breasts rising and falling with heavy pants to where his hand still stroked the hottest part of me.

"See, if you just give me a minute, I can please you, sweetheart." His eyes met mine, that gorgeous blue sparkling with an 'I told you so' look and a smirk that was just as irritating as it was enduring.

I think it's my turn to play with him.

My hands found his, entwining our fingers and pulling him forward. With his weight on me, I wrapped my legs around his waist, no doubt leaving a distinct mark across his underwear, and twisted us around.

The movement was a mess of limbs and giggles as I rolled us so I was on top of Mason. Once he'd figured out what I was doing, he went willingly, easing his limbs so I could move him where I wanted. And his smile … it was bright and soft and tender. It was his real smile. Or maybe just the most reserved one, only for special occasions.

I wanted to claim it as mine.

He was my husband, after all, his best smiles *should* be mine.

So I kissed him like he was mine. Gently and without the usual fervor of scratching an itch. I kissed him like I had all the time in the world with this man and we wouldn't go back to the pranks and the stubborn arguments when all this was over.

Satisfied, I pulled back, intending to slide down his briefs, but his hands found my face, holding me in place just a few inches away.

"You're never going to stop surprising me, are you?" he murmured, stroking my cheek with a tenderness that stuttered my heart, made the very vital organ forget how to function completely.

"I need you, Mason."

Simple words. That's all they were. They didn't mean anything more.

And given the way Mason slid his briefs down to pull out his cock, I knew he didn't take them as more than what I meant.

Without a word, Mason's hands went to my hips, gently guiding me onto his cock. We both let out a sigh of relief as he filled me, my body slumping down onto his. One of his hands stayed on my hip, while the other fisted into my hair, not tight or pulling, just a way to hold me close.

We lay there in silence, the only noise our labored breath and raging hearts. But there was a sort of peace in the moment. Connected and settled.

And then, with the ease of something habitual, we began to move. We didn't say anything, we didn't even look at each other, but we were in unison. Our bodies moved, chasing warmth at a slow and easy place. Mason's head cradled into my neck, lips grazing over my skin, not really kissing but just there, like he knew I needed the touch and he needed it just as much as me.

At some point, Mason rolled us over, maneuvering on top of me and placing my legs on his shoulders. He bent me in half, leaning into me to capture my lips for a brief kiss.

"I need you too, Ashley." Another kiss, this time accompanied by him rolling his hips, hitting so deep inside me I could cry.

I wrapped my arms around his neck and pulled him closer. It wasn't close enough. I scratched at his chest and tugged at his hair, my hands restless as my second orgasm started to build and build and build. It was a slow climb, a slow ball twisting tighter and tighter and the only relief I had was holding onto Mason like my life depended on it.

"Let go, sweetheart, I've got you."

Curse this man's smooth Southern accent and the way it coaxed me into coming.

This orgasm was a sweet release, not explosive but comforting. Like he'd sucked away all the tension in my body and I could finally relax. And with the last shudders of my release, Mason found his own, sinking into me with a final thrust and collapsing down to press kisses into sweaty skin.

"You can't be too stubborn with me anymore, okay?" he whispered, trailing the kisses from my neck up to my cheek.

"Hmm, I think that's asking a lot of me," I murmured, the orgasm blissfully diluting my desire to argue with him. In fact, he could probably ease a lot of my stubbornness with orgasms if he could keep up the good work.

"I'll always return the favor." Mason started to pull away and I tried to grab at him to keep the peace I'd found in his arms, but he just laughed and pushed my arms away.

"Shush, sweetheart, I've been dying to know what we taste like together." Mason cupped one hand under my cunt and pulled out of me. The loss had me grumbling. I was perfectly content to lie there for a few more minutes. But then Mason sank to his knees and pulled my ass to the edge of the bed.

"Can't give you kids, if you don't keep this in there," her murmured, his fingers scooping lines of come dripping down my thigh and shoving it back inside me. He teased my G-spot with two gentle strokes, before copying the motion with the mess on my other thigh.

He pulled back, admiring his work and I sank into the bed, relieved he wasn't going to do anymore. As hot as him shoving his come into me was, I don't think I could take any more stimulation.

"God, I've been starving."

Mason's mouth was on my come-filled cunt, his tongue teasing my clit before pushing his come deeper inside me. My brain completely stopped functioning, I was literally babbling nonsense of more and fuck and feels good falling out of my mouth as I dug my fingers into his hair.

And Mason just kept going, moaning into my pussy like it was the best meal he'd ever had.

Even if I was held at gunpoint, I couldn't tell you if I came multiple times or if it was just one time that never really ended.

"Fuck that's good." Mason pulled away, standing up with a shit-eating grin, looking down at me with satisfaction. I'd have loved to hassle him, but my brain was disconnected.

"I can't believe you did that," I whispered once I could finally find words between heavy pants. It was hard to catch my breath seeing Mason with our come shining on his lips.

"What do ya mean?" Mason pulled his underwear back on and then headed to the restroom. I waited until he returned, a wet washcloth in hand, to explain.

"You just ate me out after coming inside me." It was a wild thing to say out loud.

"I told you I would."

"Sure, but I didn't think you actually would. I thought it was just … I dunno, talk."

"I'm not too proud to say I never talk shit I don't intend to follow through with." Mason returned to the bed, wiping down my thighs before helping me into my clothes. "But that'll never be the case with you."

"Don't you find it gross?" Clothes on, Mason took my hand and pulled me to stand in front of him.

"No. Do you?"

"No."

Our chests were just a breath apart. I could smell my come on his lips.

I liked that he smelled like me.

"Good. Then there's nothing wrong with it." His head tilted to the side. "Unless you're upset you haven't gotten a taste yet."

Yeah, I was.

But instead of admitting that out loud, I slid my hand around his neck and pulled him into a kiss.

Savory was the best word to describe how we tasted together. Umami if I was being pretentious about it.

My stomach grumbled. A long and loud gurgle that ruined the moment. Except Mason only chuckled, pulling away to place a kiss on my forehead before wrapping an arm around me.

"Since you were my dessert, it's only fair I make you dinner."

40

Cinnamon Tea

Mason

Last night was a fucking dream. I'm not sure how much I'd actually gotten through to Ashley, but nothing about us felt fake, that's for sure. We were on the verge of something real, something that was gonna last. And fuck I don't think I've ever been more excited for something in my life.

So when the morning came, I was a little reluctant to start the day. I wanted to stay in our bubble, stay in the bed I shared with my wife, and keep my dreams tucked away, safe and warm.

Except the feeling of my briefs being tugged down popped that bubble in the most enticing of ways.

My eyes fluttered open to my wife kneeling at the side of the bed, her left hand wrapped around my cock, rings sparkling on her finger. She'd braided her hair back in that little crown thing again, all ready for the day in her pretty little dress and her husband's cock in her mouth.

And holy fuck, she was waking me up with a blow job.

"Ashley," I groaned. My whole body was instantly on fire as she slowly sank her mouth over my dick.

"Mhmm?" The vibration of her throat was gonna kill me. I'd just managed to keep from coming immediately when fucking her, but I was gonna need a lot more practice before I could handle her mouth.

"Sweetheart, it's too much." But fuck if I didn't slide my hand to the nape of her neck to guide her motions. She moaned in approval and I gave up the fight, as if I stood a chance of telling her she couldn't do whatever the hell she pleased with me.

"Fuck, if we're doing this, can I stand and have you on your knees for me?"

Ashley's eyes met mine, big and beautiful green that sucked my soul out of my body. Then she twisted her tongue over my head and my soul was completely gone. She'd stolen it and took it with her as she let my cock fall out of her mouth and she settled onto the floor.

"Christ, you can't indulge me like this too often, sweetheart. Having too many dreams come true in a row will ruin me."

"You dreamed of this?" she asked as I climbed off the bed and stood in front of her, her eyes glued to my cock.

"Are you kidding me? Of course, I did. After every one of your little pranks, I'd dream of you coming over to the Pub, all sheepish-like. You'd bat those pretty eyes at me and ask if you could apologize for all the trouble you'd given me. You'd take us somewhere private and get down on your knees, letting me fuck that smart mouth of yours. Then you'd smile up at me, licking my come off your lips, and ask if I forgave you."

Ashley looped her finger around the band of my briefs and pulled me closer. She smiled up at me, mischief and desire darkening her eyes.

"And do you forgive me?" Her breath tickled my cock and she pressed a kiss to the aching flesh.

"Fuck, sweetheart, there's nothing to forgive." My hand went to the nape of her neck and I stroked the little pieces of hair that had already fallen loose from her braid. "You can do any goddamn thing you want to me and I'll thank you for it."

The color of her eyes shifted just a shade, thought roiling like a storm behind all that green. Her tongue peeked out of her lips and traced a vein n my cock before twisting over my head.

"Then let me do what I want," she said. Without warning, she yanked me by my briefs, pulling so my cock sank deep into her mouth. She paused there, taking slow breaths through her nose. Each second teased at the ache, knotting me up inside. She could probably make me come if she sat like this for long enough.

But then she started moving and I saw stars. Her mouth glided over my cock, occasionally sucking in so her cheeks hollowed out. And all the while her tongue caressed the sensitive skin on my head, stroking and tracing.

"Shit. I'm real damn close, sweetheart. Either stop now or let me know if you're swallowin' or not."

Ashley hummed around me, quickening the bob of her head. I dug my hands into the neck of her dress so I didn't ruin her braids and spilled into her mouth as soon as I got that permission. Because fuck, if my girl couldn't get me worked up quicker than a cat on a hot tin roof. Ashley took her time swallowing, slow gulps as her tongue passed over my sensitive cock. I was either going to pass out or come again and I wasn't sure which.

"Hmm, I guess I should be thankful you don't take long when I'm on my knees," Ashley teased, a lightness in her voice as she carefully pulled away. There wasn't a single drop wasted.

Knees still wobbly, I picked Ashley up by the armpits and tossed her onto the bed. Before she had a chance to squirm away, I took her hips and brought her onto her knees, the hem of her sundress just covering the swell of her ass.

"Mason, what're you —" she started grumbling. But her voice stumbled as my knees hit the floor.

"You can't get me all riled up like that and expect me to not eat you out, sweetheart." I slid my hands over her ass, pulling up the skirt of her dress before yanking her panties down to her knees. The scent of her arousal made my mouth water. "Besides, my wife got *so fucking* wet sucking me off. I've gotta reward that, right?"

"But I —" I ran my fingers along her pussy and her ass pushed back. "I was trying to keep up even."

"Even?" I chuckled. "Sweetheart, two to one is the minimum."

"But I came three times last night and I wanted to … do something for you." Ashley had buried her face in the blankets, grumbling but staying perfectly still. I pressed a chaste little kiss to her ass.

"I appreciate that, sweetheart, I really do. But there's something called an orgasm gap where cishet women don't reach climax as often as other groups. And I'm not letting you become a statistic." My lips trailed down, kissing ass to thigh as my hands maneuvered her legs apart just enough for my lips to coast up to her cunt. We both groaned as my lips met hers.

There was something about the taste of her first thing in the morning that was soothing. Like this was a common occurrence and I could take my time. I explored her cunt, tracing my tongue over her until I had her shape memorized and she was shaking. Then I focused on her clit until she came apart.

A simple process really. Repeated actions accompanied by breathless moans.

I wanted to start all my mornings like this.

"Are you done or are you gonna overstimulate me again?" Ashley grumbled, pushing her ass against my face to knock me backward. Laughing, I gave her a little smack before pulling her underwear back up.

"I have a feeling you'd get mad at me if I took it any further." Arm around her waist, I pulled Ashley off the bed to stand in front of me. She turned, her eyes narrowed in a stern look that didn't have any bite in it with the way her cheeks flushed.

"We have to get to work. This was supposed to be a quick little … thing." She was still grumbling, like she needed to act unhappy about the whole thing to keep her dignity. It was awfully cute.

"Yeah, all right. Let's get ready then." I tucked a stray hair behind her ear and kissed her cheek. These were my mornings now, little arguments, her being stubborn and pretending like she doesn't enjoy my antics, the eye rolls. It was perfect.

41

Pan Au Cholcolat

Ashley

I was confused. Lines were blurring and I couldn't get my footing in this new ... whatever it was.

Mason and I were legally married and having sex on a possibly regular basis. He called me his a lot. He did sweet little things to make my life easier like sneaking away from the Pub to help during my morning rush to help. And every time I looked at him, bubbles floated around in my chest.

It was like we'd hit a newlywed phase without taking any of the steps a relationship should go through. And it was throwing me off balance.

So instead of heading home after I sold out during lunch, I went to the community garden to think and check on my strawberries.

The garden was something Ms. Taylor had set up next to the church-turned-community center last year at the urging of one of the old lady gang members. I couldn't remember which one, they all were a blend of grouchy and their raspy voices were hard to tell apart sometimes. But the garden had actually turned out to be one of their better ideas. It was a decently sized plot next to the church that had been plowed and fertilized before opening up to the public. At the entry gate, there was little library equivalent for seeds and a comically large, tape-covered QR code that led to a *very* thorough document that contained community rules and basic gardening tips. Whoever Ms. Taylor had gotten to set this up, they knew what they were doing.

Unfortunately, Clive did not respect all the work that had gone into the garden. Regularly the garden latched was found up and the garden rummaged through with various parts of the chain fence dented and scratched up.

My strawberries were not spared during Clive's last tirade.

I took a picture of my ruined little bush and sent it to the girl chat.

Me: Look at what your precious Clive has done

Zoey: Wasn't him, no proof

Olivia: There's no way it was anyone but Clive

Zoey: It could have been raccoons

Shea: NC does have the highest population of raccoons

Olivia: Seriously?

Olivia: I'm fact checking this

Olivia: I'm only seeing one Quora post about it, so let's take that with a grain of salt

Olivia: Also Terminex is saying the only state there aren't any raccoons is Alaska. Are there native Hawaiian raccoons?

I left the girls to discuss the possibility of raccoons in Hawaii and tried to assess if there was anything that could be done to save my strawberries. The berries remaining weren't ripe and there definitely weren't enough to make any jam, not even a test batch.

Without letting myself dwell on it for too long, I pulled my phone out again to text Mason a picture.

Me: Think you can lasso Clive and drag his ass away from the garden?

Mason: For you, anything

Mason: But you should garden in the back yard instead, pretty sure Clive can't get through a 6 foot, wooden fence

Me: I dunno, he seems pretty clever

Me: Plus I'm not sure it'd be worth the hassle to set up. I just wanted to grow some fruit to try making jam

Mason: I'll build you a garden

I sat with the offer for a moment. I hadn't really taken the time to look into what building a garden would take. I certainly had the yard space, but I didn't even have the time to care for this one deer-sacked bush let alone a whole garden. And Mason didn't exactly have much free time either.

He didn't have much free time and he still offered to build me a garden for a hobby I was just considering.

Mason: Come by the Pub when you're done at the garden

Me: Why?

Mason: Because I miss you

Me: I saw you a few hours ago

Mason: Don't shame me for missing my wife

I slid my phone back in my pocket and tried to ignore the way my heart was thundering.

This is what I wanted when I moved to Snowfall, Mason and a future. I had it right in my hands, for the next three years at least. I could enjoy it while it lasts. Three years is a long time, I might find reasons to hate him again by the time our contract is up.

I mean, it's Mason, after all, he's bound to stop being sweet and do something idiotic any moment now.

42

Affogato

Mason

"What're you grinning about?" Travis asked as he rounded the bar to fix up somebody's order.

"My wife texted me first today." I knew I looked like an idiot. I've had a comically big grin plastered on my face all day. There was no helping it though, my wife was actually starting to feel like mine. And after all these years of repression, I was giddy as fuck and about to cry.

"If you're this excited about her texting you first, I'm worried about the longevity of your relationship."

"Ah, shut up and let me be happy." I nudged Travis just enough to ruin his pour for the cappuccino he was making. He glared at me and dumped the cup into the sink.

"I'm just saying a first text is not something you should be romanticizing. And I'd very much like the new place to be successful, if only so I can work a shop Ashley's set up." Travis had talked nonstop about Ashley's register system and process notes. He was so obsessed with them that he'd taken it upon himself to get a quote for getting it set up in the Pub. Had it been anyone but Travis, I'd be suspicious about how they felt about my girl. But Travis was so work-focused, I don't think he'd notice if the perfect woman for him walked into the shop and winked at him.

The bell over the door rang and I looked up, eager to see my wife or settle for the woman for Travis. But it was just Bailey, and Ashley mentioned she'd just gotten together with some museum donor or something. I couldn't tell ya why, but I didn't think he suited her. Her free spirit needed a tight ass to balance her out.

"Hey, Bailey. How ya doing?"

She sat on the stool, letting out a heavy sigh. "Oh, fine. Just … well it always feels like I've missed out on too much when I come back, you know?"

"Can't say I can relate. Sorry. Caramel macchiato?"

"Yes, please. Oh, I don't think we've met. Bailey Hartley." Bailey pushed up on her stool and held a hand out to Travis. He looked at me, then back at the woman, blinking rapidly.

Interesting.

"Right, Travis Sutton." He shook Bailey's hand while I fixed her drink. She struck up a conversation, somehow getting Travis to talk about Jayson and what sorta things his kid likes. Talking about his kid eased the tension in his shoulders.

Hope I'm not the one to break the news to him that she's not single.

The bell rang again and I thought surely this time it'll be Ashley.

But of course it wasn't. It was my ex.

I would say Dani and I parted on good enough terms that she could stop by without ruffling feathers. We'd dated from freshman year of high school to freshman year of college. She'd been my first girl and back then, I figured she'd be my only. She'd been supportive when I'd lost my parents, as I struggled to get along with my uncle when he drank, but she somehow assumed that after 18, my attitude on drinking would change. She wanted to get wasted at college parties, drink whatever was offered to her, while I stood by like a bodyguard. And of course, I'd do anything to protect her and keep her safe, but the anxiety of that responsibility coupled with the way she didn't give a single shit about what watching folks drink did to me meant I had to cut ties.

And of course, when I sat her down to do that, she accused me of complaining about taking care of her, said I was calling her a burden when other girls were doing the same thing.

That was the last time we'd talked too. Until the other day when she stopped by and made my wife all upset.

Though I suppose I did get a good conversation out of it.

"Hi Mason," Dani said, giving me a bright smile as she stepped up to the register.

"Hello, Danielle, how can I help you?" I tried to straighten my shoulders and look presentable when what I really wanted to do was toss her out.

"Oh no, not my government name," she teased, giggling like we were making some sort of inside joke. From the corner of my eye, I caught Bailey making a gagging motion and Travis chuckling.

"Long time no see, Dani," Bailey said once she'd pasted over a fake smile. "I'm bi now, did you know?"

I raised an eyebrow, confused by the lie. Had Bailey come out, Shea would've thrown the biggest party Snowfall had ever seen. Plus a betting pool on those two would start up.

But then I saw Danielle's reaction and I got it. Her eyes went wide and she scooted back. It wasn't a big movement, but it was obvious enough.

"That's wonderful, good for you," she said with a big smile and all the insincere cheer of fried cotton candy.

"I'm in a relationship with a dude though, so you don't have to worry your pretty little head," Bailey grumbled, rolling her eyes. Travis' gaze narrowed on her, clearly trying to work out what was happening and how much of what Bailey had said was the truth.

Dani's shoulders eased and she reached over the counter to place a hand on my arm.

"That's wonderful, right, Mason?" She gave me a little squeeze and I was considering all out banning her from the Pub. My arms were crossed, so my hand and wedding band were right below where she was touching me.

Plus that biphobic shit was not welcome in here. I was gonna need to pull one of the girls aside to see if that shit was something new or something my dumbass couldn't recognize back in high school.

"Could you get your hands off my husband, please?"

I looked over to the door to see Ashley, my stunning wife, arms crossed and her knees red from sitting in the garden, glaring at Dani. Jealousy was written all over her face and I knew I shouldn't, but I was grinning like a fool again.

Turns out Ashley had a bit of a possessive streak. And I liked it. I liked it so god damn much, I loved it. I loved her and I loved being hers.

I stepped away from the counter, Dani's hand falling away, not worth the energy to shrug off. Then I went over to my wife. I wrapped her up in my arms, squeezing her a little too tight as I picked her up and swung her around.

"Ashley, I ..." I set her back down and she tilted around me to glare at Dani some more while the words caught in my throat. I knew now wasn't the time, but she'd just claimed me in front of my ex and a good deal of folks here for dinner. The words were gonna spill out my mouth and probably scare her away. We'd just gotten past the 'this is more than a fake marriage' stage. If I fucked this up now, I'd be a mess of a man. If I scared her away now, if she decided she didn't like how fast we were going, if she called it quits for any reason, I could easily see me not being able to get out of bed.

So I kissed her instead. I kissed her to smother the words on the tip of my tongue. And when she melted into me and kissed me with the warmth of a homecoming, I thought she might feel it. Thought that even if she wasn't ready to acknowledge it, she still felt that love, right within reach whenever she was ready.

"I uh ..." she pulled back, the words coming out with little giggles. "I think that was a little excessive."

"Nothing's too excessive for you." I would've kicked myself in the ass if I could for getting so close to the truth. But when her cheeks turned red and she started biting at her lip, all I could think about was how cute she was when she was about to act stubborn.

"Well, we put on a good show, I guess," she mumbled and tried to pull away. I yanked right back and nestled her into my chest.

"It wasn't for show," I whispered, pressing a kiss to the top of her hair.

And then before she had a chance to overthink those words, I took her hand and guided us over to the bar.

"I don't think y'all have ever met. Dani, this is Ashley, the love of my life and baker of the best peanut butter cookies in the world. Sweetheart, this is Dani, my ex." It was small, but I caught Ashley's smirk over how I described her versus Dani. But it was true, Dani was just an ex. There was no pining for the past or regrets. There was just Ashley.

"Nice to meet you." Ashley gave Dani a tight smile and a small nod before joining Bailey at the bar.

"God, I missed you," I mumbled, pressing another kiss to her head and giving her a quick hug before heading back behind the counter.

"You saw me this morning," Ashley grumbled.

"Aw, cute," Bailey said.

"Don't encourage him. It'll make him insufferable."

"I have to agree with Ashley here. Mason let's compliments go to his head. Dude was just smiling like an idiot because Ashley texted him first this morning. Actually, Ashley, will you tell him to change his registry system? He'll listen if you say it." Travis went on complaining about me as a boss, every so often looking to Bailey with some type of softness. But I was focused on Ashley and how when he mentioned her texting me, her eyebrow raised. I just gave her a wink.

I turned around to face the register and take Dani's order, but she was already out the door. Thank god for small blessings.

43

Chess Pie

Ashley

It was Bailey's last night in town, so of course we were crowded into the back booth of Rosie's diner with shakes. This time though, my milkshake wasn't spiked.

When I told Mason I was going out after closing with the girls, he asked if I'd be drinking. I saw the flash of anxiety and said no without thinking anything of it. It was an easy thing to do that saved him hours of anxiety. There was no point not to.

What worried me was how easy it was to fit him and his needs into my life. It'd only been a few days since we'd crossed that line and already he felt like a staple to my life. We shared the same bed, we bickered over breakfast, we played board games after dinner, and he stayed up late reading my bodice ripper books and occasionally asking me to explain historical references.

It was scaring me how simple it was.

"Were you guys surprised about me and Mason?"

The table clattered to silence, all the girls blinking at me with the shock I would have expected when Mason and I first pretended to get together.

"What do you mean?" Rosie asked, voice soft like she was afraid of stepping on a landmine.

"Well, I know there was the betting pool and everything, but did you all really expect Mason and I to get together eventually?" I was answered with a chorus of yeses and a single no from Shea. All the others gave her various odd looks and she slunk down in the booth, taking her milkshake with her.

"Don't give me those looks. I bet that it'd never happen because I knew she was headstrong and whatever struck her wrong about Mason in the first place wasn't bound to change."

"I guess that's true, but there'd always be moments Mason acted like a smitten fool when you were brought up," Roxie said.

"Mhmm, like when I spilled coffee all over myself at the Pub last year. He easily could've grabbed one of the shirts for his shop, but instead, he went and stole yours," Olivia pointed out.

"And he never called the sheriff on you for breaking into his place," Zoey added.

"And he got a band to serenade you," Bailey crooned.

"Okay, but that's all ... that's circumstantial and all about him. What made you think I'd fall for him?" I asked, having a hard time grappling with all the pranks and antics they were presenting as flirting or as anything other than Mason just trying to get under my skin.

"Mostly just the lady doth protest too much thing," Roxie said.

"And since you never told us why you hated him, we kinda assumed it was just because your businesses were in direct competition. And that sorta thing just adds tension," Olivia said, keeping her focus on her fries.

"I thought you were just being petty over the Pub not being a pub," Zoey said.

"Well it was kind of about that," I mumbled. There wasn't really any sense in hiding how Mason and I met now that we were married and sort of together. And maybe telling them would give me more clarity on what's happening now.

"Actually, I met Mason the night I signed the lease for Tost-Ka."

Elbows were slammed to the table, drinks and food pushed aside, and a loud, unison 'what' rang out.

"What do you mean you met that night? I saw you the next day!" Shea shouted.

"Oh no, what happened then?" Rosie said.

"When you say you met, do you really mean bang?" Roxie asked.

"Yes," I answered, looking up at the ceiling to take a deep breath. When I looked back at my friends, they were all wide-eyed and various shades of pale. Except for Roxie, she was bent over laughing.

"I went to this bar or line dance place —"

"The Bank in Mayberry?" Bailey asked.

"Yeah, I didn't realize it was in Mayberry though. I thought it was in Snowfall."

"Oh no," Rosie whispered.

"Right. So I went out because … I didn't have anyone to celebrate signing the lease with and thought I might as well treat myself to a drink. Mason approached me at the bar and …

I don't know. Something about his Southern accent, that smirk, the way I was finally building something of my own, the Hallmark life I was embarking on. It all went to my head. We hit it off and I went home with him. The next morning I had to rush out to get back to the hotel for check out and shit, so we didn't get a chance to talk or exchange numbers. And the next time I saw him was on Tost-Ka's opening day.

"When I realized I'd slept with the competition, competition I hadn't realized existed because of the stupid name, I felt like an idiot. All that time between our hook-up and the opening, I built us up in my head. I was convinced we'd get together, have some sort of easy romance, get married, have kids, the whole happy ending. So when I found out he'd 'conveniently' left out that he owned a cafe, I was pissed. All those stupid girlie dreams were broken and I was mad at myself for even having them. Embarrassed even."

"Oh sweetie," Rosie crooned, wrapping me up in her arms. On my other side, Olivia did the same. Zoey, Shea, and Bailey leaned over the table to pat whatever part of me they could reach.

"It's insanely wild he didn't mention owning a cafe too," Olivia assured.

"You are far from the first woman to be charmed by a sweet accent. I met somebody at a bar in Charlotte with the most charming British accent and let them do all manner of things to me."

"Ooo, like what?" Bailey asked, sitting back before something dawned on her and she frowned, adding, "Wait, is this one of the times you went to Charlotte without visiting me?"

"Irrelevant."

"So yes," Shea said.

"Shut up. Ashley is venting about Mason being an idiot. Go on, Ashley."

"Wait, but why *didn't* he tell you?" Zoey asked.

"Because the Banks not in Snowfall," Bailey answered.

"Sure, but like, if someone said I own an auto shop, the first thing out of my mouth would be 'me too'. It's wild he didn't bring it up, especially when he's trying to get in her pants."

"Right?" I gestured to Zoey, almost knocking over a few milkshakes. "He says he didn't want to dull my excitement over signing for the shop, which like, fine. But still!"

"Oh, he was just looking out for you," Rosie said.

"Or he just didn't want you two to end up *just* talking shop," Roxie countered and I aggressively pointed at her.

"Exactly! It made me feel duped when I saw him again."

"What *did* he say when he first saw you again? Was it at that town hall meeting?" Olivia asked.

"No," I grumbled, knowing the answer was going to make me look like a petty bitch.

"Ash, not a single thing you've done to Mason these past few years has phased us. You literally broke into his apartment and I took after your lead and stole a car," Zoey pointed out.

"So you admit, you stole it," Olivia shouted.

"I didn't break in, I knew where the key was," I mumbled under my breath.

"Because you'd already been to his place!" Rosie shouted as she connected the dots and lightly smacked my arm.

"Yeah, yeah. I fucked the man who became my husband three years later. Sue me."

"Get back to the first reunion," Shea urged, she'd gone from sinking in her seat to elbows on the table as she slurped her milkshake, looking like a kid during story time.

"Ugh. He came by the shop opening day. He'd walked straight over from the Pub and by then I'd talked to enough town folk to know a man named Mason owned it, I'd just hoped it was some other Mason. But there he was, my competition walking in with that stupidly charming smirk, obviously thinking we'd just pick everything right back up, and I just — I was already overwhelmed with the shop, things we busy, I ignored him."

"That's it?" Zoey asked.

"I mean, when she follows it up by police taping his patio, you can't really say that's it," Shea said.

"Where did you even get that tape?" Rosie asked.

"Amazon."

"Hmph, vile company," Rosie grumbled.

"Don't get distracted," Olivia chided. "So then what? You ignored him when he stopped by and then he tried to talk to you after town hall and ..." Olivia waved her hand for me to continue where she left off.

"And ... he tried to ask me about that night, about why I hadn't left my number and how he liked what I'd done to the shop. He was perfectly nice and civil and just as charming as I remembered and I was so pissed at myself and him, so I took it all out on him. I insulted the Pub, the decor, the menu, literally anything I could think of. So he fought back and I maybe sorta thought it'd be funny to see if he'd notice the giant ass puddle we were walking towards. He didn't, but he did realize I guided him into it. And then it was just … the thing. He got me back for the puddle by painting the sidewalk in front of my shop, and so on and so forth."

"God I wish I caught him stepping in the puddle," Shea said through laughter.

"He does make a funny face when he's connecting the dots." It was cute too. Endearing. My stupid, idiot husband was endearing.

"Okay, well you were attracted to him and already thinking about what your future would be like three years ago, so you just … had a three-year fight and then got married. That's not really quick," Olivia said.

"Yeah, Stephen decided to move in with me in like a month, so getting married in a couple of dates after three years of foreplay doesn't sound too crazy."

"It's kind of romantic, don't you think? You two did your worst to each other and still fell in love," Rosie swooned, resting her head on my shoulder.

A lump stuck in my throat. It was true, I was probably the shitiest version of myself to Mason for years and he still wants me to some capacity. How was that possible?

"I don't think Mason was ever his worst version of himself to me though." The confession spilled past my lips, nausea twisting my stomach.

"What?" The table erupted.

"He literally unplugged your fridge and ruined your prep work one time. I know jack shit about baking, but I'm pretty sure that's a big deal," Roxie said.

"And like, it was funny, but the mariachi band when he *knew* you'd be in bed is pretty fucking shitty," Shea added.

"And he really should have just told you he owned a cafe too. Or when he realized it was you opening the new shop, left a letter or something," Olivia said.

"You guys were just talking about how he was smitten with me ten seconds ago."

"Well, yeah, he is. But he also did that stupid pick on the girl he likes thing, which is sorta ick," Zoey said.

"He did have the opportunity to talk or write to you several times," Rosie pointed out. "Oh and if he wrote to you, it would have been like in Pride and Prejudice. What a missed opportunity."

"But I was the one who wouldn't listen when he tried to talk. Fuck, even if he did pull a Mr. Darcy, I probably would have torn up the letter before reading it."

"Sure. But you would've taken it out of the trash and put it back together an hour later," Roxie said.

She was right, my curiosity would have gotten the best of me and I would have melted for him the same way I did when he got jealous over Grant. Or when he proposed. Or when he told off my parents.

"Wait, Shea, why didn't you tell her about the Pub being a cafe?" Zoey asked, turning to the woman in question.

"Yeah, that is kinda weird you didn't point that out during the showing," Bailey said.

Shea sank back into her seat, taking her milkshake with her. Without her lips leaving her straw, she mumbled something none of us could hear. To her left, Bailey nudged her.

"Ugh, fine. I was a little hungover and just kinda forgot to warn her about other shops in the area. *Plus* when we first talked, Ashley said it'd be a bakery. That wouldn't have been in competition with the Pub, not really."

"I changed it because I was worried I wouldn't get as much business if I had such a narrowed market."

"That was stupid. Where'd you get that idea?" Roxie asked.

"My mother was … worried about my career change."

"Now that sounds like bullshit," Shea muttered, sitting back up in her seat.

"How was your parents' visit?" Rosie asked. I wasn't sure if I was grateful for the subject change or not. But I suppose anything was better than hashing out my discombobulated feelings for Mason.

Especially since I knew the only way to settle things would be to talk to the man himself.

44

Bombon Coffee

Mason

I didn't know much about Mayberry's community. It was a little more suburban than Snowfall since it was right on the highway, so I figured there wouldn't be the usual small town gawking when we were working in the shop.

Turns out I was wrong.

As Ashley and I started really setting up shop, folks would be peeking in through the window, a couple of people even trying the door despite the several signs we had up about our opening being in July.

"Think we should just cover the whole window up?" I asked Ashley after a group of teenagers pressed their whole faces up against the window. Ashley looked up from the test batch of scones and the kids immediately scattered.

"Nah, let them look," she said, a light laugh lifting her voice. "It'll drum up more hype."

"Sure, but they're leaving a whole mess of marks on the window," I grumbled.

"It's fine. It's supposed to rain soon anyways." She tilted so her head rested on my shoulder for a brief second before returning to work. It was such a simple thing, but fuck if it didn't have my heart pounding like a jackhammer.

"Right," I said, trying to clear my throat of all the emotion getting stuck there. "Um, I think the cookies with the jam might be a little much work for this shop if it's gonna be as busy as we hope. We'll want more streamlined recipes."

"I know." She took one of the aforementioned cookies from the cooling rack on the counter and shoved it in my mouth. "These are for us to take home."

God I love my wife.

Three sharp knocks on the door had us jolting apart like caught teenagers. I turned to the door, still chewing on the cookie, ready to yell at whoever interrupted the moment.

But instead of kids fooling around, it was a tall, lanky gentleman with a lanyard that read 'press' in all caps. There wasn't a logo or anything else on it, just 'press'. Like maybe the dude bought it himself at a Party City.

"I do not like the look of this dude," I grumbled. Meanwhile, Ashley was already wiping her hands off as she walked to the door.

"We need good press, remember." And then the door was opened and the man strutted inside.

"Hello, hello. Pleasure to meet you, Mr. and Mrs. Foster." The man tipped an imaginary hat at me and shook Ashley's hand. "My name is Abraham Murphy. I write with the Mayberry

Wrap Up and I was hoping you'd have a minute to speak with me about this shop y'all are opening so I can do a little expose."

"Expose?" I repeated, walking around the counter to join them. We were nearly finished with what we'd planned on getting done tonight and I wanted to go home, not be interviewed by someone who used words like expose.

"I'm sorry, but we were just about to wrap up. We can schedule something in the next few days though." Bless my wife and her ability to read my mood and avoid annoying people with her heavenly customer service smile.

"This'll be quick, I promise. I've just got a couple of questions." Before we had the chance to reply, he'd pulled out his phone and hit a big red button. "Alana Burnett mentioned the two of you applied for the small business grant for married couples, yes?"

"Yes," Ashley replied hesitantly.

"But you two weren't dating at the time of the tour? In fact, she described your relationship as somewhat antagonistic. And when I followed up with some folks in Snowfall, they said the same thing. And yet the two of you went viral with a proposal video just a few days later."

"What're you getting at?" I stepped up to the man and his eyes went wide, scuttling backwards.

"Nothing, nothing, sir. I was just repeating the facts. The timeline is a little ... convenient is all. Doesn't seem like it was a case of love at first sight."

"Well it was, but I guess happily ever afters would sound convenient if you start at the ending," I grumbled. Ashley put a hand on my shoulder, giving me a light squeeze before pulling me back.

"What my husband means is it might not've been love at first sight, but we've been dancing around each other for years now. Once there was a practical reason for us to be together, I … stopped being stubborn about it, stopped resisting. It may look like things just got started, but we've been working towards this for years."

"Oh, yes. I'm sorry, I didn't mean to imply anything," the man said with a slimy smile. "Just trying to find the most interesting part of the story is all. You two have a nice day."

The little bastard slid out of the shop, tipping his invisible hat again.

"I don't like that guy —"

"I think we should reevaluate our contract," Ashley interrupted.

"Say what?" I checked out the window to make sure that guy wasn't lingering just outside. With the coast clear, I took Ashley by the elbow and guided her back behind the counter. She looked relieved to be back at her workstation and have something to do with her hands.

"Well, I made the contract thinking our relationship wouldn't … change. But it has and I want to sit down and discuss it."

"Discuss it," I repeated, trying to parse out what she meant by that and what it *really* meant for our relationship. She didn't sound scared or resentful of the change, so that was probably progress. "When you say discuss …"

"Oh my god, Mason, why are you making this so difficult," she groaned as she started tossing the cookies into a box.

"I'm not trying to be difficult, you're just not explaining it in a way I can understand." I grabbed one of the cookies before she could toss it among the rest. They'd still taste good, but with the way she was piling them in, there was gonna be jam on all over the bottom of the top layers.

"Since we're sleeping together, we should discuss what our relationship is going to look like moving forward." She snapped the box closed and started stomping off to the back.

"Oh, I see." I followed behind her, turning off the lights and locking the doors. "My wife wants to have the label talk."

Ashley kept on walking, barely pausing to snatch up her bag before going through the back door. Amused, I took my sweet time closing up the rest of the shop. I made sure all the counters were wiped down, triple-checked the ovens, and even walked back to the front to make sure it was all cleaned up.

Then, whistling the whole way, I locked up the shop and joined Ashley in the car.

"That was deliberate," she grumbled from the passenger seat, arms crossed over her chest.

"It was indeed. Just cause we're married, doesn't mean we can't poke at each other every now and then."

"Well, I'd rather you not do it when I'm trying to have a serious conversation."

"Oh, really? Sorry, I didn't think it was serious by the way you stomped out there." Ashley made some grumbling noises but didn't say anything. I squeezed her thigh so she knew I heard that. "So what you said about this not being love at first sight..."

"Oh please, don't tell me you believe in that."

"Hmm, maybe not literally. But I think you can tell if it's possible or not. I certainly knew I could fall for you standing at that bar."

"Please!" She laughed, throwing her head back and putting her hand over mine. One squeeze. Like a sign she wasn't laughing at me exactly, just the 'stupid' shit coming out of my mouth. "You don't really believe that, do you?"

"I do. And I think you do too, you're just being stubborn again."

"You flatter yourself."

"All right, let's make another bet. We'll redo that night and if you feel the sparks, you'll have to admit it."

"Admit what?"

"That you felt it back then too." I moved my hand from her thigh to around the headrest, turning so my face was just inches from hers. "Because I know you did."

Her breathing slowed, pretty green eyes batting up at me as the stubbornness made its way to arousal.

"Okay," she whispered. Somehow, any little word of agreement from her, spoken in a whisper, made my mouth water for her pussy. I was nothing if not a simp for my wife. "But either way, we'll talk about the contract, right?"

I pressed a soft kiss to her forehead and said, "Of course, sweetheart."

45

Peanut Butter Cookies

Ashley

When Mason suggested redoing the night we met, I should have asked follow-up questions.

But when we got home, he wanted to eat me out and I was not in a place where I could deny that.

So now I was sitting at that little bar/line dance club in one of the very few skirt suits I had left, waiting for Mason to come hit on me.

It was ridiculous. We drove here together, he even kissed me outside the door before we went in.

But despite the silliness, it was kind of exciting. We got to pretend like none of the awfulness between us existed and I could pretend my anxiousness about what we were didn't matter.

"Any chance you're looking for some company?"

I turned in my bar stool to see Mason leaning against the bar, in the same cowboy hat and boots he'd worn that night. Just as ruggedly handsome as he was back then too.

"I could be convinced." Mason gave me his little smirk, biting at the corner of his lips like he was trying to fight a laugh.

"I do like a woman who makes me work for it."

Flutters in my chest, schoolgirl giggles, all of it was there just like that. It should be embarrassing how right this man was about knowing love was possible at first sight. Because all those little fantasies I had with my small glimpse of him in this dim barlight came right back to me, this time without the excitement and rose-colored glasses of the unknown. And somehow, without those things, I wanted him just as badly. Or maybe even more.

"Well, I can certainly do that. If you've got three years, I can really put you through the wringer."

The grin that broke out on my husband's face was incredible. Dimples and flashing teeth and it was all mine.

"Do your worst, sweetheart." Mason pressed a kiss to my cheek before settling onto the bar stool beside me.

"A kiss and a sweetheart? Mighty forward aren't you?"

"Sometimes when you know, you know." He shot me a wink before waving down the bartender and ordering a drink.

"What's your line with that?" I asked, nodding to the pint placed in front of him.

"Hmm, wild of a stranger to assume I have some sort of line on drinks. You've been stalking me, sweetheart?"

"Mason, come on." I nudged his arm.

"Wow, you know my name too. I'm starting to think I should call someone. Though you are awfully pretty for a stalker. The suit is an odd choice, doesn't really fit in with the bar atmosphere." Through all his talk, Mason was grinning like an idiot. I bet he'd been thinking up these lines all day, expecting me not to play along.

"You're right," I said, waiting until he took a sip of his beer before continuing, "And I know you keep a key under your mat for the apartment over your restaurant."

Mason keeled over laughing, beer spurting out his mouth.

"God damn it, Ashley," he muttered, grabbing a napkin to wipe off the beer on his pants.

"What? I was just playing your game."

"You weren't and you damn well know it. If you were playing along, you would've brought up your shop, then I could've been like 'Oh I have a cafe too, but honestly, I wanna talk about you more'," he grumbled.

"So you were gonna tell me this time?"

"Well, yeah." He turned on the stool to face me, taking my hand in his. "I swear, I didn't think it would matter all that much. I just wanted to spend the night getting to know you. And you know, based on the way you talked about yourself, I got the impression you'd want to talk shop."

"So you didn't want to ruin your chances of getting laid?" I asked, half teasing and half desperately needing to hear him confirm it out loud.

"Ash, you are like the fourth woman I've ever been with. No, I wasn't just trying to get laid."

"Fourth, huh?" I turned in my seat to face the bar, hemming around like he didn't give me the exact answer I needed.

"Okay, what's your number then?" His foot hooked around the rung at the bottom of the stool and twisted me around, hands on my hips to keep me in place.

"I don't think that's a polite thing to ask a woman you've just met." I straightened my back and Mason's playful smirk returned.

"Yeah, all right. Guess there's nothing good coming out of that information anyways." One squeeze on my hips before he took my hands in his and settled them in my lap. "The drink line is one beer. I've tried some hard liquor but I end up feeling guilty, even if I'm not driving. It just doesn't sit right. But one pint." He shrugged. "It's the level that doesn't feel harmful."

"Would you ever want me to not drink?"

"No." His answer was quick, like maybe it'd been given more than a few times. Mason straightened and opened his mouth to speak, but I pulled his hands closer.

"You can ask me not to drink, okay?"

"I don't want to ask you that. That's not fair."

"If drinking was an important part of my life, maybe. But it isn't, so you can ask."

Mason sat with that for a while, his eyes searching mine, softening when he found whatever it was he was looking for.

"How about a compromise?"

"Hmm, I'll hear you out."

"That's all I could ever ask of ya," he said, smiling. "How 'bout you always make sure you have a DD that can call me if anything happens? And if there's any time I don't want you to drink, 'cause it's raining or anything, I'll tell ya?"

"Deal." I shook our hands and Mason laughed.

"You take your deals seriously, don't you?"

"Of course."

"And that's why you want to revisit the contract?"

"Yeah," I murmured, looking down at our hands. It might be too soon to revisit the contract, I mean, us sleeping together could just be a matter of convenience.

But it didn't feel that way.

"What if we just tear it up?"

My eyes shot up to Mason, wide and scared. Because what the fuck did he mean by that?

"Don't jump to assumptions. We can keep the prenup stuff, the business-specific things. But everything else, stuff about pretending, just rip that up. We're married, we're together, we don't need all the rules and stuff. And we can just talk whenever something comes up. Or more like we can argue and then talk."

"I don't know, I …" I liked having everything clearly written out. I liked knowing what was coming and how to plan for it. I liked the sort of equality a contract made.

"Do you trust me, sweetheart?" he asked, squeezing my hands.

"The last time I trusted you, you left out a pretty important detail," I snarked, but we both knew I was all bark.

"Never again."

46

Turkish Coffee

Mason

We slept at the apartment after our date. We'd talked more, danced some, and Ashley made several snarky comments that nearly had me rolling on the ground. Then we went to my place, just like we had that night, and fucked.

Except fuck wasn't the right word to describe it. It was slow and quiet and when rain hit the window, I was so consumed with her I didn't bat an eye.

Making love to my wife was sure as hell the best anxiety distraction I'd ever had. Much better than experimenting with coffee techniques, taste testing the coffee, and getting more anxiety from the coffee.

It was the perfect evening.

Until about 2:00 a.m. when thunder hit and my nerves caught on fire.

I clung to Ashley like a kid holding his teddy bear. The apartment didn't have the best AC, so she kicked and turned in her sleep, but I couldn't bring myself to let her go. If I couldn't literally feel her breathing, I couldn't breathe.

After a few hours, I gave up on sleep and checked my phone. Specifically, the weather to see when this nightmare would end.

Turns out Snowfall was under a severe thunderstorm warning with potential flooding. Fucking great.

A quick scroll through socials said all the shops down Main Street were closed because of the weather, so I called off my staff and made my own posts. Then I looked down at my wife. She'd be pissed if I made the call without her. She'd also be pissed if I woke her up before her alarm went off. The woman valued sleep more than anything else and a man could only take so many pillows to the head.

"Ashley, sweetheart." I wrapped my arm around her waist and pulled her into me, she immediately snuggled in with a satisfied sigh. "No, Ash. You gotta wake up, just for a minute."

I pulled away, so she had to roll on her back. Her eyes fluttered then narrowed.

"What're you — wait are you okay?" The shift from sleepy and stubborn Ashley to concerned Ashley was distinct. She sat up, sheets pooling around her waist, and grabbed my shoulders. "What's wrong?"

"Oh." I was a little taken aback by the way she was assessing me. "It's storming pretty bad, so most folks are already calling it. I've called my staff off and stuff and I wanted to see if you were okay closing too."

"That's all?" she asked, one eyebrow raised. Her hands ran down my arms, warming my skin.

"Yeah, I figured you'd be pissed if I made the call for you. But you won't get any customers today anyway, so there's no sense in —"

"Mason." She said my name so softly, with so much care and concern that it could have been an 'I love you' for the way it shook my heart. "What's wrong?"

"Ah, I may have undersold how bad storms are for me. I um … fuck, I'm gonna be a bit of a mess today, sweetheart. I can handle it, but I'd do much better if you stayed here with me today."

Ashley's face wrinkled as she thought, eyes never leaving mine. Her hands fell to mine and gave me two squeezes.

"Okay." She let go of my hands and crawled out of bed. I sat, stunned that she agreed so quickly and that she wasn't immediately going back to sleep. She'd slept in my shirt and her underwear, her ass blessedly poking out as she walked around looking for pants. It was distracting, watching her walk around the apartment like it was a usual thing.

But then she found a pair of leftover sweats and walked out of the bedroom. I scampered out of bed to follow.

"What're you doing, Ash?"

She was in the kitchen, pulling out coffee mugs. Once she moved to my press, a retired one from the Pub that more buttons and levers than what she was used to, I stepped in.

"Mason, let me make you coffee," she grumbled, hip-checking me.

"It's just … coffee's sort my thing and yours isn't exactly …"
I trailed off and Ashley simply rolled her eyes before moving to
the fridge. But since I'd been living with her for a while now, it
was empty.

"I'm gonna go downstairs and grab stuff for breakfast, all
right?" she said as she shut the fridge.

"You can go back to bed, sweetheart. I know you like your
sleep. I'll be fine."

Ashley stopped halfway to the door and turned back to me.
Then she walked right up and smacked my arm.

"Hey!"

"Don't hey me. You're shaking and your shirt is damp from
all the sweat. You're not fine and I want to help. So let me."
Ashley rested her hands on her hips, a challenge in her eyes.

"You don't have to, sweetheart. I'm gonna … I'll be fine. Like
I always am."

"You don't have to settle for fine today. You have a wife who
is going to make you the best fucking hash you've ever had and
distract you all day. Or we can talk more about it if you want. But
if you *don't* let me help," she paused to poke at my chest, "then
we're gonna fight. Because I saw all that gardening shit you think
you've hidden in the garage and if you think you can get away
with building me a garden and *not* let me help with something
you actually need, then you've got another thing coming."

I took the finger still resting on my chest and brought it to
my lips for a kiss.

"Oh yeah? What're you gonna do to me if I don't listen?"
There was no use fighting the smile. This was Ashley showing
she cared about me, cared enough to fight me. And god, I'd

been waiting so long for this, I was having trouble believing it was real.

Thunder crashed and I flinched at the sound, my body tensing as my ears strained to hear anything outside, specifically car tires.

Then Ashley's arms were around me and I was able to relax some.

"Looks like shoving you outside would be punishment enough," she mumbled, her hold tightening. "Why didn't you tell me it affects you this much?"

"Well, it's kind of embarrassing to be a grown man afraid of thunderstorms." I rested my forehead on hers, keeping my eyes closed so I could concentrate on her and not the way my heartbeat ramped up with every thunder strike.

"You're not afraid of thunderstorms."

"I appreciate you trying to lie for me, sweetheart, but —"

"Shut up." She pinched at my stomach. "You're not afraid of the storm, you're anxious that somebody might get hurt. That's a pretty common concern."

"I suppose." I squeezed her tighter.

"Besides, we live together, we're married. How did you imagine you'd hide this? Were you just going to pretend to have a cold and not leave the bedroom?"

"I honestly hadn't considered it."

"Idiot," she grumbled, hugging me tighter for just a second before pulling away and walking towards the door. "I'm getting us food. You fix up the coffee however your picky ass wants."

"Ashley." She stopped, hand on the door and the words just tumbled out of my mouth. "I love you."

Her face shifted, eyes going wide and blinking so rapidly that I was getting concerned. But then her cheeks started to redden, her feet shifting in place, her fingers fiddling with her rings.

"Really?"

My heart squeezed, remembering her saying something about her not being in a serious relationship before. And knowing I was the first man to tell her I loved her was a heavy thing, a comfortable weight.

"Yeah. Really."

"Oh." The fiddling continued and Ashley's face got an even brighter shade of pink.

"You don't have to say it back. If you remember, I like a woman who makes me work for it."

47

Blueberry Cheesecake

Ashley

I should have expected Mason's thing with storms to be worse than he led on. It was such a typical man thing to do, underplay their fears so they look strong. As if I would have thought any less of him for worrying about people he loved when he had a trigger raging on outside.

And the people he loved included me.

Mason loved me.

Breakfast ready, I set our plates on the small kitchen table and sat across Mason. He murmured a word of thanks, but I just sat there, staring at my food, trying to process it.

Mason loved me.

We were married.

We were business partners.

We lived together and had been sleeping together for a week or so.

And I ...

"Ashley." I don't know if it was the stress of the storm or just the situation, but Mason's accent was heavy as he said my name. "I told you you didn't have to say it back. Stop thinking so hard. It's stressin' me out."

"Asking me to not think about it isn't fair either." I stabbed into my hash, glaring at my husband.

"Then think out loud."

"You love me." I pointed my egg-laden fork at him like it was an accusation.

"I do." He laughed at my distress and I considered, for the briefest moment, that opening the windows might make him shut up. It was a cruel thought that I immediately shook away. I had zero desire to inflict pain or even inconvenience on Mason anymore. Which was a big enough shift in our relationship, but Mason just had to throw love in too.

Bastard.

"So what? Does that mean we're dating now?"

"No, sweetheart. We're married. Remember?"

"Mason, take this seriously." I kicked at his leg under the table. He parted his legs and closed them around my foot trapping me. I yanked at my foot, but he held strong

"I do take this seriously. You're my wife and I love you. Doesn't matter if we got married for any other reason. Right here and right now, we're no different from any other married couple."

"Except I don't —"

"But you could." He said it so confidently I almost gave him shit for it. But then he slipped with a flash of lightning. His hold on my foot dropped and he reached over the table to take my hand. "Right?"

"I —"

On the table my phone flashed, the ID reading Mayberry Police Department. I met Mason's eyes for the briefest of seconds and saw the panic grow. I squeezed his hand and took the call.

"Hello, Ashley Bowen speaking."

"Ah, good morning Ms. Bowen. This is Sheriff Montgomery with the Sheriff's Department in Mayberry. Sorry to call first thing in the morning, but I've got some bad news about your Mayberry storefront."

"Not a problem, sir. What's wrong?" I squeezed Mason's hand one more time before getting up from the table and walking into the bedroom so Mason didn't have to overhear the conversation. Logically, this call wasn't going to be about someone we know being hurt. The storefront wasn't staffed yet and it was so early in the morning, most of the shopping center's other stores weren't open yet either. But I knew that wouldn't help much with Mason's trauma.

"Well, there was a car accident outside the front of your shop and with the rain and how fast someone thought they could drive through an *almost* empty parking lot, one of the cars crashed into your shop."

"Shit."

"Yeah. We've got it boarded up for now, so you don't have to worry about coming out here in the storm. But you will need to come by the station to get the police report for insurance and whatnot. Make sure you check your policy 'for you come by, some companies have specific forms they want us to sign and a bunch of other nonsense. This one place had a —"

"I'll be sure to check our policy today. Is everyone all right? And what sort of damage was done?"

"The drivers are mostly fine. The one who went through your shop is probably looking at an overnight stay, but nothing serious and nothing you'll be liable for. As for your shop … well, the windows and door are gone. I don't know nothing about structural integrity, but that's certainly in question. The car was damn near all the way in the shop, so all your interior will need fixing along with the counter and tables and stuff."

The officer kept listing the damage and as he spoke, my brain started doing mental gymnastics, estimating how much of this would end up being out of pocket.

The answer was too goddamn much.

* * *

"Do you want me to go in first?" Mason asked at the back door of our shop. Today's weather was sweltering, the humidity after the storm making the heat and my anxiety all the worse.

Depending on how bad the damage is, we were fucked. The grant was the only thing that let us afford this place, this sort of setback could dissolve the venture entirely. All that time and money would be wasted. And my thing with Mason would …

"I told you, we'll be fine. Stop worrying, sweetheart."

"If you tell me to not worry one more time, I'm kicking you right in the dick."

Mason immediately held his hands up and backed away.

"Let's just get this over with," I mumbled, pushing through the back door. The back and kitchen were blessfully untouched. But then we entered the dining area.

It was completely destroyed.

And amongst all of the damage was a man in a construction hat, presumably the building contractor we were told would have a quote for the damages for us. When he noticed us, he meandered over to the counter and tossed two hard hats our way.

"Get those on, just in case," he said before holding out a hand to Mason, then me. "Heya, folks. Freddie Jackson, the building contractor. Nice to meet you."

"Nice to meet you," Mason and I said.

"So, I've got a real base quote for ya. Basically, the owner is responsible for building structure. So that's all that exterior shit, the windows and so on. You'll have to redo all the signage you had put up though. And you'll be responsible for all the stuff you've added inside, of course. So your tile, the showcases, the fancy coffee maker. This is a quote for my team to do the work." He handed a sheet of lined, yellow paper with scribbled numbers to Mason and before I even opened my mouth, Mason handed it right to me.

"We'll look it over and let ya know. Do you have a schedule for dealing with all of that yet?" Mason asked, tilting his head to the plywood that was our windows and door.

"Oh yeah. It's actually not all that complicated and nothing's specialty order, so we'll have everything done by next week. If you decide to do repairs yourself or with another team, we'll need to coordinate schedules."

While they continued to talk, I ran numbers. Pulling up our contracts and insurance policy to estimate what would be covered and then researching any grants or other emergency aid that we could apply for. Nothing would be enough. Especially if we didn't want to change our opening date.

"Mason, there's no way we can do this."

Silence.

I turned around and Mason was just standing next to the contractor, looking down at the ground.

"Mason, I know it sucks but ... we can't cover this much. It was a stretch for us to get this shop to begin with. There's no way we can afford these costs on top of all the profit we're missing out on from closing my shop to be here. And we most certainly can't afford another month or two of rent on this place without it making any money. The only thing I can think to do is sue the driver who crashed, but I don't want to be that person. Plus I can't represent myself in this state, so we'd have to hire an attorney and that'd be a whole other cost we can't —"

Mason walked over to me and grabbed my shoulders, shaking just enough to snap my senses out of the cyclone I was whirling in.

"I told you, it'll be fine. I've got it covered."

"Covered? Mason, unless you have a secret stash of money you didn't tell me about, then you don't have it covered."

The second I brought up a secret stash of money, Mason's eyes flicked away and he bit his lip.

"Excuse me?" I practically laughed the words out.

"I still have most of my folks' life insurance money saved up. I only touched it for college, so it's a decent amount. Enough to cover all of this for sure."

"For sure? What do you mean for sure? I haven't even given you a number yet."

"I've got enough. Trust me."

"Mason, this is literally a business transaction thing, you can't just 'trust me' on this."

"Fine, I've got nearly 100k saved up." He didn't look at me as he confessed, his voice soft. His tiny little confession was almost drowned out by Freddie running from the argument, the door slamming on the way out.

"100k?" I repeated. Mason hummed, still looking at the floor. "With a 100k, you easily could've afforded this place on your own. You didn't need me."

"No, of course I need you, sweetheart. I just … didn't need your financial assistance necessarily."

"Ha." It wasn't a laugh, just a huff that was spelled the same. "Was it all a ploy to just — fuck, get in my pants? Get my fucking help running this shop? What?"

"No! I just … you wanted the shop, I wanted the shop, and I sure as fuck wanted you. It was a way to all our goals."

"All our goals? See, the only goal I was aware of was running a successful shop so that we wouldn't end up bought out by a conglomerate. *You* had something else in mind this whole time. Again, you conveniently left out some pivotal information."

"It's not that pivotal. Had I rented this place on my own, I'd sure as hell be in trouble now. I didn't — Ash, where are you going?"

I'd snatched up my things and made my way through the back, shaking off Mason's hand when he tried to grab mine.

"I am going home. To *my* home. I am going to pack up your things and leave them on the porch for you to pick up." I pulled the handle of the back door, but Mason slammed it shut, hand over my head.

"Ashley, you don't — that's too far. I get it, I fucked up. I — I put what I wanted over you having all the information, I guess. But are you really just going to immediately throw me out?"

"Yes." I yanked at the door and Mason stumbled back.

God bless the fact that we came here separately after the morning rushes. I'd bemoaned having to drive since that'd become Mason's thing, but now I was grateful.

"God damn it, Ashley. Why can't we just take an hour apart and talk about this after we've calmed down? You like logical shit, right? Doesn't that sound like the most logical thing to do?" Mason had followed me outside, the hard helmet tilted back on his head like he'd tried to run a hand through his hair having forgotten the hat was on.

"Well, you wanted to tear up the contracts. That sounds like a pretty fucking logical thing to do now."

We stared at each other for a long while, Mason searching for something he wasn't going to find. Fuck him for having the audacity to tell me he loved me while still keeping shit from me. Fuck him for trying to trick me into loving him or whatever the fuck his plan was.

"I'll talk to you tomorrow," he finally said before heading back into the shop.

"If your shit gets ransacked by Clive, it's on you."

48

Guillermo Coffee

Mason

I tried calling Ashley three times later that day. I don't know what kind of delusional I was to think she'd be calm enough to talk in under 24 hours, but I needed some sign of hope. But of course, I didn't get hope, I got her voicemail.

So for the first time in weeks, I slept alone.

Check that, I didn't sleep a fucking wink. My stomach was eating me alive and I had to google how many Tums were too many.

The answer was 15.

I was a fucking idiot. I should've known it would be a big deal to her, I should've fucking told her when I signed the contract that I had a decent emergency fund, I should've just looked her in the eye and said I just wanted one fucking chance at everything she was turning down for stubbornness sake.

But instead, I left something out, I proposed a whole scheme, and now she wanted to rip out my guts and feed them to Clive. I'll have to wait another three whole years before she's willing to even consider hearing me out.

I don't know why it was him of all people, maybe because he gave me the idea in the first place, but Dennis was the first one I texted. And since Ashley mentioned tearing up the contract, I shared the whole fucking shebang with him.

> **Me:** You can't tell a soul about this, but the other month when you mentioned fake dating Olivia, it gave me an idea. There's this small business grant for married couples and I thought damn, it'd be nice if Ashley needed that to get the

> shop, then I might finally figure out how to get her to stop being pissed at me so we could fall in love and shit. And then she did need it and the realtor even brought up the grant first. It was all set. We got married, got the shop, and

> I was finally getting through all her stubbornness only for a car going through the new shop to screw it all up. The damages were more than what we could cover without going into my savings and she put two and two together that I didn't

> need the grant or the marriage scheme to get the shop and she's pissed and doesn't want anything to do with me. And it's been a fucking night and I'm already miserable sack shit. Help.

> **Dennis:** Dude, you need to break up texts into readable chunks, that is a scrambled mess of nonsense. It's gonna take me a second to read through

Dennis: Okay, you're fucked, man

Dennis: And how the hell did my one comment about fake dating send you to a fake MARRIAGE?

Me: Well what other options did I have?

Dennis: Fair point

Dennis: Have you tried telling her what a desperate dumbass you are?

Me: Sort of, as soon as she figured it out, she immediately took off. I told her we should just take an hour and talk later but she didn't want to. She isn't answering my calls and I'm afraid to drive by and see my shit packed up outside

Dennis: Look, I don't think I'm the best equipped to help ya, you should talk to Shea

Me: I assume the girls have already talked and decided I'm a piece of shit

Dennis: You're not a piece of shit, just a dumbass

Dennis: Do the Darcy apology thing

Me: What?

Dennis: That movie you proposed at, O made me watch it during the flight

Me: That would require her having a sister in trouble and money I do not have to spend because I need to fix up and possibly run an extra shop on my own

Dennis: No, do the letter thing

Me: Didn't the letter thing not work?

Dennis: Look, I said I wasn't the best equipped to help ya. But it's worth trying, right?

> **Me:** It is, thanks, man

> **Dennis:** And when you drop it off, don't let her bait you into a fight

> **Me:** I'll do my best

I tossed my phone to the side and went to grab a notebook and pen. Then I sat at my kitchen table and stared at the ceiling for god knows how long before I started to write.

49

Dark Chocolate Truffles

Ashley

I tried my hardest not to look towards the Pub all morning. It was easy for the first few hours. I had people to attend to, dishes to restock, and coffees to make. I was busy. But then the crowd died down and my eyes drifted.

I'd seen Travis come out a few times to clean off patio tables, but otherwise, the Pub's attendants were hidden by the foggy glass.

Whatever, it didn't matter. Mason had lied about needing the grant to get the shop. He lied about needing me. The only thing left to discuss was the annulment of our fake marriage and the dissolvement of our business.

In fact, I had the documents all ready to go. They just needed to be delivered.

I should just put them with the pile of his shit on the porch. Not my fault if it all gets rained on or picked at by wild animals. It would serve him right.

What was he even thinking getting into this ridiculous scheme? At least I had the excuse of being in desperate need of growing my business to justify staying in a town that didn't need me. Why did he do it? To feed some fantasy that started three years ago? To get a free trial of me?

The bell over the door rang and my body tensed, flipping into customer service mode. "Hello and welcome to Tost-Ka."

The man who walked in wasn't somebody from town, but it wasn't odd for a tourist to tumble in during off hours. What was odd was the way he looked from the desserts to me and nodded, his eyes narrowing like a predator.

Great. The worst part of working a public job to top off my already shitty day.

"Hello, sweetie," he whistled as he came up to the registrar. I bit my tongue to keep from cringing.

"Hello, sir, how can I help you?"

"Well, how about you tell me what's good?" He leaned against the counter, eyes tracing my chest, and winked. "Besides you, of course."

Rolling my eyes will only make it worse, it'll only make it worse.

"I recommend the cinnamon rolls. They're my most popular. Scones are better if you're in a hurry though." As I gestured to the display case, the man's eyes didn't leave me. Or more specifically my chest. This dude was as subtle as a bull in a china shop.

"I'll take a cinnamon roll. For here. Maybe we can talk some since the shop's empty. I'd like to get to know you." The man leaned over the counter and placed a hand on my bicep, rubbing his thumb over my bare skin in a way that made it impossible for me to hide my reaction. But the man just kept going, pulling me ever so slightly closer to him and adding, "I'll make sure you get a big tip out of it too. I've got a lot to give."

"Get your hands off my wife." All of a sudden, Mason was behind the man, growling like an angry bear. And seeing his stupid face made me relieved.

The man let go and immediately made for the door, mumbling something about not seeing any rings. Because of course, the only reason he would have backed off was because I 'belonged' to another man. Fucking typical.

"Thanks for chasing off a customer." I had no desire to listen to that man attempt to flirt with me, but I sure as hell would have taken his money.

"Does that kind of shit happen a lot? Fuck, I don't wanna know. Imma hire somebody to help you out with the shop, even just having some kid to run the register with you should discourage that kind of bullshit, right? And let's get some cameras installed while we're at it, just in case."

"Oh fuck you. Did you just come in here to rub the fact that your store makes enough that you can save money?"

"No, that's not what I meant. I just … that dude was touching you. I'm worried." Mason had dark circles under his eyes. His usual cowboy hat was missing and his shirt was buttoned wonky. Good. Let him be the fool for a change.

"He wasn't hurting me and if he did I could handle it. Without you. Because you lost your right to worry over me."

"One fight isn't gonna make me stop worrying about you. You're still my wife."

"Under false pretenses," I shouted, tossing the first thing within reach at him, which happened to be an unfolded to-go box. The cardboard flopped off of him and dropped to the floor. Mason picked it up without a word and set it on the counter.

I tossed it in the trash.

Mason bit his lip, clearly trying to fight a comment. Eventually, he swallowed it down and pulled something out of his pocket.

"I'm sorry, Ashley. Really fucking sorry. I shouldn't have … baited you into a marriage. I thought … I thought it was the only chance I'd get and I jumped on it. You make me desperate, sweetheart. I need you and —"

"Pft, no one needs me." I crossed my arms, wanting to roll my eyes but I was glued to the envelope he pulled out. Did he make his own annulment documents? Or was he trying to renegotiate the terms of our contract to save the business end of things?

"What do you mean by that, sweetheart?"

"Don't call me that. It's demeaning," I deflected. Mason's eyes narrowed on me, jaw twitching.

"Sorry," he gritted out. "What do you mean by no one needs you?"

"The town, you. I'm not necessary here."

"That's a load of fucking bullshit and you know it." He tossed the envelope down on the counter and started pacing, hands in his hair. "Look, I know I'm a dumbass, but you don't gotta be Einstein to see you think anything that isn't perfect is a failure because your mom instilled some stupid shit about success into you. You overlook every other good damn sign you're doing well if just one thing has gone wrong."

"Don't insult my mother," I said, not able to fight the accusation. Because maybe I did measure my success by my mother's standard. I'd changed the shop from a bakery to a cafe because of her and I'm sure there were other things. But either way, it was none of his business.

"I'll insult her when she's hurting you. Because you *are* successful. Look at this place." He waved a hand around the empty shop.

"There's nobody here," I deadpanned.

"It's the middle of a work day. Of course, no one's here. But you always have a line in the morning and the display case is nearly empty. *That's* success, right?" He slammed his hands on the counter in front of me, looking into my eyes with so much determination that, if I was a little less stubborn, I would have looked away from him.

"I think you're stretching. But it doesn't matter, my success isn't tied to yours anymore. In fact, I've got the annulment papers in the back, let me go —" As I turned to head to the office, Mason grabbed my arm. I turned, putting every ounce of hate and frustration in my glare. He let go and took a deep breath.

"I don't want an annulment, swee— I don't want it. I want you, I *need* you. Just read this and you'll understand." He tapped at the envelope on the counter.

"No, I don't think I will, thank you. And you don't need me. I'm sure you'll forget all about this silly affair in a week." I grabbed the envelope and opened the cabinet below the register where I stored the trash.

"You wanna bet?"

"What?" Was Mason on something?

"If I can prove I need you, show that I'm a fucking miserable piece of shit without you, will you read the letter?"

My finger ran over the envelope. It wasn't exactly thick, but there was definitely more than one sheet of paper in it. And Mason wasn't the kind of person to pull a one-word-per-page bullshit.

He put in the effort. Like he always did.

"Fine." It was a moment of insanity. Or maybe just plain old curiosity. But I closed the cabinet and instead opened the register to set the letter under the bill holder. "If you somehow magically break down without me next week, I'll consider reading it."

Mason let out a long sigh before pushing away from the counter. He walked around in a circle once, fingers threading through his hair again.

"I guess one week of fighting the urge to pretend everything's okay is better than waiting another three years," he murmured to himself. Then he turned to face me, shoulders dropping, the exhaustion no longer hidden by competing emotion. "I'm sorry, Ashley. I miss you, I love you. And I guess I'll see you later."

And then he walked out.

50

Strawberry Lemonade

Mason

> **Me:** Hey guys, I got y'all's number from Dennis. Ashley and I are fighting, so she's alone in that big house and I'm worried about her. Could y'all go over for a visit, play games or gossip or whatever she wants?

> Just don't bring us up, I'm sure she doesn't want to talk about it.

> **Rosie:** Of course, Mason. I can be over in an hour or so, what about everybody else?

> **Shea:** God, I feel that. Being alone at home sucks. I can be there whenever

Olivia: Oh no, what happened? Does it have anything to do with the accident at the shop?

Shea: Oh yeah, is there anything we can do to help out with that? I know how to lay tile

Zoey: Where'd you learn that?

Shea: I helped out with a bunch of remolding projects while doing my real estate classes

Olivia: How many odd jobs have you had?

Shea: I honestly have no clue

Roxie: Shit, I'm not in town, y'all give her a hug for me

Shea: Not in town? Where are you?

Bailey: I'm not in town either, lol

Bailey: But FaceTime me! Maybe we can find one of those online games to play

Zoey: Mason, what kind of games does Ashley have?

Me: Literally every board game on the planet

Olivia: I don't think that's right, but we'll work with it

Shea: 1, let's not drop Roxie just suddenly being out of town

Shea: 2, do we think she has that game Eli told us about, Olivia? The one with the mansion and multiple endings?

Rosie: Rox, where are you? Should we be worried?

Roxie: No, I just had a really stressful day at work and I've been having issues with my landlord fixing a leaky faucet and I just needed to blow off some stress

Shea: [I could fix that gif]

Roxie: 😊 if you can come over tomorrow, I'd happily accept your help

Me: And if you could, make sure she feels needed, that'd be much appreciated. Not being able to go to Seattle with y'all really bummed her out but she's too stubborn to say anything

Rosie: Oh poor thing! Of course, we'll give her all the love she needs

Roxie: Fuuuuccckkk, I picked the wrong night to go out

Shea: We'll give her some extra hugs for you

Me: And if any of you happen to have to drive by the Pub on your way home, could you bring my shit Ash left on the porch?

51

Cinnamon Rolls

Ashley

"Mason, if it's you, I swear to —" I shouted as I made my way to the knocking door and stopped as soon as I opened it. Because it wasn't Mason. It was my friends.

"Roxie is out chasing dick because she's stressed, but hi," Shea said, stepping into the doorway to hug me. Then she let go and hugged me again, presumably the second one was from Roxie.

"We don't know if she's with a man," Rosie chided. "But we do want to hang out. Is that all right?"

"Well sure, you're always welcome. But why are you —"

"Mason said you have board games. And there's this haunted mansion game Eli was talking about that sounded really cool," Shea said, slipping past me and into the house. Rosie, Olivia, and Zoey all gave me hugs before we went into the living room.

"Holy crap, why is this box so fucking thick?" Shea shouted, sitting on the floor next to the board game shelf.

"Oh shit, that's a lot of Jenkins," Olivia mumbled, going up to the bookshelves and tilting her head to read the titles.

"Why haven't we been over here before? Your place is huge," Zoey said, plopping on the couch and stretching out.

"I guess we've always hung out at the diner to make room for my odd hours," Rosie noted.

"And you have milkshakes at the diner," Shea pointed out before slamming the box on the coffee table and sitting on the floor. "All right, let's figure out how to play this behemoth."

"I've never gotten a chance to play it. So we're gonna have to pop out all the pieces," I said. Shea sighed as the lid slid off and there were several sheets of cardboard pieces to pop out. She started handing sheets out as the other two joined us around the table.

"So why did Eli recommend a game with a million pieces?" Zoey asked.

"It's got different endings or something. I dunno."

"Yeah, so based on what tiles we lay down and the cards we pull, we get a different event that changes the gameplay," I explained. Shea tossed the instructions to Zoey and Zoey immediately passed them to Olivia.

"Sweetie, do you want to talk about the pile of Mason's things on the porch?" Rosie asked, leaning into me to whisper the question while Olivia started reading out the instructions.

"No, that's his problem. Though I am curious how long before Clive starts rummaging through them."

Zoey set down her sheet and asked, "Has anyone seen Clive go up stairs? Can deer climb stairs?"

"He can go over curbs, I don't see why steps would be a problem," Olivia said.

"But wouldn't porch steps be too narrow? Or like not long enough?"

"I think you're overthinking it, Zo," Shea said. "Dogs can go up steps like that just fine. Though I think Clive is too food motivated to fuck with Mason's clothes."

"Hmm, guess I could put some carrots in the pile."

"Ashley," Rosie cautioned, voice soft. I knew Rosie didn't like being called the mother of the group, especially when she clearly took on a lot of parenting duties in her own family. But fuck if she didn't sound more motherly than my own mom. "You don't have to talk about it if you really don't want to. But we're here for you if you do. Just like you've been here for all of us."

"Absolutely," Olivia added. "I don't think I would've been able to get my business up and running as fast as I did without you. Seriously. You know more about the codes in the city than anyone, possibly even more than Ms. Taylor."

"Now I don't —"

"And I think I would literally die without your cinnamon rolls," Shea said and Olivia and Zoey nodded along aggressively. "But also, I'm eternally grateful you talked me out of doing blue hair."

"It would've looked terrible and like you were a Tumblr girl having a breakdown," I mumbled, shifting in my seat to shake out the uncomfortable feeling of being complimented.

"Oh my God, I would have," Shea said, laughing.

"And could you imagine how much legal trouble Zoey would have gotten into if Johnny knew she didn't have you at her side," Olivia said, nudging Zoey with her elbow.

"I don't think Johnny's smart enough to figure out how to sue anyone," Zoey grumbled. "But it was reassuring knowing you had my back."

"Did Mason tell you guys to say all this shit?" It was embarrassing.

"He said you might be lonely is all," Rosie said before tilting her head toward my hands. "But you're wearing the rings, so I think there's still some hope left."

I fiddled with the rings. There wasn't any real reason I kept putting them back on. Habit, maybe. But the thought of pulling them off right now twisted my stomach. They were just symbols of a con scheme. They didn't matter. They *shouldn't* matter.

Fuck it.

"It was all fake!"

Silence.

Then Shea was on the floor laughing, rolling onto her side so she was nearly underneath the coffee table.

"What do you mean, fake?" Olivia asked.

"How many fake relationships can one friend group have before we get a sitcom?" Zoey asked.

"No," Rosie cried, giving me the biggest sad eyes I'd ever seen.

Shea kept laughing on the floor.

"When we went to tour that shop, the realtor basically said the only way we could afford it was if we got married for the small business owners grant. So we..."

"Wait, wait, wait. I'm calling Bailey," Shea cried from under the table. I could hear a faint ringing before the call was picked up and Shea immediately said, "Bailey, it was a fake marriage!"

"What?" Bailey shouted. Shea crawled out from under the table and set the phone down in the center before making a 'go on' motion with her hands.

"Oh my god, you're so dramatic," I grumbled before resituating on the couch to explain. "It's simple. There was an open storefront we were both interested in. But the owner was considering renting to Starbucks and they were bound to outprice us. The city council or whatever disqualified a bunch of other grants because they wanted business, so the only grant available was for married couples. So we did that."

"Did that, she says," Rosie said, aghast.

"But like, you're legally married, right?" Zoey asked.

"Mhmm."

"Is that why you did the courthouse wedding?" Olivia asked.

"And why you couldn't come to Seattle with us?" Bailey asked.

"No, I couldn't come to Seattle because I can't afford to close the shop. Especially during the summer." I curled my legs up and wrapped my arms around them. Rosie set a hand on my shoulder and gave me a light squeeze.

"You could have told us. I know you wouldn't have accepted help, but we understand what it's like owning a business," Rosie said while Zoey nodded along. "My parents ... well I don't think they wanted to inherit the diner and it showed in how they treated the restaurant. I took over straight after high school and I still wasn't making any real profit until a few years ago."

"And I only have the flexibility I do because I have zero competition in town. Most folks are fine waiting an extra day or two for me to fix their car just so they don't have to deal with going out of town."

"I wouldn't have been able to afford it if I hadn't been living with my parents until recently," Olivia said. "Honestly, I would've said I couldn't go if I hadn't been able to work some on the trip."

"And once you and Mason get things settled with the new shop, we can go again. And this time I wanna go to Portland too," Shea said.

"Oh yeah! There was this ice cream shop Stephen recommended that we didn't get to go to."

"There's not going to be a new shop," I interrupted before Zoey and Shea had a chance to plan any further.

"What do you mean no new shop? You two are going to get back together, just like all the other fake relationships," Shea said, waving a hand at Zoey and Olivia.

"I don't think that's fair to —"

"I went on like one fake date with Stephen. It wasn't so much fake dating as pretending we were closer than we were at the time," Zoey argued and Shea threw her hands up in mock surrender.

"We're not opening the shop and we're certainly not getting back together. When the car ran into the shop, Mason revealed he had *way* more money than he led on. He didn't need the grant or me. He's just a big lying bitch who leaves out whatever's inconvenient to getting what he wants. I hate him."

My mini rant was met with awkward silence, the only sound was the popping of pieces from the cardboard sheets.

"What?" I asked, looking around at the women who all distinctly looked away. "What?"

"Well, sweetie, you don't really hate him, do you?"

"Of course I do. He lied to me."

"Eh," Zoey said, stretching out the sound. "I'm kinda on Mason's side, what he did wasn't *that* bad. And like, he clearly just wanted a chance with you."

"To fuck me, you mean."

"Well he's definitely been smitten with you this whole time," Olivia argued. "But what he did is shitty. I mean, maybe not divorce shitty because his heart was in the right place. But he should still, I dunno, show some sort of genuine apology."

"Oh my god, make him pay for a trip to Seattle," Shea suggested.

"No. He left out crucial information. Twice. He doesn't get to do anything with me."

"Did he apologize for that first time? Or did you refuse to talk about it and not give him the chance?" Shea asked, one eyebrow raised. I flipped her off.

"He apologized. I … fuck, I understood why he didn't say anything back then. But it was still shitty. And this was just — he could have asked me out at any point in time these past three years if that's what he wanted."

"Like hell, he could have," Zoey laughed out.

"Ash, don't lie. You're a stubborn bitch and we love you for it. But he could have done a whole song and dance number about how much he loves you and you would have criticized every second of it and never considered what he said."

"I would have listened. Eventually."

"Has he told you he loves you?" Bailey asked, shouting over the phone. I had a feeling she had to shout even on speaker to be heard over all of us.

"… yeah. He told me the other day."

"And do you believe him?"

I didn't say anything. I didn't have to.

I did believe Mason loved me. And if I stopped being stubborn about everything for just one minute, I'd probably realize I loved him too. Because of course, that's how it would go. When Mason wasn't being an idiot, he was sweet. He cared about this community and the traditions of the town. He wanted to build a family with the same love and care that I wanted. He could catch when I was mentally breaking down and I could soothe his triggered anxiety.

It was stupid how much one little miscommunication rattled me. But I didn't know how to force myself out of this stubbornness.

"So what's your thing gonna be?" Shea asked.

"What?"

"Everybody's got their thing, their sore spot. Olivia's was letting go of a goal she'd worked for all her life that didn't make her happy."

"Hey!"

"Zoey thought her craziness needed to be fixed."

Zoey just shrugged at that, not as outraged by being read out by Shea.

"Mine is gonna have something to do with my homophobic blood parents."

"Blood parents?" Bailey asked.

"Well, I'd consider your folks my family."

"Aw."

"Bailey, whenever that guy decides to take it a step forward, is gonna have a freak out about structure because her little hippie heart doesn't like when others try to enforce control."

"I don't think Greg is like that."

"Ignoring. Roxie, if she finds anybody she wants to commit to, is definitely going to carry some sort of shame about her body count. *Especially* if it's somebody that never went through a slut phase. And Rosie will hopefully find a man that will fight with her to put herself first, which she won't do."

"Well, now," Rosie grumbled, picking off invisible lint on her shirt.

"So what's your thing gonna be?" Shea set down the game pieces and leaned onto the coffee table to stare at me.

I bit at my lip. Shuffled in my seat. Pushed out a few more pieces. Then finally gave up stalling because Shea had read everyone else out, so it was only fair I confessed.

"I hate feeling like an idiot. Like *really* fucking hate it. My mom ... perfectionist isn't the right word, but she wanted to set me up for success. And anything less than that was ... not acknowledged. So I guess whenever I feel stupid I go hard in the opposite direction."

The girls all hummed and nodded their heads. Shea collected the pieces and started setting up the game.

"So let's sleep on that," Shea said definitively, clapping her hands once all the cards and tiles were laid out, "And let's play this game."

We all shuffled around, getting closer to the table and claiming our characters. Then we all stared at Olivia expectantly, the instructions still in her lap.

"Oh. I didn't really understand the instructions. We're going to have to find an online tutorial or something."

52

Long Black

Mason

Turns out that breaking down without Ashley was incredibly easy.

After I'd texted her girls, I spent the rest of the evening aggressively cleaning the Pub and stayed up late doing inventory. But no matter what I was in the middle of, I always found myself looking across the street at Ashley's shop. And I knew full well that she wasn't there.

At some point, the kid who was helping me out this evening asked if I needed to go to the hospital because I was acting so weird.

And now I was lying in a bed that didn't feel like mine anymore, completely unable to fall asleep. I kept putting my phone away to try, then give up after five minutes and doom scroll.

Then Ashley's name flashed on my screen and my heart jumped into my throat.

"Everything all right, sweetheart?" I asked as soon as the call connected. The only thing she could possibly be calling me about at this hour was an emergency. Fuck, the only thing she'd call *me* for was an emergency, regardless of the hour.

"Yeah. I … I didn't think you'd pick up. I just wanted to say thank you for telling the girls to come over."

"Fuckin' hell, Ash. You scared the shit out of me." I sat up, pressing a hand to my heart willing it to settle down.

"Sorry, I figured you'd be asleep and I could just leave a message."

"Why not just text me then?" I asked.

"Well, I just …" Ashley drifted off and the call filled with sounds of sheets shuffling and the bed squeaking. "Fuck it, maybe I wanted to hear your voice before going to bed and thought the voicemail would fulfill that desire, all right?"

"Well I'll be," I whispered. "Does my wife miss me?"

"No. You don't have a wife. We decided to tear up the papers, remember?"

"I suggested tearing up the contract. *Not* our wedding certificate. I wanna keep that forever." I could picture her in our bed, rolling her eyes. God, I miss her.

"What're you doing up anyways?" she asked.

"It's hard to sleep when I'm not in our bed."

"You mean *my* bed."

"Stop pretending, sweetheart," I teased, getting giddy from the simple fact that she'd called me. "We both know that's our bed. Just like that's our home, the one you picked out for us to raise our family someday."

"That's not —" she started, but I wasn't going to let this line go.

"I said stop pretending, Ashley. We both knew it that night, what we could have. And I'm sorry my dumbass made it take longer than it should have. But we're married now and no matter how many times I screw up, I'm not letting us get off track again."

"Mason." It was so hard to tell how she felt with just the sound of my name. I needed more cues to understand if the softness in her voice was from hesitation or affection.

"Tell me about your girls' night," I said, scared to hear what else she might say.

"It was … nice. Much more comfortable than going to the diner to hang out. We're considering doing a regular game night."

"Oh yeah? What'd you play tonight?"

"This game Eli recommended to Shea. It has multiple endings, so we can play it again next time."

She went on to describe the game and how their playthrough went. I didn't interrupt, but I liked the idea of her including me in that we. We'd host one hell of a game night together, especially once we got the second shop up and running so we could have mornings off.

"Sweetheart," I interrupted eventually. "It's getting real late and you're gonna blame me tomorrow when you're running on too little sleep."

"Oh shit. I didn't realize how late it was."

"That's what happens when you're talking to your husband." I could practically hear the eye roll. "Goodnight, sweetheart. I love you."

"… night, Mason."

53

Creme Brulee

Ashley

I was exhausted and had too much on my mind to deal with work. The only blessing was that while it wasn't enough, I did fall right asleep after Mason said good night.

With all my frustration about feeling played like a fool, I'd forgotten how nice it was to have Mason around the house. The way he warmed the bed, the way we talked about our days, the soothing timber of his voice. We'd shared a bed for such a short amount of time but fell into a routine with so much ease.

Shea was right. I needed to fight my knee-jerk reaction to lash out at Mason because I felt dumb.

And just as I thought that, Mason stepped into my shop with the heaviest bags under his eyes, shirt unevenly tucked, and a much thicker beard than he had just the other day.

"You look like shit," was of course the first thing I said. Mason gave me a bit of a smile as he walked up to the counter, but it didn't reach his eyes. It didn't even summon his dimple.

"I told you I don't sleep too well without you. I don't wanna get used to sleeping without my wife."

"It's not real," I said, another knee-jerk reaction that hurt to say aloud. And hurt even worse when Mason shrunk, face dropping and eyes going distant.

"Right. Shoulda've known not to have too much hope after last night. Gotta work for it after all," Mason said with a lifeless chuckle. "Well, can I get my usual, please?"

"Usual?" I repeated because even since our scheme started, he didn't exactly come by the shop and order off the menu.

"Ah, right. Guess I got another stupid secret. I've been having Louis come over to get your stuff for me." He scratched at the back of his head, eyes downcast.

"For how long?" Mason just hummed in response. "Mason, *how long?*"

"The whole time," he mumbled.

"Three years? Louis has come in here for three years, at least once a week, to get you my food for you?" My heart was rising into my throat like it was being filled with helium.

"Yeah. I guess it's safe to assume any dumb shit I haven't told you already has to do with how I'd do just about anything to be close to you even when we're fighting." His eyes finally looked up to meet mine. Then his eyes dropped to the neck-lace. He leaned forward, hand outstretched to tug at the chain and pull the pendant out from under my dress. Mason ran his fingers over the rings knotted there. "I never told you about this ring, did I?"

I couldn't very well speak with my heart in my throat, so I just shook my head.

"It's a family ring, on my mother's side. It was hers and then my nana's before her. It supposedly has been around since my family immigrated from Ireland, but I'm not sure if I buy that story." Mason set the pendant down gently before pulling away and my brain scrambled.

"Mason, you should have never given these to me." My hands went behind my neck to undo the necklace, but Mason grabbed my elbow.

"Don't you fucking dare."

"But you should give these to somcone you actually want to be your wife." The words came out in a whisper. As upset as I was that Mason made me out to be a fool, I didn't want him with anyone else.

"I already did. Aren't you listening, sweetheart? I want you, I always have. I'm just a dumbass that went about it in the most complicated way possible. I guess love really does make you act like an idiot, huh?"

Love makes you act like an idiot.

It was idiotic of me to accept a wild rom-com plot as a business deal. It was especially idiotic to keep taking steps into a relationship while pretending I had the safety net of a deadline for the marriage. But it was probably most idiotic that I knew I could fall for him that first night and when I did fall for him, I didn't notice it until after I kicked him out of the house.

"Mason, I —"

I wasn't ready. The words were too sticky in my mouth to get out.

Plus, he did do a shitty thing. I could make him sweat for a little longer. After all, it'd only been a couple of days since he bet on his misery. I could plan on exactly how I wanted to confess so it'd be a picture-perfect ending.

"I'll call you tonight. If I'm in the mood."

Mason let out a little puff of a laugh before knocking twice on the wood countertop. This time his smile met his eyes, the blue sparkling with hope. Hope I gave him.

So without another word, I packed up what I'd thought was Louis' usual order and slid it over to Mason.

54

Peanut Butter Fudge

Ashley

My heart was pounding as the phone rang. I supposed since we skipped the talking phase of our relationship, it only made sense that calling Mason would give me butterflies. Except he was my husband and it felt stupid for my stomach to be in knots like this.

But I was taking the steps to not see feeling silly as a bad thing. Just in baby steps.

"Ashley," Mason answered, his voice oddly ragged.

"Mason?" I asked, hesitant. "Are you still cleaning up the shop or —"

"Nah, Travis closed tonight, so I took a nap and was just … in the middle of a dream," he rushed to say. Which I supposed made sense, but the last time he answered a call slightly out of breath I thought he was getting together with his ex.

"What were you dreaming about?"

"I'm already in the dog house, I don't think answering that will go over well," he said, chuckling.

"If you don't tell me, I'm going to assume you were dreaming about someone else and you'll never get out of the dog house."

"Sweetheart, you can't talk to me like that when I'm this hard and you're not here."

"Talk like what?"

"Like you need to mark your claim on me."

"Well if you don't like it, say so now and I'll go rip up your letter and drop off the annulment paperwork." The idea of Mason thinking of another woman ruffled my feathers. And the idea that he did it subconsciously was even worse. If he didn't want me to claim him all the way down to his subconscious thoughts, then he could fuck off now. I wasn't going to confront my issues of feeling stupid for anything less.

"Don't you fucking dare," he growled over the phone. "I love the ever-loving shit out of you claiming me as yours. The problem is you should never feel like you need to."

"Well ... I did."

"Hmm, guess I need to fix that."

"Yes, you do." Despite being alone in the room, I puffed out my chest like I was issuing a challenge. And maybe I was. Best we got all my knee-jerk reactions out of the way now before Mason officially moved in.

"All right, get that purple toy out then."

"Cocky much? Who says you describing a dream will turn me on?" I said, reaching over my bed to dip into the bedside table where that specific toy was stored.

"I'll make it worth the trouble, sweetheart, I promise." There was some shuffling on the other line before he continued. "Every dream I've had since I met you, sexual or not, has been about you. From simple shit about just living with you to our wedding. And yeah, several of those dreams have been about fucking you. I've lost count of how many times I woke up hard as fuck because I went to bed thinking about how you screwed me over that day."

"What'd you go to bed thinking about tonight?" I asked, trying to ignore the way my heart fluttered at him dreaming about our wedding. For all his gruff cowboy appearance, Mason played the pining, lovesick boy so well. Where would we have been if he hadn't hidden it all these years?

"That for all we know you could be pregnant right now."

"*That's* what led to your sex dream? Guess that solidifies the whole breeding kink thing," I joked.

"Breeding kink? I don't think it's a kink to want kids with the woman I love, who *also* wants kids."

"Sure, but you seem to get an awful lot out of shoving your come back inside me."

Mason groaned, a knock sounding like he'd leaned back and hit his head on the bed frame.

"Yeah, I do. That's where it belongs. And don't you dare pretend like it doesn't get you all hot and bothered too. Your pussy grips my fingers so tightly, like you wanna keep me inside you forever."

"Sometimes I do," I admit before shimmying off my bottoms and clicking on the dildo portion of the toy. The second the vibrating started, Mason groaned. "Sometimes I think I'd enjoy our relationship much more if I took you home and sat on your face before you have a chance to say anything stupid."

"Fuck, yes, sweetheart. Feel free to drag me off any time, even on the rare occasions I'm not acting like an idiot."

"You have your moments," I murmured. I should have considered Mason's willingness to eat more when kicking him out. That would probably solve most of my knee-jerk reactions, the simple reminder of the things his tongue could do to my body.

"Care to elaborate on that?"

"Fishing for complements?"

"Begging, sweetheart." His voice was so vulnerable, it made my heart ache, made me completely forget all the stupid reasons I didn't immediately tell him to come home.

Mason cleared his throat.

"Sorry, sweetheart. Didn't mean to get you all riled up and then dump a bucket of cold water on you. Let me tell you about the dream"

"Right. You're the one who made this a sex call, so make it sexy, cowboy."

"Cowboy, huh? You think just cause I know how to work a rope, I'm a cowboy?"

"Well, the hat too."

"Hmm, remind me to give you a proper lecture on the history of cowboys. The real shit, not the stuff they put in those bullshit Western movies."

"So you're just a stereotypical cowboy and not the real thing?" I teased.

"Those are fighting words, sweetheart. You keep that up and I won't make you come."

"Make me? Last I checked, you aren't here. I have to do all the work."

"Physically, sure. But it's my name you're gonna be screaming as you come."

"Hmm, we'll see about that. How'd your dream start?"

"Mmm, we were in Tost-Ka. You'd called me over to try a new recipe but instead of taking me into the kitchen, you took me back into your office. You sat on your desk and told me I had to earn my treat."

"Such a good submissive cowboy."

"I like pleasing my wife, ain't nothing wrong with that."

"Tell me how you'll please me then." I'm not sure if I meant how he had pleased me in the dream or how he'd please me when I forgave him at the end of the week. It didn't really matter which.

"I got down to my knees, of course. Ran my hands up your thighs to push up your cute lil sundress up only to find you ready for me. Bare and wet."

I hummed in response, raking the toy up and down my thighs, imagining it was his hands touching me. And despite the ups and downs of the conversation, the side tracks, my body instantly heated.

"And since you went through the trouble of getting ready for me, I didn't make you wait. I grabbed you by the thighs and pulled your ass to the edge of the desk and ate. Fuck, I know it's only been a few days, but I'm fucking starving for you, Ash. There is nothing that tastes as good as your pussy."

"Not even those peanut butter cookies?" I teased as I brought the tip of the toy to my clit, circling it the way Mason did with his tongue.

"They're incomparable, sweetheart. I love your baking. Anyone with taste buds would love your baking. It's a reflection of all the effort you put into it. But your pussy is mine alone. It's a base part of you, the most intimate part of you, and I'm fucking desperate for it."

My heart stuttered.

"Mason, you're not very good at dirty talk." My voice came out crackly. Why the hell was him talking about eating me out causing an emotional reaction?

"I'm just following what your books do. What's wrong with it?"

"Is that why you read them?" I asked, sitting up in bed and turning off the toy. This phone sex thing wasn't working for me right now, Mason was too sincere. His words didn't dull the heat, but they shifted it into something too tender for phone sex.

"I like learning more about you, Ash. I'd read them even if they didn't have the sexy bits."

Maybe I was pregnant. That would certainly explain all the emotional ups and downs of the night.

"Mason, put your cock away. This isn't working."

"Sweetheart, I can do something different —"

"No. I'm just not … I'm not in the mood for phone sex. You didn't do anything wrong. This time."

"This time. You sure about that? Because it sorta feels like I failed at turning you on. And I'll be honest, I'm hitting my limit of feeling like shit because I keep failing you. And I thought the sex was the one non-issue between us."

"Mason." I said his name softly because I was breaking inside just a little too. All my stupid stubbornness was hurting him. I should just tell him I love him now and to come home. What was the point in waiting?

"Sorry. I told you I'd prove my life is miserable without you and now I'm complaining about it. Don't mind me, sweetheart. I love you and I hope you sleep well."

And then the line went dead. I sat, pants-less, staring at my phone.

Fuck his week of misery. He fucked up and made me feel stupid, but I wasn't going to let that prolong my misery.

Me: I want to tell Mason he's an idiot and I love him in the most dramatic, over the top way possible

Shea: Fuck yeah

Rosie: Is the idiot part completely necessary?

Me: Yes, we're both idiots in love and that needs to be made very clear

55

Nitro Brew

Mason

I needed a better plan to apologize to Ashley than just proving I needed her to function.

For one, it wasn't having much of an effect on her. Last night's call left me feeling like shit. I kept sticking my foot in my mouth saying unnecessary shit and ruining the mood. Of course, she gave up on the whole thing. I'd gotten her to call me, two nights in a row, and I couldn't even make it worth her time.

And then on the other hand, given that I was a miserable sack of shit, work was not going ... well. Since I hadn't been sleeping well, my ability to remember folks' orders and how to make said orders was shit. Over the morning rush, I fucked up around 20 orders and people were not happy. Some folks went so far as to dump their drinks out on the counter.

I probably spent an hour just cleaning up after angry customers.

So it wasn't a big surprise that come lunchtime the place was empty. Word must have gotten around that I was providing some shit service and was best avoided.

Which was fine by me. My misery didn't need company, it needed a solution. One that would prove to Ashley that … I don't even know what I needed to prove to her anymore. Obviously, she had a hard time believing the people around her needed her, but proving that line of thought didn't apply to me wasn't something a week of sleeplessness would prove. That was something I'd have to show up for, consistently. I was willing to do that, but she'd have to be willing to let me in.

Then there was the actual root issue and not the thing she threw out off-hand, though that didn't make it any less important. She hated feeling stupid. And me scheming my way into a relationship with her made her feel fooled. I could apologize all I want and promise to never intentionally do it again, but that was another thing where it'd take time to prove.

So what could I do to prove our possible future was worth her giving me that time?

"Mr. Foster," a sharp voice said, accompanied the front door bells as Ms. Taylor stepped into the Pub.

"Hello, Ms. Taylor. How can I help you?"

"Hmph, how can he help, he asks. Like you don't know the disturbance you've caused."

Great. News had made its way to Ms. Taylor, which meant —

"Emergency town hall. Now." And then, just as quickly as she entered, she was gone.

God fucking damn it.

I had two choices. I could ignore Ms. Taylor and let the town say whatever bullshit they wanted to say without me present to tamper down their comments and suffer any consequence Ms. Taylor decided to dish out. Or I could go and sit through it.

Either way, I was going to be miserable. But if I didn't go and Ashley did, she'd be given all the blame for my shitty behavior. And like hell I was going to let that happen.

So begrudgingly I locked up the shop and headed to the community center.

Apparently, I was the last one to be collected. Which is exactly the kind of drama I should have expected Ms. Taylor.

Despite it being in the middle of the workday, the pews were filled to the brim. Folks were crowded inside, shouting and grumbling about the Pub's service these past few days. Their complaints ranged from my general attitude to the frequent wrong orders. But they all had one thing in common, they placed the blame for all of it on Ashley.

"All right, what the hell is this?" I asked, stepping through the crowded aisle and up to the front where Ms. Taylor stood behind the podium.

"Mr. Foster, language," she cautioned.

"Your coffee sucks!" someone shouted from the crowd.

I turned to figure out who was speaking, but at this point, everyone had sat down, so it was hard to tell. What I did see was Ashley sitting in the front with Shea, Olivia, and Roxie. Guess Ms. Taylor wasn't able to close down everyone's businesses.

"If you'd have a seat, Mr. Foster. Perhaps by your *wife*." Ms. Taylor waved in Ashley's direction. Ashley paled, her eyes widening at the way Ms. Taylor said the word wife. Shea nudged her with an elbow and Ashley shook the look away.

Doing my best to look simply annoyed by Ms. Taylor, I took up the space by Ashley and squeezed her hand. She smelled like flour and I was wondering what she'd been baking when she leaned in to whisper, "What do you think this is about? People seem to be pissed about stuff happening at the Pub. But do you think they found out that we —"

I interrupted with another squeeze of her hand.

"No, they're just pissed at me."

"They are not. They clearly think something else is going on. What if that Mayberry press guy started —"

Ms. Taylor banged her gavel on the podium.

"We're here to discuss certain relationship troubles disrupting the normal flow of business in Snowfall." Everyone's eyes went to us and I felt Ashley stiffen beside me. "Over the past few days, the following has been noted. Mr. Foster's truck has not been parked outside the Foster home. There is also a large pile of men's belongings on the porch. Mr. Foster has shown several signs of sleep deprivation, including bags under his eyes, mistaking customer orders, and replacing all of the coffee in the Pub with decaf. He also canceled last night's trivia event, a mainstay event for residents."

"Oh my god, are you all seriously so pissed I've had a couple of bad days that you —" I started, already seeing where this was going.

"Mr. Foster, language. You will have an opportunity to speak after I've listed all of the disturbances."

"There's more?" Ashley balked.

"Meanwhile, the shop the couple owns out in Mayberry has been put on hold, meaning we will no longer see the economic benefits of drawing customers into Snowfall."

"A car went through the shop!" Ashley exclaimed, her friends shouting similar things.

"And you, Mrs. Foster, have not appeared to be bothered one bit by whatever it is that's distressing Mr. Foster. Which has led several community members to believe that *you* are what's causing the problem."

"Excuse me?"

"Ma'am, are you accusing my wife of something?" I stood up, damn near ready to fight. I was exhausted and miserable and I couldn't handle any more shit piled on.

Unfortunately, my outburst was a domino falling and other folks stood to shout their complaints.

"You gave my wife decaf and she made me sleep on the couch."

"I look forward to trivia all month and you canceled it just hours before."

"That pile of clothes is unseemly."

"The coffee tasted like shit today!"

"It's all her fault, she's making you miserable."

"Mason is a good man, stop being so nitpicky with him!"

"She doesn't even want to give him children! What's going to happen to the Pub?"

"If you're going to get divorced, get it over with."

I turned back to Ashley as the comments got nastier and nastier. Her shoulders had slumped, her lips pressed straight. She was going into that lawyer mode, stone-faced. Olivia, Roxie, and Shea tried to talk to her, but she kept shaking her head at whatever they were saying.

No one needs me.

God, this proved her right, didn't it? She might've made progress with her friends on their game night. Hell, I think we were taking some steps forward with our calls. But what the hell kind of good would it do if she still sees her shop, an extension of herself and the happiness she was seeking here, as second fiddle to my place?

And god forbid we get back together and have any other spat just for this sort of thing to happen over and over again. Ashley would always face the brunt of the small town gossip, no matter the case. I couldn't stand her having to face that. Even this was too much.

"It's my fault." The room went silent, all eyes turning to me. "I did something stupid and hurt her feelings. Ashley has every right to kick me out, divorce me, or whatever she wants. If you're pissed that I'm a sad sack of shit because she broke up with me, you can take it up with me. And keep her name out of y'alls mouths or I'll ban you from the Pub, divorce or not."

Then I walked right out.

I passed through screams and accusations and a general air of dramatization. But it didn't fucking matter. Ashley didn't want me for damn good reasons, I dragged her into a mess desperate to change her mind, the least I could do was know when to call it quits and keep her from being miserable too.

I stepped outside, the doors closing behind me and blocking out the ruckus that had become the town hall. I looked up at the cloudy sky, trying to find some sort of calm in the quiet.

But then the door opened behind me and I just focused on not crying at whoever decided to come pick a fight.

"Look, if you have a complaint about my coffee, complain about it at the —" I turned to see Ashley, arms crossed, cheeks red, and eyes water.

"What the fuck kind of answer was that? We're getting divorced, is that right? Last I checked, you were the one refusing an annulment. Where'd that conviction go?"

"Ashley, I'm sorry. I just … I can't see you like that."

"Like what?"

"Miserable. Considering quitting everything. Stewing in criticism that shouldn't matter. I had enough of that when your mom was in town. I'm not gonna let the town shit on you for my mistakes."

"So what? You're giving up?"

"Well, if it's between both of us being miserable and just me being miserable, you should know what I'd choose." Ashley was a few steps above me on the church steps, our eyes almost level. And I couldn't read a damn thing in them. And shit, that hurt. For all the progress our relationship had made, for all the new things I'd learned about her, she could still hide things. Though I guess I'd done that too. "I've made you miserable enough already. I think it's time for me to cut that out, don't you?"

Ashley's face remained stoic as she reached around her head and undid the clasp of her necklace. Then she shoved it into my chest.

"Fine."

"Fine?" I repeated, a little dumbstruck as I clutched the pendant and rings to my chest. I know I'd said the words, but the rings being back in my hands made it real. Made my heart shatter. Fuck, I'd been so stupid.

"Yeah, fine. You don't want me to be miserable, I can't argue that I stand a better chance of that without you. So take back the rings you wanted me to keep so bad the other day."

"Ashley." She tried to walk around me and I grabbed her arm. When she turned to look at me, her eyes were watery, cheeks an angry red. "I'm sorry if I embarrassed you in there. I'm sorry I did something thoughtless and desperate to get you in the first place. I'm sorry for all of it. But at least this way no one will bother you again."

"Including you?" she asked like it was a challenge. And hell, it would be. Seeing her across the street and not walking over to pick a fight or do anything to get her to talk to me. Not driving to her house after work. Fuck sleeping in my bed was already a challenge with the recent memory of our night there.

"If that's what you want."

Ashley stared at me for another beat, eyes narrowed. Then she huffed and walked away.

56

Peanut Butter and Jam Cake

Ashley

"He's a little fucker," I shouted to my phone on the counter.

"All right, straight for the jugular, huh," Shea said over the speaker. I'd called her over the others partially because not everyone had been at today's town hall. But also because she mentioned how much she hated being alone in her apartment. So I needed a rant and she needed company, it was a win-win.

"He just decided to give up after setting up the whole marriage shenanigan, after three years of supposed pining and chastity, after —"

"Wait a second. Chasity?"

"Yeah, he didn't sleep with anyone between the time we had our one-night stand and the whole marriage shit," I explained, angrily spooning flour into a measuring cup.

"Damn. He really is an idiot in love, huh?"

"In love? The away he shows his love is to keep making decisions for us without asking me first. He decides the only way we'd ever get together is some wild marriage of convenience thing and just does it."

"All right, Ash. To be fair, it's not like he could have just asked you out. You've thrown several cleaning rags at the man just for entering your shop. How would he have asked you out like that?"

"Shut up, Shea. We're shit-talking my husband." Another angry scoop of flour.

"Well, your husband just basically confirmed you're getting a divorce in front of the whole town, so …"

"That's because my husband is an idiot and he thought I couldn't handle being a part of some small town drama."

"They were being pretty bitchy."

"They were. I felt like shit. Shea, would you ever consider taking Ms. Taylor's place?"

"Holy fucking hell, that is some grade-A sacrilege you just said."

"What do you mean sacrilege? She has to retire at some point."

"Retire? It's not a job."

"Wait, it's not a job?" I asked, pausing in the middle of leveling the sugar. "So people are just letting her run around, ordering people to do shit, and it's not even like an official position? Why the fuck is everyone listening to her then?"

"I dunno. Because it's Ms. Taylor," Shea said like it was just a forgone conclusion that everyone needed to put up with that woman's dramatics.

"That's fucking insane. Are there any sort of community center bylaws? Let's get this bitch in check."

"Woah, love the energy, but if you go after Ms. Taylor, you're gonna be in for a world of trouble."

"Hmph, I'd like to see her try to fight me on fair grounds. She disrupted the whole town's businesses just to air some drama? It's fucking ridiculous. If she really wanted to do better by the community, she could have had a private meeting with the two of us instead of inviting everyone to air their grievances at us."

"Yeah, that was a shit show. I'm sorry folks went off on you like that."

I took a deep breath, fighting the knee-jerk reaction to pretend it didn't suck to hear people say I was making Mason miserable and being a general bitch to him. It hurt like hell and Mason hit the nail on the head when he said I was considering that everything I'd done so far was a failure. But all that was blown out of the water when Mason decided to give up on us.

"Yeah, it fucking sucked. But I'm more pissed about Mason now. And his stupid, dumb ass ruining my planned confession."

"Right, what're you gonna do about that? Should I cancel the mariachi band?"

I paused to think about the various stupid arrangements the girls and I made last night, including a mariachi band that I paid extra for them to go during off hours so Mason would be awakened at 12:01 on the promised day I'd read his letter.

"Is it bad that I kind of want them to go just to get back at him for declaring we're getting a divorce?"

"I mean, you did give him the rings back," Shea pointed out.

"Shut up," I grumbled, whisking the dry ingredients together a little more aggressively than necessary.

"Mm-hmm. What're you making anyways? Is it worth braving the storm for?"

I hadn't been paying much attention to what I was baking. It didn't really matter what it was since I was only baking to keep myself occupied. But when I looked down at the mixing bowls and the gathered ingredients, I realized my default baking item had changed. No longer did I make cinnamon rolls in a daze. Now it was peanut butter cookies.

"That little fucker," I grumbled. "I'm making his favorite cookies."

"Aw, you're so in love," Shea crooned before singing, "Mason and Ashley sitting in a tree, K-I-S-S-I-N-G."

"Shut up. This is so fucking stupid. He doesn't deserve a big romantic gesture. I'm just gonna finish these fucking cookies then drive over there and take my rings and him back."

"Hell yeah! But are you sure that's a good idea? It's coming down pretty hard."

I looked out the window to a curtain of rain. And I thought of Mason, curled up on his bed, head in his hands, a sweaty mess. Alone and miserable. With no cookies or anyone to keep him company.

"God damn it. Fine. Fuck the cookies. The dough needs to chill anyways. Talk to you later, Shea."

"Go get your man! But also drive safe. There're a lot of areas where the roads flood."

57

Breve

Mason

Nights like these made me wish I could drink.

Tonight's storm was bad, because of course, the first storm after letting Ashley go would be bad. I felt like shit, I couldn't sleep, and I missed her so damn much already. I'd put her necklace on and just clutched it as I lay in bed, staring at the ceiling.

It was my own fucking fault. I knew it. But dear fucking lord, did it hurt. And I couldn't even concentrate on what I could've done differently because the storm made my brain sound like television static.

The static was so loud that I almost missed my phone ringing. But the light from my phone was just different enough from the lightning to catch my attention.

"Hello," I said, answering without checking the ID. It didn't matter who was calling, I'd take just about any company at this point.

"Mason, I need your help." Ashley's voice shook me out of the daze and I sat straight up, swinging my legs over the bed, ready to walk straight out of the apartment.

"What's wrong? Are you okay? Are you hurt?" I asked in quick succession.

"Shit," she hissed. "I'm fine, Mason. Really and truly fine. I thought I'd be able to get more than a sentence out before you freak out."

"Of course, I'm going to freak out when my wife calls me at night, in the middle of a rain storm needing help."

"… your wife, huh?" Ashley said after a long pause. A pause in which all I could hear was rain on metal like she was sitting in her car.

"Slip of the tongue. Just tell me what you need help with."

"Hmm." She paused again, taking her sweet time tormenting me with worry. "This is going to be a big ask. But you have a truck and Zoey's already closed and not answering her phone."

"Where are you?" I was out of my bed and dressed faster than if there was a fire in the apartment.

"On Clairmont. I was trying to avoid a large puddle and got stuck in the mud. I've got my flashers on and I'm right near a light. So I'm perfectly safe, I just need a tug out of the mud or something."

"Okay," I murmured, pausing at the door with my keys in hand. I tried to take a few calming breaths before I drove in the rain for the first time. It didn't work. "Right. I've got a tow strap in my emergency kit. I'll be right there. Stay in the car and —"

"Mason, just … stay on the phone with me. Put me on speaker while you drive so we can talk. I know how big of an ask this is for you. I wouldn't have called you if anyone else was available."

"Strangely, that doesn't make me feel any better," I laughed, quickly locking up the apartment and heading down to my truck.

"Don't be so dramatic. You'd be my first call if it wasn't raining."

"Oh really?" I didn't believe it one bit. Not when I was still wearing her rings.

"Okay, I'd probably still call Zoey first. But she's literally a mechanic. You can't blame me for that."

"I suppose that's fair. I'd rather you put your safety first than my ego." I got into my truck and set up the Bluetooth so that when Ashley spoke next, her voice poured through the speaker and nearly drowned out the rain.

"Well, I'll never pass up on an opportunity to knock your ego down."

"That's my girl," I murmured to myself as I carefully pulled out and hit the road, a nice 10 under the speed limit and the AC cranked up to help with the sweats.

"Although given how stupid you act sometimes, I could probably sit back and watch your ego dwindle without lifting a finger." There was a snark to her tone that was softer than her jabs in the past. It was lighter, the kind of poking fun at each other friends do. And I'd take that over nothing at all.

"You do know how to make a man feel special. Teach you that at law school?" I teased.

"Actually, yes. Sort of. I took a seminar for women in law to stand up against the patriarchy or something like that. There were a lot of worksheets on intimidating men who questioned your knowledge."

"And let me guess, you memorized all of them?"

"Of course. Some part of me must have always known I'd meet a man who needed to be checked."

"Checked, huh? Sure you haven't just been checking me out?" I teased.

"Don't flatter yourself, Mason. You have the charm of a bull."

"Hmm, a bull you like to ride though."

"God," she groaned, though her voice shook as she tried to fight back giggles. "When are you gonna run out of terrible come-ons?"

"Dunno. Would you like to find out?" It was too easy to fall back into flirtatious teasing. And by the following silence, I knew Ashley felt it too. Except unlike me, it didn't fill her with a warm comfort.

Fortunately, the silence didn't get a chance to stretch as I turned to Clairmont and saw Ashley's little sedan on the side of the road, emergency lights flashing.

"I see ya, sweetheart. Stay in the car while I turn around."

"No, I think I'll get out and stand in the middle of the road. Actually, hold on, I think I've got a black hoodie in the back somewhere," Ashley snarked. And although I couldn't see her clearly through the car window, I knew she was rolling her eyes.

Slowly, I turned my truck around and pulled up in front of Ashley. I grabbed the tow strap from the emergency kit and braced myself to step outside. Once my door was open, Ashley's quickly followed. I tried to wave her off, but instead, she pulled out an umbrella and stepped up to me. Under the heavy pounding of rain on plastic, Ashley held her arm out awkwardly high to cover me, her free hand going to my arm.

"How're you holding up?" she asked, squeezing my arm as she assessed me.

"Better than getting my car stuck in the mud, that's for sure."

Ashley pinched my arm before pulling away. She only moved a bit so I was still covered by her umbrella, but the loss of her touch stung.

God, I was a fucking mess.

"Right, well get back in the car and I'll take care of this. When I give you a —"

"Shut up. I'm not going into the car. You're out in the rain, something extremely taxing for you, to help me. The least I can do is hold an umbrella over your head while you work," she huffed, taking my arm to lead us over to the bumper of my car where she let go.

"It's actually not all that taxing with you," I murmured, looking down at the yellow strap in my hands. It was true though. Had she not stayed on the phone with me, drowned out the rain with her snark, I wouldn't have made the drive. Without her, I probably would have pulled out of my parking spot and stopped right there. I still had a thin layer of sweat on my brow and my legs didn't feel very stable, but I was doing considerably better than I normally did during a rainstorm.

When I finally got the balls to look at Ashley, her eyes were on my neck. She stepped closer, finger hooking underneath the chain to pull out the necklace, *her* necklace. The pendant holding her rings flopped out of my shirt. Ashley hummed, stepping even closer to tuck the rings away, tapping gently against my chest where they rested.

"Right. Get to it then, cowboy." Her hand moved to my shoulder, giving me a rough pat before pushing me towards her car.

Holding my tongue, I got to work hooking up her car to mine. The whole time Ashley stood beside me, shoes covered in mud, holding the umbrella over my head. At first, she stayed quiet, watching, then a car drove by and my shoulders tensed and suddenly Ashley had a lot to say.

"Those strawberries we moved into the backyard are starting to sprout. Since they were transferred so late in the season, I didn't have much hope. But I might have enough for a shortcake. Maybe one jam test. I haven't done much research on jam recipes though. I think there's somebody who sells jam at the farmer's market, but it's at the same time as the post-church rush. Maybe I'll ask Shea to go and get a couple of samples for me."

Ashley kept on talking as I hooked the two cars together, even following me back to my car door.

"All right, sweetheart. I see what you're doin'. But time go back to your car, get it in neutral, and —"

"Yeah, yeah. I know. Zoey has given us all very thorough emergency car lessons. If it had been a tire change, I would've been completely fine." She waved me off before going to her car. Once she was in, I got into my truck and started it up. Eyes on the rearview mirror, I waited until Ashley stuck a hand out her window, flipping me off, before I switched into drive and slowly pulled us onto the road.

When we were a good dozen feet away from the mud, I parked and looked up at the mirror to make sure Ashley was good. Instead, what I saw was her ducking out of her car and heading straight to the tow strap.

"Ash, I can do that. Get back in your car," I shouted, jumping out of the truck. She flung her hand wildly at me, her umbrella tucked between her shoulder and neck as she unhooked the tow strap.

"You can't tell me what to do," she grumbled, pulling the hook loose and moving to my truck.

I grabbed the strap from her.

"I'm not telling you what to do, I'm just trying to keep you safe." I undid the strap from my truck and tossed it into the bed. "And I know you hate me, especially now, but I'm still gonna look out for you. Even if you find it annoying."

Ashley's nose crinkled but she didn't respond, she just crossed her arms and stayed standing beside me. Knowing Ashley, this was the start of an extremely stubborn argument. And while her presence was helping me weather the storm, I couldn't handle an argument at the same time.

"Look, I know this is also gonna make you pissed, but the quicker you agree to it, the quicker I'm out of your hair. I wanna follow you home and make sure you get there all right."

"No," she said immediately, her jaw setting into lawyer mode.

"Ashley, look, I'm not inviting myself over, I don't need to come inside, I just —"

"I'm not going home."

"Well, where the hell are you going?"

"None of your business," she said, straightening her shoulders before turning around and walking straight to her car. I followed, grabbing her door frame right before she was able to get in.

"Ashley."

"Mason." Ashley said my name with an exasperated sigh as she slipped into the driver's seat and handed me the umbrella.

"Where are you going?"

"Like I said, it's none of your business."

My grip on her door tightened.

"Will you at least text me when you get there so I know you're safe?" I compromised. Ashley chewed at her lip for a long moment before shrugging.

"You'll be made aware when I arrive."

I banged my head on the top of the car.

"Can I go now?" Ashley asked, one hand pushing me out of the door's way. Without waiting for me to respond, she closed the door and buckled up.

With nothing left to do, I walked back to my car, muttering curses the whole way, her umbrella in hand. In my truck, I waited for her to get on the road, half tempted to follow her wherever she was going just so I'd have the peace of mind that she was safe. But of course, my stubborn girl sat in the middle of the road, waiting for me to go first.

So I went home. And every time I checked the rearview mirror, Ashley was there. She followed my every turn and just as I thought she was going to Tost-Ka, she followed me into the parking lot behind the Pub.

I sat in my car, feeling like I was losing my mind. What the hell was she doing here? Did she come out in the middle of a storm to pull some sort of prank on me as punishment for the town hall thing? And did she really decide to keep on with it after I pulled her out of the mud?

Frustrated, I stomped out of my truck, leaving the umbrella behind, and stormed over to her car. After a few knocks and an overly dramatic eye roll, Ashley rolled down the window.

"What?"

"What're you doing here, Ash? If you've got some sort of punishment lined up, save it for tomorrow."

"That's what you think I'm doing here? To fuck shit up?"

"Well, why else would you be here?"

Ashley's face dropped for a millisecond before she pulled herself back together, meeting my eyes with steady determination. Or maybe it was just stubbornness. With her, they were the same thing. And if I questioned that one look of hurt aloud, she'd dig in further. There was no winning, only resignation.

"Fine, do whatever you want." I walked away and Ashley finally stepped out of her car. She followed me into the Pub and up the stairs to my apartment, silent the whole time. So when I opened the door, I just stepped back to let her do whatever it was she had planned.

Nothing she could do could make me feel worse than I already did knowing I fucked up my chances with her.

Seeing me resigned, Ashley huffed and stormed into the apartment, slamming the door in my face and clicking the dead-bolt into place.

Yeah, all right, that's my limit.

I grabbed the spare key from under the mat and opened the door.

"Ashley, I've had it up to here with your bullshit tonight. I love you, but every man has his limits. And —"

I stopped in the middle of the living room, stunned. In the few seconds, Ashley'd been in my apartment alone, she'd managed to find a duffle bag and was shoving as much of my shit into it as possible.

"What're you doing?" I whispered, my heart caught in my throat. Either she was packing up my shit to burn it or …

"I'm packing up your shit. Obviously." She disappeared into my bedroom and I followed. Ashley slid a suitcase out from under my bed and set it on my dresser. Then she pulled out my sock drawer and dumped everything into the bag.

"And why're you packing my shit up?" I asked, leaning against the door frame and crossing my arms. Warmth and hope were spreading in my chest as she continued to gather my belongings.

"Because it doesn't belong here. All this shit belongs in our home."

"Our home?" I repeated, barely fighting a grin. Ashley blatantly didn't look at me, focusing on the bottom dresser that crashed to the floor when she yanked it out. I stayed put, waiting for her to say out loud what was happening before I helped.

"Yes. I want this dresser too." She kicked at the fallen drawer, going up and down to toss my jeans into the suitcase. "I think it'd look nice in the guest room. I'm gonna veto the couch though."

"You wanna get rid of my couch? But that's the first place we ever made out." Ashley paused her packing tirade, cheeks flushing.

"I'm pretty sure we made out in your truck first," she murmured, shaking her head before grabbing a pair of sweats to pack. Most of my clothes were, presumably, still on her porch, so there hadn't been much left for her to grab. She stared at the empty drawer for a solid minute and I thought *this is it.*

But then she turned for the closet.

Resigned, I sat on the bed and let her futz around my apartment, grabbing bags and packing them to the brim.

It took a solid 30 minutes before she stopped in front of me.

"Mason."

"Yes, sweetheart?"

"You know how much I hate feeling stupid. And you pulling that sort of ... I dunno, the scheme made me feel stupid."

I grabbed her hands, which had been flying all around the place, and pressed a kiss to her knuckles. "I understand and I'm sorry. I won't try to —"

"Shut up and let me finish," Ashley interrupted and I did my best to not chuckle. "I know I'm stubborn and I know it probably felt like the only way to get me on a date. So ... I acknowledge my part in this. I also admit that the whole feeling stupid thing makes me act ..."

"Stubborn as a mule?" I suggested, laughing when she shot me a killer glare. I squeezed her hands to let her know I was joking and her shoulders relaxed.

"Sure. Stubborn as a mule. And I know I'm not just gonna get over that immediately and I'll work on it, but I — I should've done what you suggested and taken an hour or two then regrouped. So I know it's been a good deal more than what you suggested, but will you come back home now?" She squeezed my hands in return, eyes glued to my knuckles as she worried her lower lip. I tugged at her hands, pulling each to my side so she was forced to brace against the bed, leaning into me.

"I would come back to you if you made me wait another three years, sweetheart."

"Good. Given how hard-headed we both are, it might just end up being arguing for three years in total over the rest of our lives."

"Say it," I told her, moving closer to kiss her cheek.

"Say what?" she whispered.

"That you love me and you've missed me."

She huffed and walked out of my arms.

"I *was* going to tell you that, but *somebody* ruined my grand confession. There was going to be a mariachi band and everything," she grumbled, grabbing the suitcase from the dresser before heading to the door. I scrambled off the bed and blocked her way.

"Nuh-huh. You're not getting away that easily. Say the whole thing or I'm not going home."

Ashley, arms wrapped around the suitcase, glared at me.

"That's an empty threat."

"You wanna test that theory?" I countered. I braced myself for a long stare down, but Ashley almost immediately sighed and set the suitcase down.

"I love you, all right? I probably have for a while because you were right. I could see us having a happy ending that first night. And we've already gone through so much trouble faking a marriage, we might as well get the happily ever after, right?" Her confession was a blur of huffs and grumbles. It was the exact kind of confession I expected.

"I love you too, sweetheart." I kicked the suitcase aside and wrapped her into a tight hug. She immediately sunk into me, squeezing me in return.

"Can we go home then?"

"Yeah, let's go back home." I looked back at the bed and hummed. "But since I won't be back in this bed again, do you want to —"

An elbow hit my side.

"Shut up, Mason. We're going home. You can eat me out there."

"Sounds good, let's go."

58

Tiramisu

Ashley

One month later

Opening day for Tost-Ka at the Pub was incredible. All the girls were there with their partners, including Bailey and Greg, and damn near all of Mason and my regulars stopped by. Jessie even came in to film new content for another post and brought her family, who were possibly the sweetest people in all of Mayberry.

The only downer was Abraham Murphy walked in when Mason had stepped out to grab something at the store. He was wearing the big press lanyard again. The same one he'd flashed construction workers and other contractors coming in and out of our shop over the last few weeks as we finished setting up. He was a gnat of a person, tiny and capable of being the most annoying thing in any room.

I flashed the girls a look and they immediately abandoned their couch and armchair seats for the bar stools at the counter.

"Hello, Ms. Foster. Congratulations. It looks like you've had quite the opening," Abraham said. From the corner of my eye, I caught Shea making a face and even Rosie scooted further away from the man. He just had that sort of vibe. "Is your husband around?"

"He'll be back shortly. But I'm capable of answering any questions you may have," I said as pointedly as possible. The man grated on my nerves. Not only had he been a constant nuisance, he'd also been hitting on Regina, our lead for the Mayberry shop. He'd even gone so far as to tape a note with his phone number to the door.

Regina and Mason were just barely able to keep me from pressing charges and implementing a restraining order.

"Oh, I just wanted to congratulate him as well. I know you two had some trouble keeping this going after the incident." The implication in his tone was clear. He'd heard about the town hall and that whole debacle and didn't believe we'd really made up. To be fair, most folks in the town were hesitant. We got a good deal of side-eyed looks and whispers as we passed by. But it all stopped within a week or two.

"Mr. Murphy, if you have something to say to me, just say it. I don't appreciate your tone and I won't —" My incoming tirade was interrupted by a hand sliding around my waist and resting on my stomach. I looked up at Mason to see a fake smile plastered on his face.

I frowned at him. Mason might have kept me from filing orders against Abraham, but he hadn't once held me back from telling him, or any other man that tried to question me, off. He respected my right to yell at patriarchal bullshit.

And him interrupting me now was pissing me off.

Though admittedly my fuse had been pretty short with all the stress of opening day.

"Got something for you at the store," Mason murmured into my hair before pressing a kiss there. He pressed a plastic bag into my hands and then addressed Abraham. "Thank you for your congratulations. But Imma have to ask you to move on if you don't plan on orderin' anything. We're getting quite a line."

Behind Abraham, the girls and some actual customers had lined up. Shea took up the part of an impatient customer, tapping her foot loudly and huffing.

"Oh, yes. Sorry about that. Excuse me," he murmured before scampering out of the restaurant.

"Ugh, finally," Shea said, keeping up her act as she stepped up to the counter. "Can I get two blueberry muffins?"

"Sure thing, Shea," Mason said, chuckling as he went over the counter. While he got that, I unraveled the plastic bag to see what Mason had gotten me.

"Mason, what the fuck?" I shouted, drawing every eye to me. Fortunately, no one was close enough to see what I was holding. Except Shea, who immediately braced herself on the counter to lean over and take a peek at the pregnancy test box.

"Oh shit," she murmured before turning to the girls to whisper what she saw.

"Mason," I hissed, smacking his arm as he delivered Shea's muffins. He waved at Regina through the kitchen window and once she came out to take over the register, Mason guided me into the back. The girls followed.

"What the hell makes you think I need this?" I asked him.

"You missed your last period," he noted, that stupid little smirk lighting up his face as he leaned back against a counter.

"I've been stressed," I countered, waving my hand at the newly opened cafe.

"Mhmm, that's one explanation. That covers your short temper too."

"Excuse you?" I shouted and I'm pretty sure one of the girls gasped. Maybe Olivia.

"But it wouldn't explain the bloating."

"Do not comment on a woman's weight. I've been baking a lot for the new recipes and I have to test them."

"I'd be happy to help taste taste," Shea murmured from behind me.

"And the tenderness?"

I thought for a second.

Damn it.

I stomped into the bathroom.

59

Sweet Cream Cold Brew

Mason

Ashley, being exactly who she is, stayed in the restroom for the whole 15 minutes that the test took.

Honestly, I wasn't sure if that was how long it needed or if she stayed in there longer than necessary to keep me on my toes. But when she did finally step out, she leveled me with a glare. The girls, who'd remained in the back chattering anxiously, gasped at her entrance. They all looked at me, clearly holding back from surrounding my wife so I could get the news first.

"Yeah?" I asked, stepping up to Ashley and taking her hands. She squeezed but didn't meet my eyes.

"It's not fair," she grumbled.

"What's not fair?"

"How come you noticed first?" she asked in a whine, finally looking up at me, green eyes sparkling.

"Yeah?" I repeated, grinning ear to ear. Ashley nodded and I scooped her into my arms, swinging her around in a circle. "We're gonna be parents."

"Okay, now hold your horses," she said, her stern voice breaking with giggles. I made my way to the front of the shop ready to shout out that my wife was growing a whole human being inside her, but was grabbed by Shea and Roxie.

"Not the right move, dude," Roxie said.

"What do you mean? I wanna tell everybody."

"Mason, you don't tell anyone you're pregnant during the first trimester," Ashley explained, a soft hand resting on her stomach.

"Why not?"

"Dude, miscarriages are hella common," Shea said and the rest of the girls hummed in agreement.

"What do you mean common? What's the most common cause? Actually, let's just go home. Regina can handle almost everything. Shea, can you stay and help? Does your gynecologist take walk-ins, sweetheart? Am I allowed in? I think I've got some fish in the freezer, let's throw that out. That's a thing, right? And no more caffeine. I'll see what I've got at the Pub for decaff. We'll stop at the bookstore on our way home too. And the hardware store. They'd have baby-proofing stuff, right?"

"Mason," Ashley said my name in the softest way possible, grabbing my arm to keep me from leaving the shop and pulling me close. "We've got roughly nine months to worry about baby-proofing the house."

"He's so cute though," Rosie crooned.

"He's totally freaking out," Shea said through a laugh.

"I mean, she's the first one to have a baby, so none of us are gonna be much help," Roxie said.

"Oh, I don't think so. My youngest sister was born when I was 13. I remember almost everything about her baby years," Rosie said.

"Aw, I can't wait to buy baby shoes," Olivia added.

Ashley took my face in her hands and brought our foreheads together.

"There's nothing we need to do immediately. You can afford to take a couple more breaths before you really panic, all right?"

"All right," I murmured, moving to press a kiss on her forehead. Then I rest a hand on her stomach. "No more fish or caffeine though."

"God, you're so fucking obnoxious already."

"You love it."

"I know."

K.E. Monteith is an adult romance writer living in Northern Virginia with her two rambunctious dogs and partner. All her books can be found on Kindle Unlimited and feature anxious hot messes falling in love. You can find her on TikTok and Instagram @k.e.monteith_author

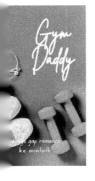

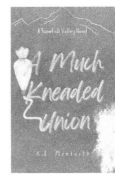